Danny angled his head and words. She didn't have to think about whether to kiss him back and opened her mouth to him. With a groan he delved deep and she clung on to his shoulders. He tasted the same, but the body beneath his clothes was now fully formed and honed with the strength of hard work into something far more potent.

Eventually he drew back and looked down at her, his expression careful.

"Do we mark this down to closure or is it something else?"

"I don't know," Faith said honestly. "I just need—"

This time she was the one who leaned into him and took his mouth. His arm locked around her hips bringing her astride his lap, making her aware of the hard ridge trapped behind the fly of his jeans. She rocked against him aware in some part of her brain that she was not thinking straight but was too into what was happening to care. She might care later, she tended to overanalyze everything, but not now, not now. . . .

BOOKS BY KATE PEARCE

The House of Pleasure Series

SIMPLY SEXUAL
SIMPLY SINFUL
SIMPLY SHAMELESS
SIMPLY WICKED
SIMPLY INSATIABLE
SIMPLY FORBIDDEN
SIMPLY CARNAL
SIMPLY VORACIOUS
SIMPLY SCANDALOUS
SIMPLY PLEASURE (e-novella)
SIMPLY IRRESISTIBLE (e-novella)

The Sinners Club Series

THE SINNERS CLUB
TEMPTING A SINNER
MASTERING A SINNER
THE FIRST SINNERS (e-novella)

Single Titles

RAW DESIRE

The Morgan Brothers Ranch

THE RELUCTANT COWBOY
THE MAVERICK COWBOY
THE LAST GOOD COWBOY
THE BAD BOY COWBOY
THE BILLIONAIRE BULL RIDER
THE RANCHER

The Millers of Morgan Valley

THE SECOND CHANCE RANCHER
THE RANCHER'S REDEMPTION
THE REBELLIOUS RANCHER
THE RANCHER MEETS HIS MATCH
SWEET TALKING RANCHER

Anthologies

SOME LIKE IT ROUGH
LORDS OF PASSION
HAPPY IS THE BRIDE
A SEASON TO CELEBRATE
MARRYING MY COWBOY
CHRISTMAS KISSES WITH MY COWBOY
LONE WOLF

Published by Kensington Publishing Corp.

Sweet Talking
RANCHER

The Millers of Morgan Valley

KATE PEARCE

ZEBRA BOOKS
KENSINGTON PUBLISHING CORP.
www.kensingtonbooks.com

ZEBRA BOOKS are published by

Kensington Publishing Corp.
119 West 40th Street
New York, NY 10018

All Kensington titles, imprints, and distributed lines are available at special quantity discounts for bulk purchases for sales promotion, premiums, fund-raising, educational, or institutional use.

Special book excerpts or customized printings can also be created to fit specific needs. For details, write or phone the office of the Kensington Sales Manager: Attn.: Sales Department. Kensington Publishing Corp., 119 West 40th Street, New York, NY 10018. Phone: 1-800-221-2647.

Zebra and the Z logo Reg. U.S. Pat. & TM Off.

First Printing: August 2021
ISBN-13: 978-1-4201-5257-9
ISBN-10: 1-4201-5257-2

ISBN-13: 978-1-4201-5258-6 (eBook)
ISBN-10: 1-4201-5258-0 (eBook)

10 9 8 7 6 5 4 3 2 1

Printed in the United States of America

ACKNOWLEDGMENTS

Many thanks to Meg Scales and her veterinarian for my newfound knowledge of all the diseases calves can get. Also, thanks to Sian Kaley for reading the book through for me.

Chapter One

Miller Ranch
Morgan Valley, California

Danny Miller gently released his horse's foreleg and straightened up.

"Looking good. Thanks for doing this, Andy."

His gelding, Applejack, snorted and tried to knock Danny's Stetson off as Andy Ferraro gathered his tools. They were in the horse barn, which sided onto the ranch house, and it was as hot as hades.

"You're welcome," Andy said. "I've built up the shoe at the back, but I'll change it out once he's walking better. Anything else you need me to look at while I'm here?"

"Nah, I think we're good." Danny clapped his friend on the back. "Come on in and have something to drink before you go."

"That would be appreciated." Andy narrowed his eyes and looked up at the unending blue sky. "It's darn hot out here. Mind you, it's better than that endless rain we had all spring."

"Which is probably why you prefer to live in Bridgeport

these days." Danny put Applejack away in his stall, made sure the door was bolted, and headed toward the ranch house.

"I'd come back if it was worth my while," Andy said. "My parents still live here, and I know they'd love it if I was closer."

Danny held open the screen door that led into the mudroom. "We could do with a farrier in the valley. You should talk to the Morgans. With all the horses they have for the dude ranch, I bet they'd love to have you around full time."

"Yeah?" Andy paused to heel and toe off his boots and wash his hands. "Ron McDonald used to do a lot of the local horses in Morgan Valley, but as he's retiring, maybe they will need someone new." Andy gave Danny a sidelong glance. "You did know he was retiring, right?"

"Yup." Danny braced himself for the inevitable follow-up question.

"I hear Faith's coming back to run the veterinary business with Dave," Andy said in a way-too-casual voice.

"Is that right?" Danny led Andy through to the large family kitchen, which was mercifully free of his siblings and parents.

"You worried about that, bro?"

"Why would I be?" Danny smiled. "She's just as entitled to come home to work for her family as anyone else."

"So, you guys won't be changing vets or anything?"

"Why would we? The McDonalds have always been awesome." Danny gestured at the refrigerator. "What would you like to drink, Andy? Something cold? A beer?"

"Seeing as I'm driving, I'll take something cold, but not alcoholic if that's okay." Andy wandered over to the window that looked out over the fenced-in paddocks.

"Grass is looking good because of all that spring rain. Wonder how long that will last?"

"Not long enough I can tell you that." Danny opened the refrigerator, took out a jug of lemonade, and held it up. "This okay? Mom made it this morning."

"Looks great." Andy's gaze went to the kitchen door. "Hey, Mr. Miller, what's up?"

Inwardly Danny groaned as his father, Jeff, entered the kitchen and sat at the table. He still couldn't get used to seeing his old man around the house during working hours. Since his heart attack Jeff had been unable to maintain his five-in-the-morning-until-whatever-time-the-work-was-done schedule. He also made sure that everyone in the family knew how much he hated his current existence.

"Afternoon, Andy. I don't know why Danny called you all the way out here just to look at something he could easily have fixed himself, but it's good to see you."

"It's good to see you, too, Mr. Miller," Andy replied. "My mom said to say hi, and that she's looking forward to seeing you back at church."

"I'm looking forward to being allowed off my own ranch, too." Jeff gave Danny a pointed stare. "My family act like I'm incapable or something."

"We're just following doctor's orders, Dad. You'll be good to go this weekend." Danny gave his father and Andy glasses of lemonade and sipped his own. "Where's Mom?"

"She's over at the Morgans'. She said that someone can start dinner if she's late."

"Will do." Danny liked to cook and with Adam staying in town with Lizzie right now, he was the backup chef. "There's no need for her to rush home. I'll text if I need any instructions."

Andy sat at the table with Danny's father. "Did you know Ron Mac is retiring, Mr. Miller?"

"Yup, and about time, too. He's getting way too old for that job."

"He's the same age as you," Danny pointed out. "And you're not willing to retire yet."

"His mind is on the golf course way too much these days and not on the job he's supposed to be doing. Dave's getting better, but he's still got a long way to go to impress me."

"No one impresses you, Dad." Danny grinned.

"True enough." Jeff sipped his lemonade.

"So, I suppose it's good Faith's coming home," Andy said. "From what I hear she's had a lot of large animal experience up in Humboldt County."

"I'm sure she'll do great." Danny chugged his lemonade rather faster than he wanted to and stood up. "I'm just going to text Mom. I'll be back in a minute to see you out, Andy."

Andy rose, too. "I've got to get back myself, Dan, so I'll follow you out."

Danny escorted his friend back to his truck, saw him on his way, and returned to the kitchen where his father was still sitting at the table. He busied himself putting the glasses in the dishwasher and put the jug of lemonade back in the refrigerator.

"Faith McDonald's coming home, then."

"So they say." Danny wiped his hands on the towel and turned to find his father's penetrating stare focused on him.

"You worried about that?"

"Why would I be?" For the first time, Danny let some of his annoyance leak into his voice. "You're about the tenth person who's asked me that this week. Why would I care what she chooses to do? I haven't seen her for seventeen years. I'm sure she's a different person now."

His father shrugged. "No need to get mad when you're asked a simple question, Son. Anyone would think you've got something to hide."

"Jeez, Dad." Danny shook his head. "You know what happened, you were right there. It's not like there was anything suspicious going on."

"Well, she did hightail it out of here pretty darn fast," his father commented. "And she didn't come back, which people might say makes her look guilty of *something*."

"Then people would be wrong." Danny met his dad's stare. "Can we just stop talking about it now?"

"Why? When the whole valley is buzzing with the news that she's finally coming home?"

"Because . . ." Danny carefully folded the towel and put it back. "Faith has a perfect right to come here, and she doesn't deserve all this stupid attention."

"She hurt you, Son."

Danny smiled. "I was seventeen. It was a long time ago. She probably doesn't even remember me."

"I doubt that." His dad hauled himself to his feet. "I'm going to take my walk out to the barn. If I don't come back within the hour, you have my full permission to come look for me. If you start fretting before that, don't expect me to be pleased to see you."

Danny took out his phone. "I'm going to text Mom back about dinner and then I'll be busy getting that started, so I sure as hell won't be worrying about you."

"Good."

Danny waited until his father slammed the back door behind him before he let out a long breath.

Faith was coming back.

He scrolled through his contacts until he found his mother's name.

In a place as small as Morgan Valley it was inevitable that they would bump into each other sooner rather than later—especially when the McDonalds were the Miller family's vets.

He tried to picture what she might look like now and couldn't even guess. They'd parted on such bad terms that even after seventeen years he still wasn't sure he'd be able to face her, or how she'd react to him. He reminded himself that they were both older and wiser, and that her defection had helped make him the man he was now, something he couldn't regret.

He half smiled as he started texting his mother.

Maybe Faith really wouldn't remember him.

Perhaps that would be a blessing,

After receiving detailed instructions from his mother about exactly how to cook dinner, Danny was just about to put his phone away when he paused.

If he had to meet Faith again, he'd prefer to do it away from curious eyes and ears. He thumbed through his contacts and started to type. He was no longer a shy teenager who sat back and let things happen to him. Maybe it was time to make sure Faith knew that as well.

Faith McDonald suppressed a sigh as she looked around the ramshackle veterinarian's hospital. After building a separate house on the property twenty years ago for his growing family, her father had left the original homestead entirely for the use of the practice and hadn't made any effort to improve it since. It was a far cry from the modern offices she and her partners had occupied in Humboldt.

"Yeah, it's a bit of a shithole," her brother Dave remarked from his position propping up the doorframe behind her. "I've been asking Dad to improve it ever since I qualified, but he wouldn't listen. What's new?"

"Sounds just like Dad."

Faith swung around to regard her younger brother. They had the same dark hair and blue eyes as their mother and had both gone into the family business along with their cousin Jenna, who now worked and lived up at Morgan Ranch.

"It's not entirely his fault." Dave shrugged. "It's not easy making money out here."

"I know, but there are things we could do to improve that and stop people having to go to Bridgeport for specialized veterinary care. We both have the skills. Dad's given me carte blanche to get the place up-to-date."

"What does carte blanche mean exactly?" Dave frowned. "Sounds like some kind of cake. And where are we supposed to get the money to make these changes happen?"

"You don't have to worry too much about that if you don't want to," Faith rushed to reassure him. "I managed our practice in Humboldt. We had twelve staff members including six vets and I dealt with all the financials."

Dave shuddered. "You go ahead. I like the 'being a veterinarian' part and hate the bookkeeping. It nearly killed me passing my finals." He jerked his finger toward the back office, which was basically a huge pile of papers. "Have you seen it in there?"

Faith came toward him. "If we are going to be partners, Bro, you're going to have to deal with some of this stuff. I can't make decisions that will affect both of us all by myself. We will need to talk things through."

"Yeah, I get that." Dave hesitated. "Can I be honest here?"

"Sure." Faith nodded. "Go ahead."

"I'm, like, not sure you're really going to stick around," Dave said in a rush. "I mean, I *want* you to, but seeing as you haven't been near this place since I was in middle school, I have some doubts."

Faith made herself meet his skeptical gaze. "I understand how you feel. All I can tell you is that I really want to stay here and build up the practice. I promised Mom and Dad that if they ever needed me to come back I would do so without question."

"Why would I believe that when you've avoided it for so long?" Dave asked.

Faith blinked. Wow, her little brother wasn't pulling his punches.

"Because I don't make promises I don't intend to keep?"

She tried not to think of all the promises she'd made to Danny Miller and subsequently broken. She'd promised to write, to keep in touch, to let him know when she'd be coming home . . .

She forced her attention back to her brother. "I will do my absolute best to make this work, okay?"

He still didn't look convinced, but there was nothing she could do right now except work as hard as she could to prove him wrong.

"There are some people in Morgan Valley who don't remember you in the most favorable light," Dave said slowly. "I'm not saying that to be mean, I just want you to know what you might be up against if you decide to stay."

"Still?" Faith raised her eyebrows.

Dave shrugged. "Folks have long memories out here.

You left, and Danny Miller stayed, so they're bound to be more sympathetic to him. And, he's a nice guy."

"Yes, he is," Faith agreed. "Hopefully, once I start working here and they get to know me again, they'll change their minds."

"I guess so." Dave didn't sound very optimistic as he straightened up and walked out into the office. "I'm just going to check on my two patients out back. I'll meet you out front."

"No problem."

Faith went into the main reception area, which was painted a pale blue and green. There were cheerful posters on the walls, and someone had attempted to set up a puppy play corner, but the whole area looked desperate for a makeover. The rest of the staff had gone home while she and Dave were taking stock of their new venture. If Faith agreed to take on the practice, her father and mother would be off on their long-anticipated golfing tour of Europe. Given the choice, she wasn't sure they'd ever come back to stay for good. But, as they'd helped pay for her to attend veterinary college, supported her decision to stay away from Morgan Valley, and never made her feel bad about any of it, the least she could do was help her brother maintain and develop the family business.

If she got it up and running and financially secure, in a year or two Dave would be able to handle it himself if he took on another vet to replace her. It was always good to have options and a backup plan.

She glanced out the window toward the parking lot and the spectacular view behind it. Leaving Morgan Valley had been a terrible wrench, and some small part of her, the little girl who'd grown up wild and free in the fields, was delighted to be home. The rest of her—the part formed by her decision to leave—wasn't so sure.

She let out a breath. Somewhere out there, after a hard day on the ranch, Danny Miller was probably about to have his dinner. From the snippets of information dropped by her parents and friends over the years she knew he hadn't left home. Like her, he'd had big plans to leave Morgan Valley. Had what had happened between them stopped him from going to college? Faith sighed. Another thing to feel guilty about, like she didn't already have enough.

"You coming, Sis?" Dave said from behind her. "Mom's cooking her famous vegetarian lasagna for dinner, and Jenna and her family are coming over to join us."

"Yes." Faith cast one last glance over in the direction of Miller Ranch and then turned to her brother with a smile. "I can't wait to finally meet Jenna."

"She's awesome." Dave's affectionate grin was more relaxed than it had been earlier. "She specialized in horses so she's a perfect fit for their dude ranch."

"So, she doesn't take work away from us?" Faith waited as Dave checked all the doors and locked up.

"Not at all. Actually, we kind of work in tandem. Sometimes I'll help out up there with the rest of the livestock, or she'll inoculate cattle for me on the other ranches. When we get to calving and lambing season, we are both flat out covering the whole valley." He winked at her. "Which is why I'm glad you're back because Dad made me take all the night shifts."

"You think I won't make you do the same?" Faith asked sweetly.

"Didn't you just say that we'll be equal partners?"

Dave walked across the parking lot to his bashed-up truck, reminding Faith that she needed to get her own form of transport as soon as possible. Her all-electric car wouldn't work on the rocky slopes and unpaved roads of Morgan Valley.

Just before they left, Dave took a last look around and then whistled for his dog, Lilo, who bounded out of the encroaching darkness and leapt nimbly into the back of the truck. The family house wasn't that far from the original homestead, but it was uphill all the way. Faith had walked down, but was glad Dave was bringing her back in the truck. The copse of pine trees behind the new house swayed in the breeze. Faith had forgotten how cold it could get in the evenings after the sun disappeared behind the mountains and wished she'd worn her thicker coat.

Light flooded out from the stone and wood structure her father had designed as his new family home. Having grown up half in the cramped century house of the clinic and half in the expansive new one, Faith had nothing but good memories of the place until her senior year had crashed and burned so unexpectedly. When she got out of the truck, she stood still for a moment to take in the scent of pine and some kind of blue flower her mother had planted along the pathway to the house.

There was an unfamiliar truck parked alongside her electric car that she guessed belonged to Jenna and her husband, Blue Boy Morgan. She remembered BB from school as a sweet-talking daredevil and hadn't been surprised to learn that he'd gone straight into the military. From what she'd heard about her cousin Jenna she couldn't quite imagine how their relationship worked, but she'd learned to her cost that marrying someone just like you didn't always work out either.

"Is that you, Faith?"

She looked up to see her mother, Amy, silhouetted against the light streaming from the open front door.

"Yes!" Faith fixed on a smile and started walking up the steps. Dave had taken his dog around the back. "I'm just coming."

Her mother gave her a quick hug and an equally assessing gaze. "You doing okay?"

"Well, it's still strange to be back, but it's also great to see you all."

"We're delighted to see you, too. Ron's really hoping you'll want to settle down here." Her mother shut the door. "Do you need to wash up and change before you meet Jenna?"

Faith glanced down at her muddy boots and grimaced. "Sorry, I should have come through the back with Dave."

"Like we haven't seen our fair share of mud on these floors. That's why we went for so much tile." Her mother smiled and motioned with her hand. "Go on up. Dinner will be ready when you are."

Faith automatically turned right at the top of the stairs and headed for her old room. Thankfully, after she'd left, her parents had converted it into a guest bedroom, and it no longer felt like her space, which was a good thing. She'd agreed to sit down with her dad after dinner and go over his plans for the practice and the financials and she was looking forward to it. Even with Jenna working up at Morgan Ranch there was still plenty of scope to expand and improve the existing business. The thought of being given a free hand to put into practice all the lessons she'd learned over the years was exciting.

Faith paused at her bedroom door. If it hadn't been for the whole Danny Miller thing, she probably wouldn't even be considering her options, but would've jumped at the chance. She sighed. But if it hadn't been for Danny Miller, she wouldn't have left Morgan Valley in the first place and gained all this great experience to run a successful veterinary business.

Her cell buzzed and she glanced down to see a text from Dave, which was weird as she'd just been talking to him.

Fyi

Faith frowned as she scrolled down to reveal the second text Dave had forwarded on to her.

Hey, any chance we could meet up in private? I think we should talk. Danny.

She dropped her phone like it was on fire and then fell to her knees hoping desperately she hadn't broken the damn thing.

Nope, there was his message, loud and clear and just as terrifying. Faith stared at it for at least a full minute before gently placing her phone on her bedside table and plugging in the charger. She'd take a quick shower, get changed, and go and meet Jenna and Blue. When she'd done all that, maybe she'd be in a better place to deal with the unexpectedly early intrusion in her new life from Danny Miller.

Chapter Two

After sending his text to Dave, Danny checked his phone at regular intervals, but there was no reply from either of the McDonalds. His mom had a strict no phones at the table rule, so he ate his dinner, talked ranch business with his brother Evan and his father, and tried not to second-guess his decision to grab the bull by the horns and reach out to Faith.

Evan had turned up late for dinner and wasn't in a good mood, which was unusual enough for Danny to ask him what was up when they reached the coffee stage.

"It's those damn Brysons again. Their lower fence is down and about thirty of their cows were in our field. I corralled them in one corner and called Doug, but he said he didn't have time to come get them."

"He's always been a jerk just like his father," Jeff chimed in. "I never liked him, either."

"I told him I didn't have time to drive them back onto his land and that he should fix his damned fences and stop relying on us to do it for him." Evan took a slug of coffee.

"What did you do with the cattle?" Danny asked.

"I left them where they were." Evan finally grinned. "If

he wants them, he'll have to figure out a way to get them back because I did fix the hole in the fence."

"I expect I'll be hearing from him tomorrow morning, then," their father said. "He's never been one to keep his thoughts to himself."

Jeff looked quite pleased at the thought of a confrontation, which didn't surprise Danny in the least. His father loved a good fight and he was bored to tears stuck at home.

"I don't know how Doug stays in business." Their father was still talking. "And, there's only his sister up there with him. I bet she won't stick around."

"How do you know?" Danny and his Mom asked at the same time, and then high-fived each other. "Women can run ranches. She can do whatever she wants."

"I suppose so," his dad grudgingly conceded.

"You need to get with the times, Dad," Evan said. "If you said that to Sue Ellen's face, she wouldn't take it well."

"She'd definitely whoop his ass," Danny added.

"I'd pay to see that." Evan set down his glass. "And, seeing as Sue Ellen has a bit of a thing for you, Danny boy, she'd probably do it for you if you asked."

"Sue Ellen has good taste," Danny's mom agreed before turning back to her ex-husband. "Now, did you tell the boys about my plans?"

"Haven't had time," Jeff grumbled. "You only told me this morning."

"I'm planning on flying back to New York next week."

"Okay." Danny was surprised she'd been able to stay for so long already. "You must have missed a lot of work stuff, right?"

She smiled at him. "To be honest, most of it I've handled online or by phone, but there's a big charity board meeting coming up and I need to be there in person for that." She sighed. "And I miss Ellie."

"When do you think you'll get back here?" Evan asked the question Danny hadn't wanted to. "Otherwise Dad's gonna sulk like a baby."

Leanne reached over and took Jeff's hand. "That's up to your father. If he wants me to come back, he'll let me know."

Danny glanced at his father's stormy expression and got to his feet. The last thing he needed when his nerves were already on edge was to watch his father lose his temper.

"I'll help you clear the table, Evan."

"But I'm not finished," Evan protested as Danny fixed him with a pointed stare. "Or, maybe I am." He started gathering up plates. "How about I load the dishwasher while you make some more coffee and deal with the pans?"

"Hey, I cooked," Danny reminded his younger brother. "So, you get to wash the pans."

A while later when both Evan and his father had disappeared into their relative bolt-holes, Danny gave the kitchen countertops a last wipe down and set the rest of the meal in the refrigerator for when Kaiden came home from the Garcia Ranch. His brother was combining his carpentry business with helping manage the ranch and was a very busy man these days.

Danny was just about to check his phone when his mother joined him in the kitchen. Personality wise he was most like her, being the quiet determined type who just got on with shit while everyone else screamed and hollered. Twenty years ago, she'd walked out on his father to teach him a lesson—a lesson Jeff had only recently learned, and he had tried to make amends for depriving his kids of their mother. They all bore the scars of that decision and even after a couple of years of her regular presence at the ranch, Danny still wasn't quite sure how to deal with her.

She helped herself to some coffee and leaned up against the refrigerator, her mug cupped in her hands. She was of average height and her hair still held a glint of the red Ben, Evan, and Daisy had inherited.

"Can I ask you something, Danny?"

"Sure." He put down the kitchen cloth. "What's up?"

"Is there something I should know about you and Faith McDonald?"

It dawned on him that she hadn't been around when everything had gone down.

"Dad didn't tell you about that?" he hedged.

She wrinkled her nose. "I think that was during the height of the divorce wars, so no."

Danny hesitated. It wasn't just his secret and he'd promised Faith. "If there was anything you needed to know that affected the here and now, I'd definitely tell you."

"You would?" She looked hopefully up at him.

"Yes, but anything that did happen went down a very long time ago when we were kids, and it's best to leave it in the past."

She sighed. "If only stuff stayed in the past, we'd all be fine." She met his gaze. "If things change on that score, you promise to tell me?"

Danny nodded. "Definitely, but we're different people now and I can't see Faith being the kind of person to hold a grudge."

"Well, she hasn't come home for almost seventeen years, so I'd say she feels bad about *something*."

Danny smiled. "Now you sound like Dad."

"You don't say." She sighed. "He's really mad I'm leaving. He seemed to think I'd come back for good."

"Hardly surprising." Danny raised an eyebrow. "You know what he's like. He complains all the time about us all being here and ruining his life, but the moment we want to leave, he gets all salty about it. He still hasn't forgiven Ben for moving two miles down the road, Kaiden for working outside the ranch, and Adam for sharing Lizzie's apartment and commuting up here to work."

"I know." She sipped her coffee. "How *would* you feel if I moved back here permanently?"

Danny blinked at her. "What about your work in New York?"

"As I said, I can manage most of it from here." She eyed him carefully. "You don't like the idea?"

"It's not up to me to tell you and Dad how to manage your lives," Danny said carefully. "Would you live here? And what about Ellie? Would she come with you?"

"You're really good at answering questions with questions of your own." His mom chuckled. "I'm not sure about living here on the ranch, to be honest. I might rent something in town."

"Are you worried Dad's not going to get better?" Danny asked flat out. "Do you think you need to be close for his benefit?"

She set her mug down on the counter. "I think you and your siblings are more than capable of looking after your own father if that's what you're getting at. I'd like to come home. I really miss this place and, seeing as I have the kind of life and financial resources to live wherever I like, I decided I wanted to make a change." She shrugged. "What's going on with Jeff certainly made me come to a decision faster, but we'd already discussed me moving back here before he had his heart attack."

"I think you should do what you want to do," Danny said slowly.

"Thank you." She offered him a smile. "That's very sweet of you." She turned to the sink. "I've spoken to all of you now and no one's told me I'm a complete fool. I'm a different person from that scared girl who let herself be pushed out of her own family and your father definitely knows it." She held out her hand. "Are you done with that mug, dear? Give it to me and I'll rinse it out and stick it in the dishwasher."

Danny was still thinking about his mother's last words long after she'd left him sitting alone in the shadowed kitchen. If his parents could find common ground twenty years after their horrible divorce, then surely couldn't he and Faith do the same?

He checked his cell phone and his heart stuttered as he saw the new text from an unknown number.

Hey, as I'm not even sure I'm staying, can I take a rain check on that?

Danny contemplated Faith's words for a considerable amount of time as he weighed up whether to reply or not. If she wasn't staying, what was the point of opening up all those old wounds? And if she was, he'd get another opportunity to talk to her at a later date. But maybe next time he wouldn't be so quick to reach out.

He turned off his phone, stuck it in his pocket, and decided to go out to the barn to finish his chores for the day. With two of his brothers currently off the ranch, his sister in San Francisco, and his dad restricted to light work, the burden of keeping the family business going fell increasingly on his and Evan's shoulders. Not that he minded the work. In fact, with his father out of the way, he could implement a lot of the new ideas he'd learned during his agricultural degree classes without constant opposition. He'd be able to improve the herd, introduce new grass and wetland management processes, and make the ranch both environmentally and economically more stable.

With that thought firmly in mind, Danny pushed away from the table and went through into the mudroom to put on his boots. Whether Faith left or decided to stay, his future was here on the ranch, and taking his family safely into the future was his number-one priority.

"We own the land, there are no mortgages on either of the two properties, and there is almost no debt—except for patient bills debt, but as you probably know that's a common problem around here."

Faith's father passed a thick accounting book over to her and sat back. They were in his book-lined study with the drapes closed while Dave and her mother watched some terrible reality show they both loved in the family room.

"You don't have your accounts online? How do you manage payroll?" Faith asked.

"Same way as I always have. I look at the book, total up the hours worked from the staff sign-up sheets, and write the checks." He shrugged. "It's not exactly complicated."

Faith ran a quick eye over the columns of figures that reflected exactly what her father had just told her.

"You do all the bookkeeping yourself?"

"I get Derek in town to help me with my taxes each year." He pointed at a shoebox. "I stick all my receipts in there and just hand them over when he asks for it."

Faith tried not to shudder at the very idea and instead concentrated on the surprisingly healthy state of the business. She supposed that because there was no competition except from Jenna in Morgan Valley, her father had something of a captive market.

"Have you ever considered taking out a loan to improve the facilities?" Faith asked.

"Well, I thought that should be Dave's decision. I didn't want to saddle him with a load of debt he didn't ask for and had to pay off when I was gone."

Faith nodded. "If I did take over the practice with Dave, I would want to change quite a few things."

Her father nodded. "I know that, and if it's something you and Dave both want to do, then it's nothing to do with me." He chuckled. "I'm not expecting any income from this place to fund my retirement, Faith. Your mom has a good pension from her teaching job, and I've done okay with my investments. I'm not worried about being stranded in Europe and having to call home for funds."

Faith smiled back at him. "I just don't want you thinking that you'd made a mistake handing over the business if I start doing things differently."

"Honey, if I sign the place over to you two, trust me, I'll skip away without a care in the world and leave you to it."

"Are you sure about that, Dad?" Faith leaned forward, her hands clasped together on the table. "I mean, you've worked here all your life and built this business into a great success."

"And now it's time to pass it on to the next generation, just like my father did for me—except he stuck around and criticized everything I did, and I'm not going to be that guy." He patted her hands. "I believe that you and Dave can make this business even better and I trust you."

The gruff sincerity in her father's voice made Faith want to cry.

"Thanks, Dad. I swear I'll do you proud."

His eyes lit up. "So, is that a yes, then?"

Faith nodded and he shot to his feet. "Wonderful! Let's go and tell your mother to pack her bags!"

Faith checked her phone again the next morning. There was nothing from Danny Miller, but why would there be? She'd shut him down and what was the point in him replying to her? At least he'd had the sense to let it go. If she was staying, and, as she was currently sitting in the local lawyer's office signing papers with her father and brother, she supposed she was, she'd find a way to talk to him soon.

Even on the short walk from her father's truck to the lawyer's office on Main Street she'd noticed a few pointed stares being sent in her direction. A couple of people had said hi to her dad and Dave and completely ignored her. Dave had warned her that she might experience some backlash from the local community, but she hadn't really taken him seriously. What had she even done? She'd left town and hadn't returned. She was fairly certain she wasn't the only person to run away from Morgan Valley.

After they left the lawyer's office her father suggested they have a celebratory lunch in town. Faith was still wondering where on earth he expected to get fed in Morgantown at lunchtime when her nose caught the scent of coffee.

"Come on, partner." Dave took her hand and led her along the raised wooden walkway to a shop with black and

pink awnings and tables set outside. "Lunch is on Dad so
we should exploit him while we can."

"When did this place open?" Faith stared in awe at the
glass-fronted cases filled with beautiful cakes and pastries.

"A few years ago. The coffee is good and Yvonne, the
owner, bakes everything here and makes amazing wedding
cakes."

Their father had already found a table and was chatting
to the waitress.

"Hey, Lizzie!" Dave grinned at her as he took a seat.
"Have you met my sister, Faith, yet? You're going to be
seeing her around a lot more."

Lizzie turned to Faith, her smile dimming slightly.
"Hi!" She immediately looked back at Dave. "I'll give you
guys a moment to check out the specials, and then I'll
come and take your drinks order, okay?"

"Lizzie manages the café side of the business for
Yvonne," Faith's father said. "She's dating Adam Miller."

"Oh, right." Faith busied herself looking at the extensive
menu. How could she have forgotten that Danny had five
siblings who were all still around, and all aware of her past
relationship with him? She reminded herself that it was a
small town and that everything would blow over once she
was accepted back into the fold.

Her father insisted on ordering champagne and telling
anyone who came over to their table about the wonderful
news of his imminent retirement. The congratulations and
good wishes he received from the townsfolk were both
sincere and well meant. It was only when Faith was brought
into the conversation that she could see a hint of reservation
in their eyes. But Dave was still not viewed in the same
way as his father was, so there was hope for her yet.

She smiled and made conversation with anyone willing

to engage with her, laughed at all the jokes and didn't answer any leading questions. To her delight, the food was excellent, and she exited the café feeling even more optimistic than she had before. Looking around the bustling, prosperous little town, her thoughts turned to a satellite clinic on Main Street looking after people's small domestic pets. . . .

"Excuse me."

Someone bumped her shoulder and she instinctively moved out of the way. "Sorry." She did a double take. "Nancy?"

"Yes?" The spiky haired woman looked her over and went still. "Faith McDonald. What are you doing back in Morgantown?"

"I'm coming back to work with Dave as Dad is retiring." Faith hesitated. "Look, I know things ended on a bad note between us, but it was a long time ago, and I'm sure as adults we can get along, right?"

Nancy raised an eyebrow. "Sure, once you get around to explaining why you dumped your best friend, broke Danny Miller's heart, and left without a word." Her gaze swept over Faith. "On second thought I'm not sure I've got the time or the interest in hearing your excuses."

"Wow, way to bear a grudge," Faith said. "I see you haven't changed a bit."

"I'm still as honest as I ever was if that's what you mean." Nancy stepped around her. "Have a great day, Faith."

Nancy crossed the street and went into her mother's store without a backward glance, her silver piercings glinting in the sunlight. It took Faith a few moments to gather herself and follow her brother and father to the parking lot. The faint look of dislike in Nancy's eyes had surprised her.

They'd been inseparable once, best friends even though Nancy was older than her, but Faith hadn't dared trust her with all her secrets and had run away without explaining herself.

Nancy liked everyone and had no compunction in telling you when you messed up, so why was Faith surprised she'd received a reprimand? And, Nancy wasn't wrong. Faith had let her and Danny down. She stared at Maureen's and made a decision.

"Dave?" she called out to her brother. "I've just got to pop into Maureen's, okay?"

"Sure, Dad thinks he left his phone at Henry's." Dave rolled his eyes. "We've got to go back and pick it up before we get to the car. We'll meet you there."

Faith went into Maureen's, took off her sunglasses, and waited for her eyes to adjust to the dim interior. The front of the store was like a normal supermarket and the back was full of stuff for the ranchers like jeans, boots, Western wear, and horse paraphernalia. As a teenager, she'd worked in the store on weekends with Nancy and had a wonderful time.

"Faith!" Maureen, Nancy's mother, who was sitting at the cashier's station, put down her phone and stared at her like she was a ghost. "I'd heard you were coming back, but—"

"Hi," Faith said, smiling. "Is Nancy out back? I'd really like to talk to her."

"She went through there." Maureen pointed to the interior of the store. "I think she said something about sorting out the jeans."

"Thanks." Faith marched toward the archway. "I won't be a moment."

As Faith came up behind her, Nancy was taking pairs of jeans off the shelves and muttering to herself.

"Hey," Faith said, and Nancy stiffened. "I know I let you down badly. It was a horrible thing to do, and I should at least have written to explain." She paused, but there was no response. "All I can say in my defense is that back then everything was so overwhelming and frightening that I panicked. By the time things settled down I was too ashamed to write to anyone and convinced that you'd all hate me."

"Well, you got that part right." Nancy set another load of denim on the floor. "But you're also right that I'm stupid to bear a grudge." She finally turned around to look at Faith. "We were just kids."

"Thank you." Faith held her gaze. "And, even though you probably think this is a worthless apology, I really am sorry for hurting you."

Nancy shrugged. "It's okay. It's not as though I lie awake every night plotting evil schemes to bring you down—well, not for the last ten years or so—I accept your apology."

"Thanks." Faith kept it simple.

Nancy pointed at the jeans. "I have to get on. I'm due back at work at six."

"Where do you work now?"

"The Red Dragon."

"That's still open?" Faith pictured the run-down dive bar on the corner of Main.

"Yeah, Jay Williams owns it. You should pop by one evening. Bring Dave."

"Maybe I will." It was Faith's turn to nod. "Okay. Dad and Dave are waiting for me in the parking lot."

"Are you really coming back for good?" Nancy asked.

"Yes, we just signed the paperwork today. I'm looking

forward to it." Faith half turned to go. "Thanks for hearing me out."

"No problem." Nancy was already reaching for the next stack of jeans.

Faith let out a relieved breath and smacked right into a solid wall of someone's chest who grabbed her arm to steady her.

"I'm sorry, I didn't see you there." She raised her gaze to the man's face and went still.

"Oh crap."

"Hey." Danny Miller looked down at her, his gray eyes full of wry amusement. "Long time no see."

He let go of her arm and took a step back, giving her plenty of room to escape. She even considered it before she told herself to act like an adult.

"H—How . . . are you?" Faith stuttered.

"Pretty good."

It was strange looking at him all grown up. He had the same gray eyes and facial features, but he'd filled out his frame and was now tall and lean. As the silence lengthened, she realized she'd been staring at him for way too long and that it was her turn to speak.

"I got your text."

"I saw that."

Man, he wasn't going to help her keep the conversation going. He'd never been much of a talker, even as a teenager.

"I am going to stay in Morgan Valley and run the practice with Dave, so I suppose we really should get together and talk."

His glance shifted over her shoulder and he lowered his voice. "Probably not here."

"I can still hear you, Danny Miller!" Nancy called out.

"Can I call you when things are more settled?" Faith asked.

"Sure."

She pointed at the exit. "Dave and my dad are waiting for me in the parking lot."

"So you said." He touched the brim of his hat and moved completely out of her way. "Nice seeing you again, Faith."

She ran. There was no other word for it. She skedaddled like prey that had miraculously escaped being eaten. She wasn't proud of herself but seeing him again so unexpectedly had jumbled up her emotions and she was terrified of saying the wrong thing.

By the time she reached the safety of her father's truck she was regretting her flight and already anticipating what she was going to say when they met again. Next time she would come prepared with her facts all in a row and, having seen him once, she wouldn't be so bowled over again. Just the shock of him, the *reality* of him after years of wondering and regretting had temporarily seized up her brain.

Faith rushed out the door like Danny was chasing her and he let out a low whistle. She probably thought he was stalking her, but he'd just come in to pick up a couple of new matching bandanas for Roman, Lizzie's son, and his new puppy, Splat.

The horror on Faith's face when she'd looked up at him had almost made him want to laugh until the emotion trapped deep inside him had welled up, and he'd been unable to say anything at all. She was still beautiful. She'd cut her dark hair short and had her ears pierced in multiple places. Funny all the things you noticed when you were desperately trying to take everything in at once, in case someone ran out on you again.

"Well, that was fun," Nancy piped up. "Almost like something from a rom-com."

"Definitely a comedy," Danny murmured. "She certainly hightailed it out of here fast."

"She followed me into the store to apologize for ignoring me for seventeen years."

"And did you forgive her?" Danny asked as he wandered over to the stand covered in bandanas.

"Kind of." Nancy lined up a set of jeans. "I mean it was all so long ago I can barely remember it, and she sounded sincere. It's not like we have to be best buds or anything. I can definitely deal with her being around."

Danny was impressed by Nancy's ability to forgive. Weird how he remembered every painful second of his and Faith's last few months together to this very day. But Nancy hadn't known all of it and hopefully she never would. Faith would need friends in Morgan Valley and he certainly wasn't going to stop anyone from coming around to her.

"She's really pretty," Nancy said as she strolled over to check out his selection.

"Yeah." Blue was Roman's favorite color, so Danny focused on that.

"I like her short hair."

"Hmm." Danny compared a Hawaiian-themed bandana with one with dog bones on it. "Which one do you think Roman would prefer?"

"You're no help, Danny," Nancy sniffed. "You could at least gossip with me."

"Not happening," he said firmly.

Even though Faith had said she'd get back to him about meeting up, he was beginning to wonder if she meant it. If she hadn't bothered to pick up the phone for seventeen years, why would she suddenly want to talk to him now? Why hadn't she come back to Morgan Valley and met him face-to-face over the years? What had changed?

Nancy was watching him way too closely. He reminded himself that she worked at the local bar and had an outstanding ability to spread gossip. He picked up the two matching bandanas and turned to the exit.

"Thanks, Nancy. I definitely think I'll go with the bones."

Chapter Three

Danny looked up as his big brother Adam came striding into the barn where he was carefully walking Applejack. Two weeks had passed since Andy had put on the new shoe and his favorite horse was almost ready to ride again. He still hadn't heard back from Faith, but he guessed she was busy getting up to speed with the veterinary business.

"Bryson wants his cows back," Adam said.

"Yeah, I know," Danny said. "He wanted them two weeks ago and Dad told him to come and get them himself."

"Evan just went by there and some of them are calving right in our field."

"Shit." Danny frowned. "That's not a problem I want to have to deal with."

"Me neither. Will you help me get them back on the right side of the fence? We'll have to take it down again to get them through, but it's easier than taking them all by road."

"Sure." Danny nodded. "Let me put Applejack away and find another horse."

Ten minutes later, Danny was astride his backup horse,

Joe, following Adam up the slope to the topmost fields of their ranch. After the torrential spring rain, the grass was tall and green and the terrain muddy. Adam whistled to his dogs and gathered them together as they approached the last field that currently held a mixture of Miller and Bryson cows.

"Where was the breach in the hedge?" Danny asked.

"Between those two trees." Adam stood in his stirrups and pointed toward the far boundary. "Evan just restrung the wire fencing so it shouldn't be too hard to get it down again. I'll start sorting the cows while you get on with that."

Danny put on his work gloves and wrestled with the fencing while Adam and the dogs worked together to separate the cows. He'd just about made a big enough gap when Adam called his name and he went over to join him.

"Two calves down here. Both Brysons." Adam frowned. "Do you want to call him and let him know he'll probably need to take these two back to the barn?"

"Sure." Danny took off his glove and found Doug's number as Adam started moving the pregnant cows back toward the newly created gap.

"Bryson."

"Hey, Doug, two of your cows have calved in our field. We'll drive the rest back through to your land, but you'll need to come pick these two up."

"I don't have time."

"Well, you can't leave them here. We're clearing this field and bringing our pregnant cows closer to home so we can keep an eye on them."

Danny waited but apart from some heavy breathing Doug didn't appear to have anything useful to say.

"Just push them onto my land and I'll come by and take a look later. Thanks."

Danny tightened his grip on the phone. "Doug, the calves have just been born. You can't just ignore them."

"Listen up, whichever Miller you are, I don't have four brothers backing up my every move. If I say I can't get to them today, I can't, so do whatever the hell you like."

Doug ended the call leaving Danny staring speechless at the blank screen.

"He's not coming?" Adam asked, his incredulous expression mirroring Danny's.

"Nope."

Adam cast a distracted glance back at the two calves who were lying at their mother's feet.

"We can't just leave them here. Doug might say he doesn't want them, but I'm sure as hell he'll try and sue the pants off us if we let them die. He's just that kind of guy."

"Let's get the rest of his cows back on his side of the fence, first," Danny suggested. "Maybe if we move the two calves over as well, the mothers will follow them?"

Adam rubbed a hand over the back of his neck as the rain started up again and dripped off the brim of his Stetson. "That'll probably work, but the calves still aren't going to thrive outside in this weather."

"Which isn't our problem as long as they're on Bryson land," Danny reminded him.

"Yeah, I get that, but I still don't like it." Adam exhaled. "I could get hold of Dad and ask him to drive the cattle trailer up here so we could load them on that."

"And take them round to Doug? That's just what he wants," Danny said. "He's so damn *lazy*." He looked back at the way too quiet calves. "Okay, call Dad. The trailer is all gassed up and ready to go. All he has to do is drive it."

* * *

Faith waved as she approached the Ramirez brothers, who were waiting for her in the barn. They'd only recently arrived in Morgan Valley and treated her just like they treated Dave, which was a pleasant change after some of the comments from longtimers she'd endured over the last two weeks. She had no idea why there was still such animosity toward her and could hardly just come out and ask exactly what the problem was. It definitely had something to do with Danny, but she was reluctant to believe he had gone around bad-mouthing her for years.

Red Ramirez, the older of the brothers, came forward to shake her hand, his expression anxious.

"*Buenos Dias*, Faith."

Faith set her bag on the mounting block and faced her apprehensive audience. "I got the lab results back for the dead calf, and I think it's going to be okay."

"Really?"

"It's not infectious. You don't have to worry about the rest of the herd."

The brothers slapped each other on the back before turning to Faith, who handed over the printed results.

"From the fecal samples the state vet determined it was a rare form of clostridium that probably just lived in the ground exactly where she was born."

"That's . . . crazy." Red shook his head. "When we found her down, we feared the worst, but it seems like it was just a freakish accident."

"Pretty much," Faith agreed. "It's still awful to lose an apparently healthy calf like that, but at least you know it's not part of a pattern of infection."

"Thank God." Red crossed himself and looked skyward. "We were freaking out and disinfecting everything and everybody who came into contact with her."

"I can imagine," Faith said. "Is there anything else I can look at for you while I'm here?"

"No, we're good, and thank you so much for coming out here to tell us yourself."

"You're welcome," Faith replied as he patted her shoulder and walked her back to her truck.

"Have your parents left for their trip yet?"

"Yes, they set off last weekend." Faith grinned. "They looked so happy to be leaving it was almost insulting."

"Well, your father has put in a lifetime of work here so I can't blame him." Red opened the door of the truck for her with an elaborate bow.

"Why, thank you." Faith climbed in and smiled down at him.

"Any chance you'd like to have a drink with me at the Red Dragon one evening?" Red asked.

Faith blinked. "Like a date kind of drink or just friends kind of thing?"

"Whatever you prefer."

Faith remembered her promise to drop in at Nancy's place of employment. "Maybe on Friday?"

"Sure! I'll meet you there around seven." Red stepped away from the truck. "You've got my number if anything comes up. I know what a veterinary schedule can get like."

"What schedule?" Even as Faith spoke her cell buzzed and she groaned. "See? I thought I'd have a few hours off before afternoon appointments began."

Red chuckled. "I'd best get on. Have a great day now, Faith, and thanks for bringing such good news."

He walked away leaving her to unlock her phone and check her text messages. The latest one had come through from Dave and was marked urgent.

While you're up at the Ramirez place can you call in
at the Millers? Jeff left a message about two calves up
at the top boundary of their ranch, which is about
quarter of a mile away from where you are now.

Will do.

Faith ignored her rumbling stomach and headed out
onto the narrow road that led down to the gate and took a
right. Even though she'd been away from Morgan Valley
for years she retained an instinctive knowledge of where
all the ranches lay and how to get to them. The lower gate
to the Millers' land was already open and fresh tire tracks
in the mud made it easy for her to locate exactly where she
needed to aim for.

She pulled up behind a cattle trailer and got out of the
truck. At the far end of the field, a trio of cowboys were
standing with their backs to her, hands on hips staring
down at the ground. It was the first time she'd been near
the Miller Ranch since she'd come home. She braced herself for a chilly reception as she slogged through the mud
toward them.

"Hey!" she called out as she approached. "Dave said
you had a problem up here, Mr. Miller."

All three guys turned around and she had no difficulty
distinguishing the grim face of Adam Miller from that
of his brother Danny, who was about the same height as
his father.

"Is that you, Faith McDonald?" Jeff Miller asked.

"Yes." She nodded at the calves, determined to keep the
occasion professional. "What happened?"

"Doug Bryson's cows got through the fence a while ago.
He was supposed to come and pick them up but didn't have
the time," Adam said in his deep voice. "We decided to

move his cows back over the property line and discovered these two had already calved."

"Yours or Bryson's?" Faith set her bag down on the least muddy bit of ground and crouched beside the first calf.

"Bryson's," Danny said.

"They look small."

"Yeah, well, Doug isn't exactly known for how well he treats his cattle."

"Did anyone call him?"

"I did." Danny grimaced. "He told me to push them into his field, and he'd get up here when he had the time."

"I don't think these two little ones have time to wait for him to turn up. They need to be under cover and warm." Faith got out her stethoscope, pressed it against the first calf's chest, and frowned. "This one doesn't sound good."

She moved over to the other one. "Neither does this one." She looked up at Adam. "I see you've got your cattle trailer up here. Any chance we can use it to transport the calves back to Doug's place?"

"That's what we were planning on doing." Adam nodded. "I checked in with Dave just to make sure it would be safe to move them, and he said he'd send you to take a look."

"To be honest, I don't think we have a choice." Faith went to stand, and Danny stepped forward to help her, his grip warm on her elbow.

"If we don't get them off this wet ground, they probably won't survive the night," Faith said. "If Doug can keep a close eye on them and we can do some tests they'll have a much higher chance of survival."

"Then let's move them," Jeff Miller said decisively. "We can take one calf between us and get it done in one hit."

"Dad . . ." Adam looked at his father. "You know—"

Jeff waved off whatever his son was about to say and stomped over to the second calf. "You take the head, Adam, and I'll get the legs."

"Fine," Adam said, sighing. "But just be glad Mom's not home right now because if she found out what you've been doing, she'd kill you."

Danny cleared his throat and gestured at the other calf. "You okay to get this one?"

"Sure." Faith put her stethoscope away in her pocket and hunkered down to take the back end of the calf. "I didn't know your parents were back together again."

"I'm not sure if they are, but they're certainly seeing a lot of each other if they aren't." Danny laid the calf gently in the back of the trailer on the packed straw. "I just keep out of it."

"And, is your dad okay?" Faith lowered her voice. "My mom said something about him having a heart attack recently."

"He did and he's in recovery. Hopefully, he'll be able to avoid any more surgery." Danny glanced back at the field. "Do you want to check out the new mothers while you're here? Maybe they will offer up some clues as to what's up with the calves."

"That's a good idea." Faith considered the large trailer. "If we sectioned off the middle, we could probably fit them in here. Receiving colostrum from their mothers is extremely important for the calves."

"I'll tell Adam," Danny said. "It shouldn't take long to load them when their calves are already on board."

He walked away to consult with his big brother, who was still arguing with his father. Adam was a head taller than Danny, but they had a similar quiet, solid-as-a-rock vibe to them as opposed to their rather more irascible father. As she waited, Faith mentally ran through a list of potential issues for the poor condition of the calves. It might just be that they'd been born too soon in a water-logged field in the coldness of a Morgan Valley night. But, from what she'd seen, all the Bryson cattle didn't look too healthy.

She didn't have a strong memory of Doug from school, although she remembered his sister, who had been in the 4-H club and junior barrel racing with her. She'd liked Sue Ellen and wondered whether she was still at home or if she had left the valley.

"Watch out, Faith," Adam called out as he herded one of the cows toward the trailer.

She quickly got out of the way and waited for them to load the second cow and make sure the trailer was secure.

Adam slammed the last bolt home. "I'll drive, Dad."

"I'll follow you," Faith said.

"You don't need to drive me anywhere, Adam," Jeff Miller said. "I'm perfectly capable of getting my own trailer down to Bryson's place."

"I know, but I don't want you getting out of the truck when you *do* get there, yelling at him and making things worse," Adam said.

Faith hid a smile as father and son squared up.

"If you're going to be like that about it, I'll take your horse back to the ranch and leave you to it," Jeff snapped, and stomped off through the mud toward the horses.

"Dad—" Adam set off after him.

Faith decided to go back to her truck, turn it around, and be ready to leave when the Millers finished arguing. She texted Dave to let him know what she was doing. By the time she looked up from her phone, the cattle trailer was on the move and heading for the gate.

She waited until it went past her truck and filed in behind, only pausing to close the gate on her way out. At this point the two ranches weren't that far apart, but the roads and tracks followed the boundaries, which meant they had to go down the slope before they could head back up. As they headed up the drive toward the Bryson Ranch, Faith couldn't help but check the place out as she drove by. From what she could see, several of the fields were water-logged and hadn't been maintained, leaving a lot of the cattle knee-deep in mud.

A collection of barking dogs greeted their arrival at the barn. Faith made sure she had her usual pocketful of dog treats and was ready for anything before she left the safety of her truck. A woman appeared at the entrance of the barn and came toward Faith, her expression puzzled.

"What's going on?"

"Sue Ellen?" Faith offered a smile that wasn't returned. "I don't know if you remember me, but—"

"I remember you, Faith McDonald. Everyone in this valley does. Running out on a good man like Danny Miller and never bothering to come home. How could we forget?" Sue Ellen met Faith's startled gaze. "Sorry, I pride myself on being honest and speaking my mind."

"So, I see. Well—"

Sue Ellen's attention slid past Faith and she smiled.

"Hi, Danny. What brings you here?"

Danny smiled back at Sue Ellen, aware that Faith wasn't looking very happy and wondering what had caused it.

"Hey, Sue Ellen. Did Doug tell you about the calves being born in our top field?"

Her cheeks went red. "He said he couldn't get the cows

back because you'd repaired the fence, but he was worried about them."

"Well, he doesn't need to worry anymore. We've brought them to you." He pointed at the trailer. "Faith took a quick look at them and they're small, cold, and probably dehydrated."

"Then let's get them into the barn and take a look," Sue Ellen said. "Doug's not here right now. He's in town trying to get his truck fixed at Ted Baker's. That's why he couldn't come and get the cows."

"I guess we can manage by ourselves," Danny said. "Faith?"

"Sure, we can." Faith put on her gloves. "Let's start with the calves."

While Faith was busy evaluating the calves, Sue Ellen came up beside Danny and touched his shoulder.

"Are you okay having to be around her?"

"It's fine."

"You know you don't have to pretend with me, Danny. I remember how sad you were when she ran off without a word." She leaned in closer. "I heard that she went off to Vegas with some rando rodeo guy. Is that true?"

"I have no idea," Danny said. "And, even if she did, that's her business."

"Oh, of course it is, but it says a lot about her character, doesn't it?" Sue Ellen studied the back of Faith's head. "She's lucky Doug isn't here. He'd probably order her off our land."

"For something that happened seventeen years ago?" Danny asked.

"Doug doesn't forget a slight. Faith refused to go to Junior Prom with him."

"Probably because she was going with me," Danny reminded her gently. "If I can let things go, Sue Ellen, I think you and Doug could, as well."

"You're too nice, Danny. She doesn't deserve it."

As Sue Ellen's voice rose, Faith looked over her shoulder and stood up.

"They need fluids." She turned to Sue Ellen. "Do you want me to set that up or—"

"We can manage, thanks," Sue Ellen interrupted her. "We don't need unnecessary vet bills."

"Okay." Faith cast another worried look back at the calves. "Warmth and electrolytes will definitely help." She peeled off her gloves and balled them up in her fist. "If you don't need me, I'll get out of your hair. I have to get back to the clinic for afternoon appointments or Dave will kill me."

She offered them both a smile and turned toward the exit of the barn. Danny looked at Sue Ellen.

"Aren't you at least going to thank her?"

"For interfering?" Sue Ellen shrugged. "She didn't need to come here and nose around. It's obvious what happened to the calves and we are well capable of taking care of our own cattle."

"We *asked* her to check the calves out," Danny said. "She didn't just turn up uninvited. Excuse me."

He went after Faith and found her just about to leave. He flagged her down and she opened her window with obvious reluctance. Even after all this time he knew she was upset by Sue Ellen's behavior.

"Sorry she's being an ass," Danny said.

"It's okay, I'm kind of getting used to it," Faith said with a tight smile. "Please reassure her that I don't intend to charge her a cent for my time."

"Faith." Danny set his fingers on the lowered window. "I'm sorry we dragged you into this."

"It's okay."

"Look . . ." Aware that he'd been slapped down once, Danny hesitated. "We really do need to talk."

She nodded stiffly. "Fine. I'll be in town Friday night. Maybe we could meet at the coffee shop?"

"Sure. I'll check in with Adam and Dad as to our schedule, but I think I'm good. I'll send you a text with a time."

Her gaze settled on his hand. "I really do need to get back."

"Okay." He stepped away from her truck. "I'll be in touch."

She nodded, shut the window, and backed up until she was able to swing the truck around to face the gate. He watched her leave, a frown on his face.

"Good riddance to bad rubbish," Sue Ellen spoke from behind him and he swung around.

"What the heck is wrong with you?" Danny asked.

She opened her eyes wide. "Wow, she really did do a number on you, didn't she? You're still defending her when she left you with a broken heart?"

"That was seventeen years ago," Danny said evenly. "I've moved on, so has Faith, and so should you, Sue Ellen. I really do not need a champion stirring up shit." He waited, but she continued to glare at him. "Tell Doug to mend his fences and keep his cattle on his own land, okay?"

He marched back to the cattle trailer and got inside, his frustration with both of the Brysons almost impossible to contain. Faith had just been trying to do her job. There was no need for Sue Ellen to treat her like that. He would've defended anyone who'd been spoken to so rudely.

Danny turned the trailer around and set off back home. Where had this rumor of Faith running out on him with another guy started? It was the first he'd heard of it, but to be fair, most people wouldn't have mentioned it to his face. Sue Ellen was famous for her so-called plain speaking and she'd definitely wanted Danny to know what was being said. Had she mentioned the same thing to Faith? It might explain why she'd looked so upset when she was leaving. Danny reminded himself that what Faith thought and believed had nothing to do with him, and that she certainly wasn't expecting him to defend her.

It was weird how he'd instinctively done it anyway. . . .

Chapter Four

"I know it's a lot to take in," Faith said patiently for at least the fifth time. "But if we all stick at it, we'll have this new system up and running in no time."

The veterinary staff didn't look quite as convinced as she was. She'd instigated a weekly staff get-together to go over new announcements, deal with any issues, and hopefully bond with her new team. Even with the enticement of Yvonne's pastries things weren't going well.

"If it ain't broken, why fix it?" Blanche the receptionist who had been with the clinic since it opened repeated. Her arms folded over her chest. "Dr. Ron's system worked just fine for all of us."

Several heads nodded in agreement.

"I get that, but with this new system, we can hold everything centrally and look up stuff like old patient notes, repeat prescriptions, new animal health guidelines from the state, and all the other stuff that crops up from one screen," Faith said.

"Actually, I like the way you can pull up the records before you go into the consulting room and know exactly what's going on. You've got all the past history on that patient right there in front of you," Trina, one of the vet technicians, spoke up. "It's organized like my college classes and easy to navigate."

Faith offered the youngest member of her staff a grateful smile.

"Maybe if you're a youngster," Blanche said. "It's all really confusing to me."

"I'll help you." Trina reached over and patted Blanche's hand. "It really is awesome once you get your head around it."

Faith resolved to grab Trina before she left and ask for her help converting the other members of her skeptical team to the new way of doing things because she was running out of ideas. Most of the staff had worked for her father for over twenty years and, while she loved them all dearly, she was having a hard time convincing them that there were better ways of doing things. Not that anyone wasn't willing to *try*; they just all thought everything was fine as it was and treated her and Dave like they were still kids with a lot to learn.

"Any more questions?" Faith asked.

Everyone shook their heads.

"Thanks so much for coming. The new schedule for the Saturday clinic and emergency callout on Sunday is up so please check it out before you leave tonight." Faith stood up. "And help yourself to the pastries so I don't have to eat them all myself."

Even Blanche laughed at that joke and everyone departed still smiling. Faith spoke to Trina, who had some excellent ideas to get the other members of the team on board. She was just rewarding herself with a chocolate éclair she'd sneaked out of the pink-striped box when Dave came in. She pointed her finger at him.

"You were supposed to be here, partner."

He grimaced. "Yeah, I know, but I got a call from Doug Bryson to tell me two of his calves had died and that I should be ashamed to call myself a vet after all the help I'd been." He sat on the edge of the table and took out the last pastry. "I was like, what calves, and he was like the two your sister brought back to the ranch, which didn't help much. Did I miss something?"

"I told you about this earlier in the week," Faith reminded him. "You asked me to help Jeff Miller when I was up at the Ramirez place. I took the calves down to Brysons' and Sue Ellen tore me off a strip, told me to go away and not to dare bill her for breathing the same air as she did."

"Oh yeah! I remember now." Dave nodded. "I called the ranch the day after, and Sue Ellen told me everything was fine, and they didn't need anything." He ate his cake in two bites and chewed thoroughly before continuing. "Maybe Sue Ellen didn't tell Doug what went down."

"Sure sounds like it." Faith sighed. "I hate it when calves die like that."

"It happens." Dave stood up and shrugged. "Should I call Doug back and ask him to talk to his sister?"

"I'm not sure if that will make things better or worse," Faith confessed as she rose to her feet and picked up the empty pink box. "Sue Ellen just hates me."

"That's because she's always had a thing for Danny Miller and he's never even looked at her."

"That's hardly my fault," Faith reminded him. "She's had seventeen years to make an impression on him without me being around."

Dave grinned. "That's the spirit, Sis."

Faith followed him out to the back of the clinic where

they checked on the remaining animals before closing up the building. One of them would come down at midnight to check again.

"Any plans for the evening?" Faith inquired as they went into the parking lot.

"I'm on call, so no." Dave paused. "Unless you're offering—"

"I'm going out." Faith put down that notion straight-away. "To Morgantown."

"That's hardly out. Are you going to see Nancy? She said she'd graciously decided to talk to you again."

"Well, I am going to the Red Dragon," Faith said. "I'm meeting Red Ramirez for a drink."

"Fast worker." Dave grinned.

"Me or him?"

"Both of you. He's a nice guy," Dave said as she got into her truck. "Be gentle with him."

"We're not going out or anything," Faith hastened to add.

"Whatever helps you sleep at night." Dave gave her an exaggerated wink. "As I said, he's a good guy so don't wear him out. What time are you 'seeing Red'? Ha ha."

As Faith had no intention of telling Dave that she'd also agreed to meet Danny she went with deliberately vague.

"I've got to do some errands in town, so I'll text him when I'm ready to meet up."

"Can you bring me back a pizza?" Dave asked plain-tively. "I don't mind when it arrives. I can eat pizza whenever."

"Sure, why not?" Faith agreed. From what she remembered, the pizza place was only a five-minute walk from the bar, and you could order online and pick up. She'd begun to suspect that if she hadn't been around to nag her brother to share the cooking and eat healthy food he would be living on pizza.

"Thanks!" Dave grinned. "Race you home! Loser makes the coffee."

Dave hared off toward his truck. It was blocking hers in, so she had no chance of winning. She sighed and settled into the seat. At least Dave hadn't inquired too deeply about the state of her love life, being too interested in securing his pizza. She was way more anxious about seeing Danny than Red. There was a lot to say and no easy way of saying it, which was probably why she'd been avoiding the conversation for seventeen years. She wasn't proud of that or of herself. She'd convinced herself that not sharing her pain with Danny was actually the best thing to do, but recent events had made her see things differently.

It was definitely time to woman up and bring him up-to-date.

Danny checked his cell and glanced around the almost empty café. He'd taken a seat at the very back where most people wouldn't notice him if they came in the main door. Despite reminding himself that he was the one who deserved answers his stomach was still tied up in knots. He'd told Adam not to expect him home for dinner and not to say anything about his absence to their father. He'd seen Faith a couple of times around town over the past week but hadn't made any effort to talk to her. It wasn't his style to be confrontational, which was probably why he'd let her get away with not talking to him for so long.

He looked up as the café door opened and saw Faith come in. She wore jeans, cowboy boots, and a strappy blue top that really suited her dark coloring. Even though she'd hurt him, she was still the most beautiful woman he'd ever met. She saw him and offered him an awkward wave as she greeted Lizzie and made her way through the tables toward him.

"Hey." He stood up and gestured to the chair that backed onto the rest of the café. "If you sit here, no one will know who I'm talking to."

"Someone will guess." She grimaced. "It's hard to keep secrets in a small town."

"Yeah, I think we both already know that."

He waited until Lizzie supplied Faith with coffee and topped up his own before asking about how she was settling in with the business and making small talk. He really had no idea how to broach the big subject and hoped she was going to do it for him. He felt like he was owed that at least.

"Okay." Faith twisted her hands together on the table in front of her and took a deep breath. "We should talk about what happened when I left Morgan Valley."

"Sure." Danny wasn't in the mood to piss around the issue. "I'd like to know why you didn't contact me after the baby was born."

"I did." Faith frowned. "I even sent you pictures. I was hurt when you didn't bother to acknowledge them."

"If you did send pictures, I never saw them." Danny studied her face. "The only thing I was told was that you'd had a baby boy and that you'd called him Marcus."

"*We* chose that name together, Danny. It wasn't just me, and *we* had a baby," Faith reminded him.

"That's what I thought, but your family made it very clear that I was to have nothing to do with you or the baby."

"I asked one of the nurses at the hospital to mail the letter when my parents weren't looking," Faith said. "When

I didn't hear back, I called the ranch and your father answered. He said you weren't around and not to call back because you didn't want to talk to me."

Danny set his jaw. "That was probably because your father threatened to take me to court because you were only seventeen when you got pregnant."

"I don't believe you." Faith frowned. "My dad would *never* do something like that."

"So, you're calling me a liar?" Danny raised an eyebrow.

"I don't know." Faith flung her hands out. "Maybe you misheard him, or he just said it in a moment of anger."

"I heard him perfectly, Faith, and so did Deputy Sheriff Rosas, who was standing right next to him at the time." He met her defensive gaze. "I was seventeen and totally convinced I would be thrown into jail if I didn't do what he said."

"Which was what? Ignore me and your son for the rest of our lives?"

"I'm not sure why you think you have a right to get angry here, Faith," Danny said slowly. "When I'm the one who was run off by you and your family."

"And you think I went along with it?" she asked.

"I didn't hear any different from you." Danny shrugged. "What was I supposed to think?"

"So, let me get this straight." Faith raised her chin. "I'm supposed to believe everything you just told me, but you can conveniently ignore the fact that I sent you a letter you never replied to."

"I never got that letter!" Danny only realized he'd raised his voice when Faith winced.

"And I never *ever* heard my dad threaten to prosecute you." She shot to her feet. "I knew this was a mistake. I should never—"

"Have tried to make things right?" Danny stood too. "If this is your idea of apologizing then maybe you'd better rethink the way you approach things."

"Maybe you should take some responsibility here as well, Danny Miller. How the hell do you think I felt being seventeen and all alone in the hospital having a baby?"

Danny stared at her and finally got ahold of himself. He never lost his temper and he couldn't believe how quickly he'd gotten fired up. "I can't imagine. It must have been incredibly tough."

"Yes, it was." She looked away from him. "I have to go. I'm meeting someone."

"Right now? You don't want to finish this conversation?"

"With you jumping down my throat every time I speak? No, I can't say that I do." Her voice trembled and he felt it like a kick in the gut. "I'm not the villain here, Danny."

"I know that—look, can we start again?" He sucked in a breath. "It's not like me to get rattled so easily and we got off on the wrong foot."

"When you accused my father of threatening to put you in jail."

Danny met her gaze. "It's the truth, I swear it."

She shook her head. "I can't believe that."

"Which is why we're in this situation to begin with because when it came down to it you always trusted your family more than you did me."

"That's not fair." Her eyes flashed fire.

"Life's not fair, Faith. My father taught me that." He shrugged. "Maybe this was a mistake and we should've left all this shit where it belonged in the past."

"Maybe it was. Good night, Danny." She turned away,

but not before he'd seen the glint of tears in her eyes. "I'll try and keep out of your way as much as possible, okay?"

He watched her walk out with her head held high, sank back down on his chair, and covered his face with his hands. For someone who prided himself on being the levelheaded member of the Miller family he'd sure gotten angry fast. His father would be proud.

"Wow."

He looked up to see Evan looming over him.

"God, not you. Go away."

"You really screwed that up." Evan took the chair Faith had just vacated. "And what the hell is this about you and Faith having a kid?"

Faith walked past Lizzie without a word and almost ran back to the parking lot where she got into her truck and locked the door. Not that she expected Danny to come after her or anything. He'd made it pretty clear how he felt about her. Away from his cool, condemning stare she fought the urge to cry. How could he think her father would threaten him like that? Her dad was the sweetest guy she'd ever met apart from Danny himself.

Although Danny certainly hadn't been sweet to her earlier. She'd always known he had backbone, but she hadn't reckoned on dealing with a man who knew his own worth and wasn't going to allow her to ignore his truth. In their teens he'd been happy to let her boss him around and been a rock when she'd discovered she was pregnant with their child. He'd single-handedly organized the trip to Vegas where they'd hoped to get married so they could return home and make their own little family.

Of course, they'd gotten that all wrong, and no one in

Vegas was willing to marry them without parental consent. And then she'd gone into labor earlier than expected and Danny had to call her parents for help anyway. After that, it had all been a bit of a blur. She vaguely remembered Jeff Miller and her parents having an argument over her hospital bed until a nurse had ordered them all to get out. When she'd finally woken up after the emergency caesarian, they'd been no sign of Danny or his father and her parents had refused to discuss the matter.

Faith took a deep, shaky breath. She needed to get a grip. Danny was right that she should have left things well alone—except now she knew that both of them had believed the worst of each other. She stared out of the muddy windscreen at the row of lights at the back of Main Street. Was there any way to fix things now? Was it simply too late?

She jumped as someone knocked on the window and turned to see Red Ramirez grinning at her. His smile faded as she lowered the window.

"Hey, are you okay? I didn't mean to startle you."

"I was just thinking too hard." Faith found a smile somewhere. "I was just about to send you a text."

He studied her for a long moment. "You want a rain check on that date?"

She nodded. "I don't think I'd be very good company tonight."

"No worries." He tipped his hat to her. "Call me when you're ready."

"Thanks, Red. I really appreciate it," Faith said as he walked off toward the bar. He raised his hand in a final farewell as he disappeared between the two buildings.

She fired up the engine and put on her seat belt. There was plenty of paperwork to get through from the past week and if Dave got too many emergency calls? Then she was more than willing to help out. Anything had to be better than sitting around thinking about her terrible meeting with Danny Miller.

"Evan . . ." Danny looked at his brother, who was now helping himself to Danny's abandoned cup of coffee. "Were you spying on me?"

"Hell, no. I just came in to get some coffee and ask Lizzie if Adam left his phone at her place. I saw him when he arrived home and he was looking everywhere for it."

"That's why you came all the way into town?"

Evan wrinkled his brow. "Man, you're super salty and suspicious today. Anyone would think you'd been hiding great big honking mind-blowing secrets from your own brother or something."

"It wasn't just my secret to keep," Danny reminded him. "And, if you breathe a word of it to anyone, I'll know it was you and I'll kill you."

"Like, really?" Evan looked interested. "But you'd make it look like an accident, right? Because otherwise you'd be spending the rest of your life in jail."

"I wouldn't care if you were dead."

"Wow, that's harsh." Evan sat back. "So, when did this all go down? It must have been when you were both in high school because Faith left for college at the end of the year and never came back." Evan paused and fake gasped. "That's why she never came back."

"Wow, no shit, Sherlock." Danny lowered his voice. "Look, you really must keep this to yourself, okay?"

"Of course I will." Evan looked pained. "You're my favorite brother."

"Only because I'm the next youngest and we had to share a room, and you imprinted on me like some kind of demented baby bird when Mom left."

"Squawk," Evan said. "What happened to the baby?"

"He was adopted."

"Is that weird knowing that somewhere in the world you have a seventeen-year-old kid walking around?"

"I try not to think about it," Danny confessed. "I just hope he's living his best life and has great parents."

There was no way he was going to tell Evan how he really felt about his unreachable son, how many times he'd wondered if he'd ever unknowingly passed the boy on the street.

"I can't even get my head around it," Evan said.

"Luckily, you don't have to."

"But I'm an uncle."

"And it's not all about you." Danny fixed his irrepressible younger brother with a hard stare. "Faith and I were just kids caught up in a terrible situation, which we tried to make the best of for all of us."

Except, he'd tried to make them into a family so they could keep the baby and screwed that up as well. He grimaced. Dammit, he couldn't leave things as they were with Faith. There were still things he needed to know.

"I have to go." Danny picked up his keys. "I ordered pizza from Gina's to pick up at six."

"Cool." Evan stood too. "Can you text Dad and ask him to tell Adam I have his phone? I forgot to bring mine with me. Lizzie's going to come and get Adam's cell from her apartment. She was going to drive all the way up there just to give it to him." He tutted. "She's *way* too nice to him. I'll go home and get things set up for dinner."

"Sure. I'll see you back there."

Evan touched his shoulder, his expression unusually serious. "Danny, seeing as I know what I know, if you ever need to talk about it to someone, I'm here for you."

"Thanks."

Despite all his joking, Evan wasn't the kind of guy who spread other people's business around. Danny trusted him implicitly. He hoped he'd never have to talk to Evan about Faith and the baby again, but it was good to know he had an option. The only other person who knew was his father, and that was never going to happen.

Danny scanned the streets but there was no sign of Faith or her truck. He headed down the street toward the pizza place opposite Ted Baker's gas station. Even the delectable scents of garlic, cheese, and tomatoes couldn't dispel his foul mood. He managed to find a smile as he checked on his order with Gina, the owner, and stood back to wait.

Mikey Baker came in from the back and went straight to his boss.

"Did Faith McDonald pick up her pizza?"

Gina checked the warming ovens. "Nope, I haven't even made it yet. Why are you asking?"

"Dave called wondering where it was."

"Then call Faith and ask her whether she wants us to deliver it to Dave, or if she still wants to pick it up herself," Gina said patiently.

"Will do." Mikey disappeared into the back again as Gina rolled her eyes.

"Dave sure does love his pizza," Danny remarked.

"Yes, he told me in all seriousness the other day that he often wished he'd dropped out of veterinary college and learned to make pizza in Italy instead," Gina said. "I told him he's welcome to come and work here for free anytime he likes."

Mikey came back. "Faith says she forgot all about it, but if you make it, she'll turn around and come right back."

"Was she on her way home?" Danny asked.

"I guess so," Mikey said.

"Then, if you like, I'll take it along with mine and save her the trip."

Gina and Mikey both stared at him, which made him realize that literally everyone in town, even the newcomers, knew all about him and Faith.

"Are you sure?" Gina asked. "It'll be ready about the same time as yours."

"Absolutely." Danny turned to Mikey. "Call Faith and tell her the pizza will be delivered and not to worry about coming back." He got out his phone and sent a text to Evan.

> Meet me in the parking lot when you're ready to
> leave. I need you to take the pizza home.

Faith went into the kitchen, which still felt empty without her mother's warm presence in it, and poured herself a glass of water. Dave was already seated at the table along with a stack of paper plates, napkins, and an eager expression which turned to a pout when he noticed her empty hands.

"Where's the pizza?"

"It's on its way." Faith took her water glass over to the table and set it beside Dave's beer. "I'm sorry, I got distracted and forgot to pick it up in person."

"Weren't you going on a date?" Dave asked.

"I wasn't really feeling it." Faith stuck to as much of the truth as she could. "It's been a stressful day."

"Yeah, what with the Brysons and the staff all talking about you behind your back." Dave folded his napkin into some kind of bird. "They all come and complain to me like I'm going to do something about it."

"Like I need more people talking shit about me," Faith murmured. "I was hoping folks would judge me by my work, not by my past mistakes."

"Oh, honey." Dave patted her hand. "This place has barely made it into the twentieth century, let alone this one, of course they're going to judge you." He paused. "Although it would be nice to know, as your brother, why you didn't come home."

"Mom and Dad never told you?" Faith stared at Dave.

"Not directly." He shrugged. "I mean I picked up that there was some dark secret, but as everyone at school said you'd run off with some trashy Vegas cowboy I didn't know what to think."

"A Vegas *cowboy*?"

"Well, you did go to Vegas, and I do remember Mom and Dad chasing after you and not coming back for about a week."

"I didn't run off with a cowboy." Faith considered her reply. Maybe it was time for Dave to know the truth. "Or, not a Vegas one. I went there with Danny. We were trying to get married."

Dave slowly closed his gaping mouth. "Okay. That makes much more sense."

"I was pregnant."

For once in his life her brother seemed completely lost for words.

"I went into labor while we were in Vegas, Danny called Mom, and they were with me when I had Marcus."

"Wow."

"He was adopted."

"And that's why you didn't come home?"

"It was part of it." Faith sighed. "I was quite ill after the birth. Obviously, I hadn't seen a doctor during my pregnancy, and I developed full-blown eclampsia. At one point they didn't think I'd make it."

Dave grabbed hold of her hand. "I had no idea."

"By the time I was well enough to return, I was supposed to have started college at UC Davis. They gave me a medical extension and let me catch up and join the classes when I was ready. After that, it was easier not to come home and face everyone. Mom and Dad certainly didn't encourage me to do so."

"I get it. I'm just sorry I didn't know any of this until now."

"There was nothing you could've done, Dave." She smiled at him. "But I appreciate the thought."

"I could've had a few words with Danny Miller, who happily went on with his life leaving you to deal with all this shit."

"That really wouldn't have been helpful."

"Oh, I don't know." Dave sat back, his usual amiable expression missing. "It sure makes me rethink my friendship with him and all the Miller family."

There was a knock on the back door. "Pizza delivery."

"Door's open. Bring it on through!" Dave shouted back. He released Faith's hand. "We can talk about this later, okay?"

He stood up and walked toward the kitchen door just as Danny emerged holding the pizza box.

"Hey, I heard you—"

Danny didn't get to finish the sentence as Dave swung his fist back and punched him right in the face.

"Dave!" Faith screeched as she ran toward the two men and just managed to rescue the pizza box, which was about to fall on the floor. "Stop it!"

Danny rubbed his jaw and stared at Dave. "What the hell was that for?"

"You damn well know, and I'm just sorry it was so late in coming."

Danny's gray gaze flicked toward Faith and then back to Dave, who was squaring up to fight again.

"It's okay." Faith grabbed Dave's sleeve. "You've made your point; now can we all act like adults rather than idiots here?"

Dave stepped back and rubbed his knuckles. "Sure, but I'm not sorry I did it."

His cell buzzed and he took it out of his pocket and turned to Faith.

"Got a call up at the Garcias'. I'll walk lover boy out, so he won't bother you, okay?"

Danny went to say something, and then seemed to realize it was pointless. He touched the brim of his Stetson to Faith.

"Sorry for the intrusion."

"It's fine. Thank you for bringing the pizza."

Dave turned to the box, opened it up, grabbed two slices, and headed for the door. "See you later, Sis."

Danny's jaw was still throbbing as Dave escorted him to his truck like some belligerent guard dog. He paused before he got in and looked at Dave.

"I guess Faith told you about what happened in Vegas."

"No shit," Dave said. "You complete jackass."

"I was seventeen, your family hustled me out of there before I could do or say anything and kept me away from her for years. You want to fight with someone? Talk to your parents."

"You don't think you bear any responsibility for me hardly ever getting to see my sister for seventeen years?"

Danny met Dave's accusing stare. "Sure, I do, and I own it. But this is between me and Faith, okay? She's a strong woman and she doesn't need you to fight her battles for her."

"I know that." Dave sighed. "Look, I shouldn't have hit you."

"Thanks for nothing."

Danny rubbed his jaw and winced. So much for his impulsive decision to walk right into Faith's kitchen and continue their discussion. Maybe he'd needed Dave's intervention to make him realize how stupidly he was behaving.

"We good?" Dave offered. "That's the first time I've ever actually hit anyone." He glanced down at his hand. "It hurt."

"Sure," Danny said. "As long as you keep all this to yourself. Faith and I have a lot to talk about, and the last thing we need right now is everyone interfering again."

"Got it."

Despite his conciliatory words, Dave still waited until Danny drove away before getting in his truck and following him down to the county road.

Chapter Five

"Dave?" Faith went into the back office of the clinic and found her brother checking up on a dog that had just had surgery.

"What's up?" He gently set the dog back into its cage.

"We just got a bill from the Brysons."

"For what exactly?"

"The two calves that died." Faith glanced down at the letter. "Doug is claiming that my negligence led to their deaths."

"That's just stupid."

"He says I should've left them in the field until he had time to get there and that by insisting on moving them, I subjected them to unnecessary stress and trauma which led to their deaths."

"Bullshit," Dave said. "Just ignore the letter, okay?"

"He says he's going to sue me if I don't pay up."

"Also bullshit seeing as he doesn't even have the money to run his ranch properly let alone pay a lawyer. Does Sue Ellen know what he's up to?"

"She was standing right there when I brought the calves

in, and she's the one who told me to leave and not to charge her a dime for my services, so I guess she does."

"Shame no one else heard that," Dave said.

"Someone did." Faith met his gaze. "Danny Miller drove the trailer down to Brysons'. What a shame you just punched him in the face. I'm sure he'd be delighted to testify in our defense."

"Dude, he said we were good about everything," Dave protested. "And, hey, how about your relationship with him? That's hardly helping."

"If Doug goes ahead and tries to make anything of this, I'll ask Danny if he'll be willing to write out a statement as to what went down. I mean, why isn't Doug suing the Millers for moving his cows in the first place?" Faith asked.

"Because he and Sue Ellen really don't like you." Dave patted her shoulder. "I'm sorry, Sis. I bet this isn't how you expected things to go when you came back."

Faith went back to her paperwork and was just about done when her phone buzzed. She checked the number, sighed, and answered the call.

"McDonald Veterinary Services, this is Faith."

"Can you come out right now? We have a calf problem," Jeff Miller said. "And don't send Dave."

Faith checked her schedule. "I'll be there in half an hour. Anything specific I should know before I set out?"

"Just get here."

Jeff ended the call and Faith sat back, her mind immediately assessing the many problems facing a newly born calf, and considered what supplies she should bring with her. From what Dave had told her, Jeff still preferred to deal with everything himself having an aversion to paying vets bills, so for him to call and ask for immediate help was something.

It seemed fate had decided she was going to be in the Millers' business whether she wanted to or not. . . .

As Faith's truck pulled into the yard, Danny walked out of the barn to meet her. She got out of the truck, turned to grab her bag, and came toward him, her expression professional.

"Hey, what's going on with the calves?"

Danny grimaced. "All four that were born seven nights ago are suffering from diarrhea."

"All of them?" Faith nodded at the barn. "I assume you've got them inside."

"Yeah. Dad found them all down in the field this morning, and we moved them to the barn."

"Any other cows in the same field?"

"Yup, because we just gathered all the pregnant ones closer to the house so we could keep an eye on them. We moved them early this year because the outlying fields are still waterlogged. We weren't sure we'd be able to get to them in time if there were any problems." He groaned. "Talk about bad timing."

"Not necessarily. At least you spotted this fast." Faith waited as her eyes adjusted to the darker interior of the barn. The far corner had been sectioned off to contain the calves and their mothers. She could smell the stench from the door. Jeff and Adam were looking over the metal barriers at the calves and were deep in conversation.

"Vet's here, Dad," Danny called out from behind her.

"About time, too." Jeff Miller was never happy, so Faith didn't take his gruff tone personally.

"Hey, Mr. Miller." Faith set her bag down and joined them at the fence. "Would you like to walk me through what you've observed so far and what was the condition of the calves when you found them?"

She listened intently as Jeff talked, aware of Danny's quiet presence on her other side.

"No problems with their mothers? All of the calves have been receiving colostrum?"

"Absolutely." Jeff waved a hand at the cows. "Look at them. All well fed and being good mothers."

"How about the field they were in?" Faith asked. "Was it properly drained?"

"Yup, we brought them in from the fields closer to Morgan Creek to avoid that very problem."

Faith nodded. "Okay if I go in and take a look?"

"Be my guest."

Even though she'd been expecting to see some dehydration she was shocked by how affected the calves were and how low their body temperatures were. She looked over her shoulder.

"Can you put some additional heat in here?"

"Sure." Adam nodded. "I'll get on that right away."

Faith was also pleased with how clean the barn was. The Millers were conscientious owners who knew the value of a well-managed ranch. After checking all four calves thoroughly she went to speak to Jeff.

"Okay, I suggest we start by administering fluids and electrolytes. I'd also suggest adding a broad-spectrum antibiotic."

"Why?" Jeff demanded.

"We can hold off on that until we have a clearer idea of the underlying cause of the diarrhea if you prefer." Faith hesitated. "Some calves in this situation have bacteria multiplying in their blood, which is why it can be helpful."

"But those antibiotics can also cause kidney damage," Danny said.

"Correct." She glanced over at him. "Which is why I'm okay to wait until we can work out exactly why this happened and successfully treat it. I assume all your cows were vaccinated?"

"Yeah." Danny nodded. "All up-to-date. This just came out of nowhere."

"Then, let's get started," Faith said. "I just need to get some stuff from my truck."

While Adam set up the heating lamps, Danny sent his father back to the house to make some coffee. He'd noticed that by the end of the conversation with Faith his father had been hanging on to the railings for grim life. The fact that Jeff didn't even object when he suggested he help out in the kitchen meant he was at the limit of his current strength. It had been a tiring and stressful morning since the discovery of the downed calves and the realization that something was very wrong. Normally, if it was just one calf, they would probably have just treated it themselves and hoped for the best, but four was a serious problem, even his father realized that.

He helped Faith deal with each calf, following her clear instructions even as his admiration for the woman she'd become increased. She was nothing like her shy seventeen-year-old self, but a confident and secure person in her own right.

"You're a great assistant," she joked as they stopped in the feed room to thoroughly wash their hands.

"Thanks, I've had plenty of practice." He hesitated. "Would you like to come in for some coffee? You've been working your ass off."

She tilted her head to look up at him and he couldn't look away as memories flooded over him.

"What?" she asked softly.

"You still do that little bird trick with your head."

"I haven't changed that much really, Danny."

"I guess not."

She lightly touched his arm. "I'm sorry I got mad at you."

"Right back at you."

Her smile was full of sweetness and he instinctively leaned in to appreciate it and then abruptly straightened.

"Okay. We'll go through the mudroom so we can take off our boots."

Dammit, she still drew him in like a bee to a flower. He really should be more careful. They were still at odds and there was no reason for him to trust her.

"Welcome back," Danny said as he ushered her through into the kitchen. There was no sign of his father, but the delicious smell of freshly brewed coffee hung in the air.

"Wow! This kitchen is amazing!" She turned a slow circle to take in the hand-finished wooden cabinets and long polished table.

"Kaiden did it."

"Your brother Kaiden?"

"The one and only. He trained as a master carpenter."

"It's beautiful." She moved over to the table and ran her hand over the surface. "I haven't seen him in town yet, but if I do, I'll tell him myself." Her faint smile died. "Although he probably won't want to talk, and if he hasn't changed, he'll have no hesitation in telling me why."

Danny shrugged. "He's been busy lately running his business and helping Juan Garcia manage his place. I doubt he'd go out of his way to be mad at you."

Faith didn't look convinced as he poured her some coffee. He went to add cream and sugar and then looked up at her.

"How do you take your coffee?"

"Just like you were going to make it." She half smiled. "I still have a sweet tooth."

He gestured to the table and waited until she took a seat before joining her.

"Is your dad okay? He looked worn out," Faith asked.

"He's definitely overdone it today. If my mom was here, she'd be telling him to sit down and let us deal with things. He's not good at giving up control."

"Who is?" She sipped her coffee, her gaze reflective. "I'm not great at that myself."

"Yeah," Danny said slowly. "I guess I realized that when you went ahead and had the baby adopted before I even got to see him."

Silence fell between them broken only by the hum of the refrigerator and the ticking of the kitchen clock.

"My parents made that decision. They said you agreed."

"Only because I was told that's how you wanted it to go down and that it was too late for me to stop it anyway."

"We did talk about adoption." Faith looked up at him. "Before, I mean."

"Yeah, we did." Danny sighed. "I'm not saying it was the wrong thing to do, Faith. I just wish I'd gotten to see him at least once."

"So do I." She reached out and gripped his wrist as if words were not enough and he covered her hand with his own. "He had dark hair and weighed around eight pounds.

I don't remember much after that because all hell broke loose and I lost consciousness."

"*What?*" Danny stared at her.

"No one told you about that either?"

He shook his head.

"I had full-blown eclampsia. Just after Marcus was delivered, I had a seizure and they ended up putting me in a medically induced coma to save my life."

"*Shit.* I had no idea."

She shrugged. "That's why I don't remember much about the decisions that were made by my parents and your father. At one point, they weren't certain if I was going to make it, which is probably why they went with the adoption solution."

"How can you be so calm about all this?" Danny asked.

"Because for me it happened seventeen years ago, and I've had time to come to terms with it." She smiled. "For you it's all new and it's obviously a shock."

"Damn straight it is." Danny set his mug down on the table. "If I'd known at the time, I would never have allowed them to hustle me away to Morgan Valley. I had a right to be there with you."

"I was kind of upset when I finally woke up and there was no sign of you," Faith admitted. "And when I tried to contact you all I got was silence. I figured you were done with me."

Danny sat back. "I was never—" He stopped talking, aware that he was treading on dangerous ground and unwilling to risk the fragile understanding they'd managed to reach. "I wish I could go back and get a redo."

"Same." She released his hand and focused on her mug of coffee. "We were both so young."

"And foolish."

She smiled. "Foolishly in love."

"I never thought that part was foolish, Faith," Danny said gently.

"Neither did Romeo and Juliet and look what happened to them." She drank more coffee, her expression strained. "What's happening with my calves?"

With his usual impeccable timing, Danny's father chose just the wrong moment to come into the kitchen and sit himself down at the table.

"We're rehydrating the calves and making sure they're kept warm. I'll come back and check on them tomorrow, but don't hesitate to call me if anything changes before then," Faith said.

"It's scours, isn't it?" Jeff asked.

"At this point I'm not sure whether it's just bad luck, or whether there's some underlying cause we're missing." She glanced from Danny to his father. "From what I can tell you've done everything right as far as ranch management goes."

"That's a given." Danny's father nodded. "We run a clean and safe ranch."

"I know it's frustrating when I can't immediately give you a solution, but as you well know diarrhea in calves is both widespread and complicated," Faith said. "It's going to be a process of elimination until we work out what's going on and how to treat it."

"I get that." Jeff fixed Faith with a hard stare. "But don't take all day."

"I won't." Faith smiled at him. "One thing I forgot to ask, have you brought in any cows recently?"

"Nope. All the calves are from Miller-bred cows."

"Okay, which lessens the chance that an infection came

in that way." Faith finished her coffee and stood up. "I'd better get going. I have a clinic in half an hour."

Danny rose to his feet. "I'll walk you out."

After Faith made one more detour to the barn to talk to Adam and check on the calves, Danny finally waved her off and watched her drive away. He returned to the kitchen to find his father still sitting at the table.

"She's a good vet. Thorough. I like that."

Danny got more coffee. "Yeah."

"Better than Dave."

"She's got more experience." Danny leaned back against the counter and studied his father. "Why did you force me to come back to Morgan Valley when Faith was having our baby?"

His father blinked at him. "Where the hell did that come from?"

"A sincere desire to know why you decided to interfere in my life?"

"You were seventeen! What the heck did you know about anything, let alone how to be a father?"

"Mom was seventeen when she had Adam," Danny reminded him.

"That's different!"

"Why?"

"Because we were married, I had this place, and you had nothing but foolish dreams." Jeff folded his arms over his chest. "And I didn't like the way the McDonalds were blaming you for everything. I told them it takes two to tango and that Faith was just as guilty as you were."

Danny winced. "Wow, no wonder they couldn't wait to get me out of Faith's life."

"You were both too young to have a child. We all agreed on that."

"It's a good job your parents didn't say the same thing to you, isn't it?" Danny countered.

"As I said, it was different back then."

Danny held his Dad's defiant gaze. "Did you tell Faith not to call again when she tried to contact me?"

"Yup."

"You're just admitting it out loud?"

"Sometimes it's easier to have a clean break than a drawn-out drama. You'd been through enough," Jeff said gruffly. "I didn't want her riling you up again and putting you off your work."

Danny slowly shook his head. "Do you ever think about the fact that you have a grandson out there somewhere, Dad? A boy who will never know this family or the life he might have had if you'd let me bring Faith home?"

"Can't say I've thought much about it." His father shrugged. "I'm not one for looking back and questioning every damn decision I make. I do what needs to be done in the moment and I live with the consequences."

"Like when you kicked Mom out."

"You've got me there." Jeff rubbed a hand over the back of his neck. "That wasn't one of my best decisions."

"Neither was siding with the McDonalds and stopping me from having a family." Danny nodded at his father. "I'm going to check on the calves."

Even as Faith ran through the list of possible reasons the calves had all come down with diarrhea, she kept hearing Danny telling her that he hadn't known she'd been sick, that if he'd known, nothing would've torn him away from her side. And the way he'd looked at her like she was the most precious thing in his world—like they were seventeen again and deeply in love.

"Stop it." Faith spoke the words out loud like she was really trying to convince herself. "Focus on the calves."

The problem with diarrhea was that it could be relatively harmless or fatal, and the time between when the calf first became sick and death could happen fast. Unfortunately, she was already beginning to suspect that if it was scours it hadn't been caused by flaws in management, but by something infectious. Working out what that was might take time, and vulnerable newborn calves didn't have that luxury.

She reached the clinic, parked up, and went in to find Dave and Jenna in the back office. Dave took one look at her face and offered her his mug of coffee.

"What's up? Are the Brysons giving you shit?"

"Not this time. I was just up at the Millers'. They've had four calves go down with scours." Faith finished Dave's coffee in two gulps.

"Four?" Dave frowned. "That's unusual for them. Did they bring in new stock?"

"Nope, and from what I could see there were no issues with where the calves were born. The field was dry, not overcrowded, and clean."

"So, we're looking at some kind of infection," Jenna said. "What do you think it is? Bacterial, viral, or protozoan?"

"I have no idea." Faith blew out a frustrated breath. "What's the chances that Jeff Miller is going to pay for extensive testing?"

"Small." Dave shuddered. "He takes every bill I send him as a personal attack."

"He might have no choice," Jenna chimed in. "If it is infectious it could spread rapidly."

Dave and Faith groaned in unison.

"Have either of you seen any other cases in the valley?" Faith asked.

"Not yet," Dave said and Jenna nodded along. "But I'll definitely be keeping an eye out for anything coming up. The last thing we need is the whole community getting hit."

"I'm going to bag up everything I wore today and keep my medical stuff separate," Faith said. "If it is infectious, the last thing anyone wants is the local vet traipsing around spreading the problem."

"Jeff would probably claim you were doing it deliberately to increase your revenue," Dave added as he reclaimed his coffee mug.

Faith couldn't help but smile. "He probably would, but I'm still going to do everything in my power to make sure he and his damn herd survive this whether he likes it or not."

Chapter Six

"Come on, Faith." Dave held the door of the Red Dragon Bar open for her. "You can buy me dinner."

"That's very kind of me," Faith retorted as she took in the crowd of locals at the bar and around the pool table. The Red Dragon looked both busy and way cleaner than she remembered it. Jay Williams had obviously done a lot to improve the place since he'd taken it on.

"Hey, stranger!" Nancy shouted out from behind the bar.

Both Dave and Faith went to answer her and then looked inquiringly back at Nancy, who grinned.

"Whoever feels the guiltiest, I was definitely talking to you."

"That would probably be me then." Faith smiled. "Dave says we can eat here?"

"Yeah, go on through." Nancy pointed to the right. "We've still got a couple of tables free."

"Thanks." Faith smiled and walked with her brother into the dining area where she immediately tried to back up.

Dave grabbed her by the shoulders. "Hold up, Sis. What's going on?"

"Millers," she whispered. "They're everywhere."

"It's just Danny and Evan," Dave objected. "They often hang out here on a Friday night."

Of course, because she'd stopped in the middle of the restaurant everyone was now staring inquiringly at her. Her gaze locked with Danny, who looked wryly amused.

"Come on." Dave took her hand and marched her forward. "I'm starving." He nodded at various people in the booths. "Hey, January, hey, Chase, hey, Ted."

Faith smiled along and was just congratulating herself on reaching her table when Danny stood up and blocked her way.

"Hey."

"Hi, Danny." She looked past him to his grinning brother. "Hi, Evan."

"It's good to see you, Faith." Danny was speaking way too loudly.

"Er, thanks." She searched his face. "You saw me yesterday as well."

Evan snorted. "Wow, you're so *smooth*, Bro."

"It's always good to see you," Danny said just as loudly. Faith suddenly realized what he was trying to do when she noticed how everyone else in the diner was hanging on his every word. "And you, Dave."

"Thanks for nothing," Dave said, and turned to Faith. "Will you please sit down and feed me?"

Danny's smile kicked up as he stepped out of Faith's way. "The beef's good and Sonali makes an amazing fried chicken."

"Good to know." She slid into the booth and hoped she wasn't blushing as hard as she thought. "Nice to see you, too, Danny."

She busied herself studying the menu as conversation around her restarted.

"Man, you're really red," Dave commented. "You should probably have a beer or something. I'll go and get a couple, while you order."

"What do you want?" Faith asked.

"Fried chicken basket with curly fries and extra honey mustard dressing." Dave rose to his feet and held out his hand. "Beer money?"

"You can pay for that yourself," Faith said. "Remember, I know exactly how much you earn."

She returned her attention to the menu. She loved beef, but after the last couple of days dealing with sick calves, she fancied something different.

"Hi! Welcome to the Red Dragon. What can I get you?"

She looked up to find a young woman with a notepad and an expectant expression on her face smiling at her.

"Hi, I'd like the fried chicken basket with curly fries and extra honey mustard dressing and the smoked chicken salad, please."

"Got it. Anything to drink?"

"Dave's just getting us some beer." Faith pointed back at the bar.

"You're Dave's sister?"

"Yup." Faith nodded.

"I'm Sonali, I work with Bella, Jay's mom, to manage the diner. It's nice to finally meet you." She glanced over at the Millers' table. "I've heard a lot about you."

"I bet you have." Faith suddenly felt tired. "Probably none of it good."

"I'm so sorry, that came out completely wrong!" Sonali

gasped. "I *never* listen to gossip and always make up my own mind about someone when I meet them."

"Good for you." Faith suddenly felt old. "Would it be possible to have some water to go with our food?"

"Sure! I'll get that for you immediately." Sonali hurried back toward the kitchen just as Dave returned with the bottled beer.

"Everything okay?" Dave asked.

"Just peachy." Faith took a very long slug of her beer and then another one.

Sonali came back with two glasses of iced water and set them on the table.

"I should've known it was you when your sister ordered extra honey mustard."

"It's my signature dish." Dave grinned. "How've you been? How was the class?"

"Excellent and informative," Sonali said. "I can't wait to add some new items to our menu and the weddings up at Morgan Ranch." She glanced over at the other booths. "I've just got to take this check over to the Millers and then I'll check on your food."

Sonali walked over to where Danny and Evan were sitting. Danny immediately stood and gave her a hug. His arm remained around her shoulders as her smile returned and she went up on tiptoe to kiss his cheek. Faith couldn't hear what they were talking about, but the way Danny listened so intently reminded her how good he had always been at making her feel special.

"Are Sonali and Danny dating?" she asked Dave.

"I think so." Dave checked his cell. "They definitely were at some point, which makes no sense when she wouldn't go out with me."

Danny laughed at something Sonali said, which made Faith glance over again. Their eyes met over Sonali's shoulder and Faith immediately looked away. She had no right to question Danny's love life when she hadn't spent the last seventeen years pining for him. She'd gotten married and divorced and learned a lot about herself in the process. Danny wasn't the kind of man who would end up single. He had far too much to give to a woman and she really wanted him to be happy. If Sonali was that woman, even though she looked a lot younger than him, she'd happily attend their wedding and cheer them on.

Not that she was getting ahead of herself. Danny hadn't exactly gone down on one knee and proposed to Sonali right in front of her.

"How long has Sonali been working at the Red Dragon?" Faith asked.

"A couple of years now. Her brother, Dev, is an architect. He's been doing a lot of work for the redesign of Morgan Ranch and the town redevelopment scheme."

"Morgantown looks very prosperous," Faith commented. "Surprisingly so for a little town in the middle of nowhere."

"Yeah, because as a community we got together to decide what we needed to do to keep people here. Before there wasn't enough housing and a lot of our school friends ended up moving away to bigger cities for the opportunities. Chase Morgan's plan is to reuse the historical infrastructure of the town and turn it into housing and build new places for his ranch hands out on Morgan land."

"All very admirable." Faith looked at her brother. "You sound quite passionate about it."

"Well, I am. I love living here and I want this place to thrive." Dave raised his eyebrows. "What?"

Faith grinned at him. "It's just nice to see you being so positive about something."

Even as Dave went to reply, their food was delivered and they both set about eating. Faith soon realized that the new Red Dragon not only looked a whole lot better but offered amazing food as well.

"This is so good," she breathed through a mouthful of tender chicken.

Dave was too busy stuffing his face to form words but nodded vigorously. Faith set about eating as fast as she could, aware that she'd been so busy she'd barely managed to find time to stop all day. Just as she was scraping the plate, she sensed someone standing beside her and found Danny looking uncharacteristically stern.

"Hey, sorry to disturb your meal, but Dad just called. He says two of the calves are in bad shape."

Faith grabbed her napkin and wiped her mouth. "I'll come right away." She paused. "Do you want to come with me, Dave, or should I take you home first?"

Danny turned to Dave. "Evan can give you a ride home if you like."

"That would be great," Dave said. "Just tell him not to go without me while I finish up these fries."

Faith left some money on the table for the meal and followed Danny out to the parking lot. Even as she walked, she went through all the possible scenarios she might encounter up at the ranch. Dehydration was dangerous for calves and sometimes could be fatal.

"I'll meet you up there," Danny called out as he strode toward his truck. "I'll leave the lower gate open."

"Thanks."

Faith got into her dad's old truck, glad that she'd been

the one driving and hadn't had to go back to the house to exchange vehicles. Every veterinarian stocked up differently. She preferred knowing exactly where everything was whereas Dave flourished in a more chaotic environment. As far as she was concerned being able to lay her hands on something that might save an animal's life quickly was worth the endless list checking and restocking.

She followed Danny out through the town and onto the county road before taking a right up to the Millers' ranch. The cow barn was all lit up while the house was almost in complete darkness. She found Adam, Danny, and Jeff gathered around the calves.

"You're too late," Jeff said. "One of 'em's already dead."

"That's not her fault, Dad," Danny said. "She came as quickly as she could."

Faith stepped over the metal barrier and went to check on the calves. One was definitely dead and the second was failing. She glanced over at the row of concerned faces.

"I'd like to try some intravenous fluids if that's okay?"

"Sure," Adam spoke up. "What do you need?"

For the next hour, Faith shut everything out except the calf and its problems. While Adam fetched some hot water for her to scrub up with, she checked the other two calves, who were well on the way to recovering.

Time passed and she became aware of how hard the barn floor was and how her back was locked into a crouched position that would take days to get the kinks out of.

"Here." She started as Danny set a travel mug beside her. "I made some coffee."

"Thanks."

He squeezed her shoulder and looked down at the calf. "How's it going?"

"Hard to tell right now," Faith said.

"I'm going to try and persuade Dad to go to bed, but I don't think I stand a chance unless you can give him an update."

"I'll come and speak to him right now."

She went to rise and groaned as her back protested. Danny steadied her as she finally straightened up.

"You good?" He ran an assessing eye over her. "You look almost as tired as Dad."

"It's been a busy week. Lots of new calves."

She walked over to where Jeff was sitting on a hay bale. "Hey, Mr. Miller. The calf is responding well to the intravenous fluids. She's not in the clear yet, but I don't think there's anything you can do right now other than get some sleep and be ready to help out again in the morning."

"You'll be staying then?"

Faith nodded. "Yes, of course."

"Good." Jeff nodded. "You sound just like your old man. I appreciate it." He rose to his feet.

"Just one more thing before you go—do you want me to send sample tissue to the state lab from the dead calf for further analysis?" Faith asked.

Jeff snorted. "Waste of money when the calf's dead."

"How about a fecal sample from the other calves?"

"Do you think that's necessary yet? We've only had one calf go down."

"That's up to you." Faith held his skeptical gaze. "But if there is some kind of infection running through the herd, the earlier we know, the easier it will be to treat it."

"Talk to Adam about it," Jeff said abruptly. "He's in charge now."

"Okay."

Faith stared at Adam, who looked almost as surprised as she did. Jeff stomped back to the house muttering, which

Faith completely understood because to a good rancher losing even one healthy calf was a disaster.

Adam waited until his father had gone inside the house before he cleared his throat.

"I'd like to do the testing."

"Great. The best thing is that they can run a multiple PCR panel to check for common viruses, bacteria, and parasites all in one hit."

"Sounds good." Adam nodded. "I just wish I knew where this infection was coming from."

"Until we know for sure you'll need to observe strict hygiene rules," Faith reminded him. "Keep everything including feeding equipment, boots, and clothing that you use in the barn away from the rest of the cattle."

"Already doing that."

Danny looked up from his position beside the calf as lights from a turning truck flashed across the open door of the barn. "That's either Evan or Kaiden. Do you want me to go and let them know what's going on?"

"I'll go," Adam said. "You stay where you are and help Faith."

Faith checked her bag and gathered up the stuff she'd need for the test.

"How much calf shit do you need?" Danny asked.

"Not as much as you'd think," Faith replied. "Ten grams should do it and I'll take it from all four calves if I can."

"Be my guest." Danny grimaced as he smoothed a hand over the barely breathing calf's flanks. "The sooner we get this sorted the better."

* * *

His father wasn't the only one impressed by Faith's handling of the calves. Danny was in awe of how she'd handled his father, who had a tendency to set people's backs up without even trying. Before his heart attack he'd regularly gotten into shouting matches with Ron Mac and other ranchers in the valley. Faith had given it to him straight in a calm and professional manner, which had left his dad no room to maneuver.

"Danny!" He looked up as Adam shouted from the door. "Incoming."

He shot to his feet as Evan and Adam came into the barn carrying a calf between them. Faith rose as well.

"Same symptoms?" she asked.

"Yup." Adam looked grim. "And there's another one in the back of Evan's truck."

"Shit," Danny breathed as he moved the railing to one side to allow them to bring the calf through. "Literally."

"Okay, you two start with fluids by mouth," Faith said. "I'll come and check them over as soon as I've got the sample ready to go."

Danny went back with Evan to get the second calf while Adam settled the first one in new straw on the opposite side of the enclosed space. To his relief, neither calf looked in as bad a way as the one he'd just been caring for, but he also knew that things could go downhill rapidly.

"Evan?" Adam called out to his brother. "If Dad's still up when you go inside, don't tell him what's happened. I want him to get some rest. He'll work it out himself in the morning."

"Sure. I'll text Kaiden to let him know what's going on." Evan nodded, his usual easy smile for once missing. "I'm going to check the field again and see if I missed anything. I'll come back and help after that."

"Good." Danny patted his brother's shoulder. "I think we're going to need it."

Four hours later in the early morning light of the dawn, the second calf died, and Faith cursed out loud.

"Sorry." She apologized immediately. "I thought we'd gotten to her in time."

Danny patted her shoulder. "You did everything you could."

"I still hate it, though." She pushed her hair away from her face. "At least all the others are stable now."

Danny urged her to her feet. He only knew how exhausted she was when she rocked and hung on to his arm. "We've got this. Why don't you go on home, sleep for a while, and come back?"

"Because I promised your father I'd stay."

"He won't know if you leave because he's currently snoring like a pig and none of us are going to tell him."

"That's not the point." She raised her chin and met his gaze. "I'm not some fragile flower, Danny. I've slept in more barns than you could probably imagine."

Despite everything he smiled down at her.

"What?"

"Still the same stubborn old Faith."

She sighed. "The one and only."

"How about I get you a pillow and a sleeping bag so you can at least be comfortable?"

She touched his cheek. "Now that would be wonderful."

He was still smiling as he walked back to the house. He wouldn't have to go farther than the mudroom, which was where they stored their outdoor gear. Kaiden was the only one currently going into the kitchen to get fresh coffee and anything else they needed. He'd already laid out fresh clothes for them all on top of the washing machine and added a stack of towels to the shower. No one would be tracking anything infectious into the main living space if Kaiden had anything to do with it.

Danny yawned hard and checked the time. Evan hadn't found any more sick calves, but Adam was already talking about whether to move the pregnant and nursing cows into another field just in case an infection had taken root in the current location. Until they knew exactly what was causing the diarrhea, it was difficult to know just how to react to the threat.

He grabbed a sleeping bag and a pillow, added a travel mug full of hot chocolate that Kaiden had also left sitting by the sink, and returned to the barn. Adam had fallen asleep in one corner and Evan was nowhere to be seen. He walked over to Faith, who was checking the calves.

"How are they looking?"

"Good enough for me to take a twenty-minute nap." She looked up at him. "If you can stay awake that long."

"I think I can manage it." He set the sleeping bag against the wall. "I brought you hot chocolate."

"My favorite. Thank you."

"Yeah, you always loved that, didn't you? I remember . . ." Danny stopped himself. "Sorry, I'm sure you don't want to reminisce with me right now."

She wrapped the sleeping bag around herself and sat down, her booted feet sticking out onto the straw. He stuck the pillow behind her neck, and she leaned back and briefly closed her eyes.

"That's heaven."

"Only the best at the Miller Ranch," Danny said. "No need for all that fancy Morgan Ranch stuff."

She chuckled. "They've certainly got an amazing operation going on up there. Jenna took me to say hi last week. I was impressed by all the changes."

Danny sank down beside her, his back against the wall, his shoulder touching hers. "Dad thinks they're sellouts."

"He would."

"I think they're doing their best to keep this valley alive." He paused. "Did you know my brother Ben does trail rides for them?"

"Ben who married that big movie star?"

"You heard about that?"

She snorted. "Everyone heard about it—even people like me who try not to notice what's going on in this particular part of the world."

"Is that part of the reason why you never came back?" Danny asked softly, aware that he didn't want Adam to wake up. "You just didn't want to remember this place?"

She drew the fabric more closely around her body. "Actually, it was part of the deal I made with my parents."

"Your idea or theirs?"

"What do you think?"

He studied her carefully. "To be honest, I'm not sure."

"Dad said that if they paid for my college education, I had to stay away from Morgan Valley."

"*Why?*"

She shrugged. "I got the distinct impression that they didn't want any more friction with your family, and that me constantly coming back would create problems for everyone."

Danny took the time to think that through. "I wish they'd asked me."

She angled her head so that she could look right into his face. "Would you really have wanted me back? After what I did?"

He sighed. "I don't know. I was angry with everyone. As far as I knew you'd shut me out, made your own decisions, and decided not to come back because you hated me or something."

She grabbed his hand. "Why would I ever hate *you*?"

"Because I got you pregnant?"

"We were both stupid and irresponsible," Faith said firmly. "We both share the blame."

"That's kind of you, but—"

She interrupted him. "Danny, you didn't take advantage of me. In fact, I think I was the one who seduced you."

He found himself smiling. "Yeah, you did."

"So, if anyone is to blame, maybe it's me for throwing myself at you."

"Bullshit," Danny said succinctly.

"Exactly." She raised her eyebrows. "Maybe we should just agree that we were equally responsible, leave it at that, and stop beating ourselves up over nothing?"

He stared at her animated face for a long moment. "You always were the smart one."

"True." She yawned and rubbed her cheek against the sleeping bag. "Now, I really need to get some sleep. Can you wake me up in twenty minutes?"

Even as she was speaking, her eyes closed, and she let out a sigh. Danny couldn't help but lean in and drop a kiss on her cheek. She smiled, making her dimple appear. Danny stood up and walked as far away as he could go before leaning up against the wall. How the hell could he still lust after someone who had kicked him in the teeth so thoroughly that he'd sworn off ever being in love again?

What kind of fool was he? With a soft curse, he set his alarm for thirty minutes and started checking the calves while both Adam and Faith slept on. How long and how far did Faith McDonald have to stay away from him to finally make him stop caring?

Chapter Seven

He'd kissed her cheek.

Faith unconsciously rubbed the spot where Danny's lips had landed as she parked up at the clinic. Even though she'd been falling asleep she'd felt his touch. For a crazy second, she'd wanted to wrap her hand around his neck and keep him close while she slept. He smelled the same. Like the boy she'd made love with in the sweet-smelling grass, whom she'd run to for comfort knowing his arms would always be open for her.

She'd left the Millers' place with the remaining four calves now in a stable condition. Jeff wasn't happy that another calf had died when he hadn't been present, and she'd left him arguing about it with his sons. There were already a dozen vehicles in the client parking lot at the clinic, so Faith knew she was in for a busy morning.

While she'd changed clothes back at the house, she'd spoken to Dave, who was out dealing with calving emergencies in the valley. He'd offered to ask Jenna to help them out while Faith focused on dealing with the scours outbreak. The state lab was usually quick to get results back and Faith could only hope they'd have something concrete to go on soon. Not that the treatment for the calves differed that much from what they were already doing, but knowing what kind of infection they were facing and tailoring that response to each individual ranch would help contain any outbreak much faster.

She went through the back door of the clinic, checked on their recovering patients, and continued into the office, which looked way more organized since she'd arrived.

"Hi!" Trina, the youngest vet tech was sitting at one of the desks typing away at her tablet. "We've got a full house this morning."

"So I see." Faith put on her lab coat. "Any particular reason why it's so busy?"

"End of the month," Trina reminded her. "Payday."

"Makes sense." Faith nodded. "What would you think if we expanded the business and held small pet clinics in town? There's space available in the new medical center."

"I love that idea!" Trina hesitated. "I was thinking about applying for full-time veterinary college in the fall, which means that if I qualify there might be a job here in the valley for me one day." She grinned. "Not that I'm making this all about me or anything."

"I get it, and I'd be thrilled to have you *when* you qualify," Faith said. "And, if you need a reference from me, Dave, or Dad, let me know."

"Thanks, Faith." Trina smiled. "I really appreciate that." She checked the time and swiped right on her tablet. "Time for your first patient. Roman Taylor's brought his new puppy, Splat, in for his shots. He's here with Lizzie. I'll put them in exam room one, okay?"

Faith sighed as she went to scrub her hands. A day without meeting at least one person associated with the Millers seemed to be an impossibility in Morgan Valley. She'd better just get used to it already.

Two hours later after checking in with the Millers, she managed to get home to eat some lunch. She'd promised to go back up to the ranch in the afternoon to take a look at the field the pregnant cows had been held in and check out the rest of the expectant mothers. She nuked a burrito straight out of the freezer and sat at the kitchen countertop in the blessedly quiet house to check what she'd missed in the news.

Her cell phone buzzed, and she picked it up.

"Hey Dad! Are you finally settled in?" Faith waved at her father who had finally mastered FaceTime.

"Yup! We're in Scotland and I'm about to get my dream come true when I play St. Andrew's golf course." He smiled. "Your mom's decided she'd rather go shopping."

"Sensible woman. How's the jet lag?" Faith asked.

"Not too bad. Neither of us are great sleepers anyway so we're just powering through right now. How's things at your end? Bankrupted the clinic yet?"

"Not quite, but I'm working on it," Faith teased. "Just dealing with the regular calving season and an outbreak of scours up at the Miller place."

Her father frowned. "I hope you've got Dave looking after that. I'm sure you don't want anything to do with the Millers."

"Dad, I'm practically falling over them every time I step out of my door. And, I definitely think it's time to mend some fences, don't you?" Faith countered.

An obstinate look descended over her father's face. "I

hope Jeff Miller is being civil or I'll have a thing or two to say to him when I get back."

"He said I was almost as good a veterinarian as you are."

"Jeff said that?" He snorted. "High praise indeed. He always told me I was an incompetent butcher to my face."

"Well, you two do have something of a history, don't you?" Faith said. "And what happened between me and Danny certainly didn't help."

Her father smiled. "To his credit, Danny Miller has turned out to be nothing like his father."

"He's always been a good guy." Faith hesitated. "That's why I fell in love with him in the first place."

"Honey, you weren't in love." Her dad chuckled. "You had a silly teenage crush on him that nearly destroyed your future."

"It was hardly a crush," Faith pointed out. "We were together for two years. That's longer than some people stay married."

"Don't get all dramatic, sweetheart. You were just kids who eventually needed your parents to step in and sort things out for you."

Something about her father's tone made Faith sit up straight. "Did you threaten to prosecute Danny if he tried to contact me back then?"

Her father frowned. "Why are you bringing this up after all this time?"

"Because I'm living here now, and I need to know the truth," Faith countered.

He shrugged. "I might have laid it on a bit heavy back then, but it was for your own good. The last thing any of us wanted was the two of you getting back together. You nearly died, Faith. We were terrified and having to deal with Danny and his father at that point wasn't an option."

"He didn't even know how ill I was."

"Good." Her father nodded. "That was the point. We didn't want him rushing back to Vegas thinking you needed saving or something. It was much better for you to regain your health while he remained in blissful ignorance in Morgan Valley."

"Better for whom, Dad? You?"

He frowned. "That's hardly fair, Faith. Everything we did was with your best interests at heart."

"So poor Danny didn't get to see his own child or have any say in what happened to him."

"He was asked his opinion and he agreed to the adoption." Her dad's eyebrows rose. "You're defending Danny now? Four weeks back and you're completely under his spell again?"

"Of course I'm not," Faith said impatiently. "It's just that I was led to believe he abandoned me in Vegas and that wasn't true, was it?"

"You were just kids." His tone softened. "One day when you become a parent, you'll understand why we did what we did."

"Except that between you, Mom, and Jeff Miller I never got the opportunity to be a mother to my own child, did I?" Faith only realized how angry she was when her voice started to shake. "You made decisions that affected both Danny and me without consulting either of us!"

"Faith, this is ridiculous." Her father's cheeks went red. "And, if I might say, so very ungrateful. I'm surprised at you. I suggest we end this conversation right now. When you have calmed down and thought things through, maybe you'll have the decency to call and apologize. Everything we did for you was done with love and with a care for your future."

He abruptly ended the call leaving Faith clutching her phone so hard it was in danger of popping out of her grasp.

"Dammit!" she shouted, and burst into tears.

"Er, hello?"

She swung around hastily wiping tears off her cheeks to see Jenna frozen at the kitchen doorway.

"Sorry," Faith managed to speak. "I didn't realize anyone was here."

Jenna came into the kitchen, her expression so full of sympathy that Faith immediately wanted to start bawling again.

"I'm the one who should be apologizing. Dave asked me to pop in and grab us some more coffee. I have a key and I just completely forgot to knock."

"You're family." Faith tore off a wad of kitchen paper and dabbed at her face. "You don't need to knock."

Jenna took the seat next to Faith. "I'm not sure if I'm about to make things worse, but I overheard a little of what was going on."

Faith winced. Both she and her dad hadn't exactly been quiet. By the end they'd both been shouting.

"How much?" Faith asked.

"The bit about you not being allowed to be a mother to your child." Jenna bit her lip. "You can tell me to mind my own business right now if you like, and I swear I'll never mention this again. But if you need to talk about anything? I'm more than willing to listen."

Faith studied her cousin's earnest face. The urge to confide in someone who was close enough to keep her secrets but not directly involved in keeping them was very tempting.

"If it helps at all, I was adopted," Jenna continued. "And,

I'll always be grateful to the McDonalds for taking me on when my own mom couldn't care for me."

"Marcus, my baby, was adopted right after he was born," Faith said. "I didn't get to meet his new parents because I was in a medically induced coma after suffering from eclampsia right after giving birth."

"That must have been terrifying." Jenna shuddered. "I can't even imagine. . . ."

"They thought I was going to die and that making sure Marcus was in a safe and secure place was a priority."

"Which makes sense," Jenna said, nodding. "But it still doesn't make it right."

Faith sighed. "And I just had a godawful row with my dad about it all. I didn't even realize how mad I was after all this time until he suggested that as a teenager, I hadn't felt things deeply, or had the ability to love someone."

Jenna reached out and grabbed her hand. "That not only sucks but it's also not true."

Faith's eyes filled with tears again. "Maybe coming back here and having to deal with the Millers every single day in some shape or form was a bad idea."

"The Millers?" Jenna frowned and then stared at Faith as her mouth gaped open. "*You had a kid with one of the Miller boys?* Is that why you didn't come back home after you graduated college?"

"That was the deal, yes." Faith nodded.

"Which one?" Jenna asked, and then slapped her hand over her mouth. "Wow, that was rude."

Faith had to smile. "Danny."

"Ah! That explains what Dave's been ranting about for the last few days," Jenna said. "I couldn't work out why Danny had suddenly become the bad guy." She paused. "You must have been at school together."

"We dated from the age of fifteen and were pretty much inseparable," Faith admitted. She generally avoided thinking about their years together because it had been so distorted by what came next. "He was such a sweetheart."

"I bet." Jenna nodded. "He still is, but there's a lot of strength in him as well. He certainly doesn't let his father bully him." She hesitated. "If you want me to take over dealing with the Millers, I'm more than willing to do so. It can't be comfortable for you up there."

"Actually, Danny and I are fine," Faith said. "We've talked and we're definitely at peace. I'm madder with what our parents concealed from us."

Jenna winced. "When I went to look for my birth parents, I discovered they were still married and had gone on to have and keep their other children."

"Wow. That must have hurt."

"It did." Jenna gave a quick smile. "But Blue reminded me that my adoptive parents not only chose to adopt, but were thrilled to have me and love me one hundred percent."

"That's how I hope it's been for Marcus," Faith confessed. "I still think about him every day."

"Does he know about you?" Jenna asked. "Was it an open adoption?"

"I'm not sure." Faith frowned. "I suppose I should ask Dad, but as he's currently furious with me I'll probably have to wait awhile."

Jenna patted her hand. "I'm sure he'll get over being angry real quick. It doesn't suit him."

"I'm not sure this time." Faith looked down at her half-eaten burrito. "I think I managed to get under his skin and he's as stubborn as I am when it comes down to it."

* * *

Danny came out of the post office with the mail stacked in a pile and took it over to his truck. He could already tell that it was going to be a hot day and had decided to come into town early to get things done before it became unbearable. From what he could see, most of the mail was agricultural supply catalogues and get-well cards for his father. He checked the list Adam had given him, relocked his truck, and headed toward Maureen's, taking the time to nod and smile at any familiar faces along the way.

Evan had come with him and immediately disappeared murmuring vaguely about stuff he had to do, leaving Danny with all the tasks to complete. As his brother had been remarkably reliable as of late, Danny wasn't too bothered by his desertion. If Evan didn't turn up, he'd text him before he left and hope he made it back to the truck.

Faith was due at the ranch to check out the fields where they'd placed the pregnant cows. He and Adam had been over them already at dawn and seen nothing obvious, but Faith might notice something they'd missed. At this point, Danny didn't care who found the answer as long as they put an end to the scours outbreak. There hadn't been any more downed calves overnight, which was at least something.

Danny stepped into the feedstore, nodded to Fred the owner, and went on through to the back where he picked up the items on Adam's very detailed list. Caring for the sick calves had made inroads into their supplies, which now needed to be replaced just in case things got worse.

"Hey Fred." Danny walked back to the front. "Have you got any more collapsible feed pouches?"

"I thought we did." Fred ambled out from behind the counter, his brow furrowed, and came to look. "I just got in. Azalea must have sold some this morning. I can check out back if you like?"

"That would be great." Danny finished his shopping and brought everything to the counter.

Fred returned. "Nothing out there, but I can order some in for you. They'll only take a day or two to get here."

Danny tried to remember how many they already had. "If you could give me a call when they come in, I'd be grateful."

"Will do." Fred checked out his purchases. "How's Jeff doing?"

"Getting better every day."

"Give him my best, won't you?" Fred sighed heavily. "I miss him coming in here and shouting at me for no reason at all. It used to brighten my days."

"I'll tell him." Danny fought a smile as he picked up the box Fred had packed the supplies in. "Have a great day."

Even though it was only just gone nine, the sun was already heating up the cloudless blue sky. As he walked back along the boardwalk Danny wished he'd brought his truck closer to the feedstore. Once he put this load in the back seat, he only had to go to Maureen's to pick up some groceries and he was done.

"Hey Maureen." He greeted the store owner, who was sitting at the front checkout desk. "What's up?"

"Hey Danny." She smiled at him. "How's Jeff?"

"Definitely on the mend." He picked up a wire basket. "Which is why I'm here buying his favorite sugar-and-dairy-free ice cream treats."

Maureen chuckled. "I bet he hates them."

"He does, but it's that or organic fruit, and he hates that even more."

Maureen was still smiling as she turned to help some

customers, leaving Danny to shop in comparative peace. He rounded the back corner and almost bumped into Sue Ellen's cart.

"Sorry, Danny!" She immediately backed up and put herself between him and the cart. "I didn't see you there."

"No harm done." Danny indicated his cowboy boot. "My toes are so used to being stepped on I hardly felt a thing."

Sue Ellen's smile was constrained as she started to back up the aisle.

"Everything okay?" Danny asked as she was usually more than willing to chat. His gaze fell on her cart. "Looks like you're planning on baking or preserving up a storm."

"What if I am?" She raised her chin. "Some of us still value homemaker skills."

"Can't argue with that." Aware that she was behaving really weirdly, Danny tried to throw her a softball. "Doug's doing good?"

"Of course he is." Sue Ellen's color rose. "Just because he's not all flashy like you Millers and Morgans doesn't mean he isn't just as hardworking and capable as you are."

"I never said—"

Before he'd even finished the sentence, she was marching away toward the front of the store. He stared after her and slowly shook his head. Whatever was going on in her life she certainly wasn't happy. He could only hope that she and Doug really were okay.

Even though he was keen to get out of town, he took his time to make sure Sue Ellen had left the premises before he went to pay. There was enough going on in his life without adding the Brysons to the pile.

He emerged into the simmering heat and quickly loaded up the back seat of his truck. Just as he was about to get into the driver's seat, he heard his name being called and turned to see Sonali waving at him from across the street. She wore a green top and jeans that were covered by a black apron with *The Red Dragon* embroidered on the front.

He smiled as she came toward him, a sealed cup in her hand. "Hey! I thought you might like some coffee on the house."

"That's very kind of you." He automatically took the cup. "I'm afraid I'll have to take it and go." He gestured at his truck. "I've got to get the shopping home before it melts."

She fake pouted. "That's a shame. I'm on my break. I was thinking we could hang out for a few minutes and chat."

"Maybe another time?" He searched her face. She was so damn pretty. "And next time, I'll buy the coffee."

"You don't have to do that." She smiled. "It's not like I can't get it for free."

Danny chuckled. "Then I'll have to be more creative. Maybe a slice of Gina's pizza instead?"

"Like a real date?" Sonali visibly brightened. "I could do that."

Inwardly Danny grimaced. "I hate to be the bad person here, but I'm not really in a good place for dating anyone right now."

"Oh." She bit her lip. "I thought we had something going before I went off on my culinary course, but obviously I got it wrong."

"No, you didn't." Danny held her gaze. "It's all on me."

She stared right back at him. "I guess it must be difficult right now with Faith McDonald coming back to the valley."

"Faith and I are cool. This doesn't have anything to do with her." He sighed. "I just think I'm too old and too boring for you. You deserve so much more."

She studied him for a long moment and then her lips twitched. "I think you underestimate your appeal."

He smiled. "Nah, you'd be bored silly in a week."

"I doubt it."

"A month, then."

She laughed and Danny was so relieved he grinned back at her. "If I was ten years younger . . ."

"You'd be younger than me." Sonali shook her head. "It's okay, Danny. I really do appreciate you being straight with me. It's a lost art among most of the guys my age."

"Then they are all fools." Danny held out the coffee. "Do you want this back now?"

"No, you keep it. I'll add it to your next bill."

"You do that."

Sonali grinned. "With interest. Give my best to your dad and Evan, won't you?"

"I sure will."

As Sonali skipped back across the street, the passenger door of his truck slammed shut and Danny noticed Evan was now in his seat.

"Hey." Danny got in and started the engine.

"Hey." Evan didn't look very happy. "What's with you talking to Sonali?"

Danny shrugged. "My irresistible charm?"

"Ha, ha." Evan put on his sunglasses. "Like you have any."

"Obviously you're wrong because Sonali did in fact bring me a free cup of coffee." Danny backed out of the space.

He hoped that Sonali's easy acceptance of his lack of desire for a relationship was as honest as it had appeared. She wasn't the kind of woman who would cry in public or make a scene, but that didn't mean he hadn't messed up.

He'd seriously thought about getting involved with her. She was smart, funny, and seemed to have taken to living in Morgantown, which was something of a surprise for someone so outgoing and vibrant.

"I'm not sure you should be making eyes at Sonali when your baby momma is back in town," Evan said.

"My *what*?" Danny glanced over at his brother.

"I'm just saying. It's not fair to Sonali."

"Like you think I'd do that to her?" Danny asked. "And for the record if either Sonali or Faith heard you talking about them like that they'd kick your ass all the way to Nevada."

"Jeez," Evan snorted. "I'm not stupid enough to say anything in front of them."

"Yeah you are." Danny turned out onto the county road that led back to the ranch. "Just be glad I'm not going to repeat what you said to either of them."

Evan settled back into his seat and stared out the window, which meant that Danny could at least drive in silence. Evan got out to open and close the lower gate as Danny drove through.

"Thanks," Danny said as the truck bounced over the cattle grid.

"You're welcome." Evan cleared his throat. "So, just to be clear, you're not going out with Sonali or Faith right now?"

"Correct." Danny found a parking space in the crowded yard. It looked like everyone including Daisy, Ben, and Lizzie were at the ranch. "What's going on?"

"Oh!" Evan checked his cell. "I was supposed to tell you. Daisy wants to talk to everyone."

Danny shut off the engine, got out of the truck, and was immediately surrounded by a pack of dogs, which now included Roman's puppy, Splat. He patted all the heads and made his way in through the mudroom where he washed up and brought the shopping through to the kitchen. It was a good job it was so large because it was currently full of his family.

His shopping bags were immediately taken from his hands and the contents put away as he was offered coffee and various other beverages. His father was seated at the table having a conversation with Adam, which involved a lot of finger-pointing to emphasize his concerns. Sometimes Danny was glad he hadn't been the oldest son who inherited the ranch. Adam put up with a lot of backseat driver advice from their dad and he was always patient about it.

Eventually, Daisy banged on the table and they all stopped talking.

"Hi!" She grinned at everyone. "Jackson and I have something to tell you."

"Someone bought your startup and you're a billionaire now?" Evan asked.

"I wish," Daisy said. "Maybe next year." She grabbed Jackson's hand. "This is way more exciting. Jackson and I are getting married."

"That's usually why people get engaged, Daisy," Kaiden, of course, had to point that out and everyone groaned.

"I meant we're getting married in two weeks right here." Daisy turned to her father. "I was waiting for Dad to be able to walk me up the aisle."

"I can manage that," Jeff said gruffly. "It would be my privilege."

Daisy's face softened and she rushed over to plant a kiss on his weathered cheek. "Mom and Auntie Rae will be coming, too."

"But, I only just got rid of them," Jeff grumbled.

"We want everyone to be here," Daisy said firmly. "But we don't want a big wedding so it will be family and special friends only."

"Which means it'll be a big wedding," Kaiden said, and rolled his eyes. "Have you *seen* how many people there are crammed in this room right now?"

Jackson laughed. "Not on my side of the family."

"You're kidding, right? Your brother is married to a *Morgan*! That's half the valley right there."

Jackson grinned and looked down at his fiancée. "To be honest I don't care how many people are there as long as I get to marry Daisy."

All her brothers fake-groaned while the women sighed happily.

"We can manage the reception here, right?" Daisy looked over at her dad.

"I don't see why not. There's plenty of space." Jeff looked around. "It was good enough for me and your mother."

Silver, Ben's wife, spoke up. "If it's okay with you two, Ben and I will deal with the catering. It can be our wedding gift for you."

"That's really sweet." Daisy went over to give Silver a hug. "Yvonne's already working on our wedding cake and she says she can easily fit us into her schedule if the numbers don't get too high."

"We can talk about it later," Silver said as Ben nodded his approval.

Danny leaned back against the counter, his arms crossed over his chest, and contemplated his brothers and their partners. He loved being part of such a big family, but sometimes it felt lonely. After the debacle with Faith he'd thrown himself into his ranch work and eventually persuaded his father to allow him to pursue an agricultural management degree, which he'd recently completed. He'd been looking forward to taking the ranch in a new, more sustainable direction. Now he was wondering whether putting all his love and effort into a place he would never inherit had been worth it.

Even as that treacherous thought ran through his mind, he instantly rejected it. He had a deep and satisfying life outside the ranch. It wasn't as if he'd never gone out with another woman since Faith had left. But being hurt so badly so young had really done a number on his ability to trust another human being. He was always waiting for the moment when everything went to shit, and it usually did.

"Danny?" He blinked as Daisy touched his arm. "Are you okay?"

"Of course, sweet pea." He kissed the top of her head. "I'm really happy for you."

She studied him seriously. "Do you have anyone special you'd like to bring to the wedding?"

"Not right now." He smiled at her.

"I thought you were going out with Sonali?"

"Nope. We agreed we wouldn't suit." That wasn't quite accurate, but it would do for now.

"That's a shame. I really like her," Daisy said.

"She's awesome," Danny agreed.

"Danny . . ." His sister hesitated. "Is this because of Faith coming back?"

Jeez, how many times was he going to have the same conversation? Did everyone he knew think he was incapable of moving on?

"Not at all. We're good."

"Adam said you seemed to be getting on really well with her."

"Because she's up here doing her job and I appreciate that." Danny met Daisy's anxious gaze. "I'm not a teenager anymore and we're both capable of being civil to each other."

Daisy went to speak again, and Danny talked over her.

"Can we just drop the subject and get back to celebrating you and Jackson getting hitched? It's way more interesting."

"Okay, fine, but you know where I am if you ever want to talk things through." She went up on tiptoe to kiss his cheek and then went back to Jackson's side.

Danny waited until everyone was busy chatting before turning away and sneaking out to the barn where he immediately went to check up on the four calves. He wasn't sure what was up, but he had this sense of being apart from everything—as if he was an outsider—and he didn't like it at all.

"Hey."

He turned to see Faith silhouetted in the light streaming through the barn door. She carried her bag and had an old pair of coveralls on that looked big enough for her brother, Dave.

"Am I too early?"

"You're good." He straightened up and waited for her to approach him. "What's wrong?"

She frowned up at him. "Why would you think anything was wrong?"

"You look like you've been crying."

"Thanks for pointing it out," Faith said. "Like I needed to be reminded that my eyes are red and puffy."

"What happened?" Danny knew it was none of his business, but he couldn't seem to stop himself.

"I guess I owe you an apology." She looked past his

shoulder and half smiled. "I talked to my dad earlier and he flat-out admitted he deliberately kept you away from me in Vegas."

"He just admitted it right out?"

"Yeah, he was almost proud of himself." Faith shook her head. "I got really mad with him. He told me not to call back until I was ready to apologize."

He grimaced. "That sucks all around."

"You're being nice about him keeping us apart?" Faith asked.

"I suppose he thinks he did it for the best." Danny hastily qualified his statement.

"Of course he does." She sighed. "I didn't realize how mad I was about everything until he suggested that what we felt was just a stupid teenage crush."

"It didn't feel stupid to me," Danny said, his gaze locked with hers.

"Me neither," she whispered.

He didn't seem able to look away as he lowered his head until his mouth met hers. . . .

A shrill whistle made him jerk backward.

"Shit," Danny muttered as Faith touched her fingers to her lips. "I'm sorry, I—"

Evan came into the barn surrounded by dogs. "Hey, Faith. Sorry you got the short straw and had to deal with Danny. Everyone else in the family is stuck in the kitchen celebrating Daisy's soon-to-happen marriage."

"Oh!" Faith backed up a step. "I really didn't mean to interrupt your family occasion. I can always come another day—"

Danny grabbed her hand. "You're good. Why don't you come out and walk the field with me while Evan lets Adam and Dad know you're here?"

* * *

Even though part of her knew she should just leave, Faith allowed Danny to march her over to the fence-lined pasture. Not only was she interrupting a family occasion, but also she'd let Danny kiss her. If Evan hadn't interrupted them, she was pretty sure she would've kissed him back. Was her father right about something after all? Did Danny still have a strong hold over her?

"So, here's where we originally gathered the pregnant cows together." Danny pointed to the left. "It's a well-drained field on level ground protected by trees from the worst of the wind coming off the mountains."

Faith forced herself to pay attention to the terrain, her eyes automatically searching for problems.

"I can't see anything obvious," Faith said as Danny opened the gate for her and they both went through. "Were the sick calves born close to each other?"

"Not particularly." Danny had let go of her hand and was now standing a good three feet away staring out at the remaining cattle. "We're thinking of moving the rest of the herd into the adjacent field just to make certain there isn't an environmental element to the infection."

Faith glanced back at the barn, but there was no sign of any emerging Millers.

"Danny."

"What?"

"Are we going to talk about what just happened?" Faith asked.

"Not if I can help it."

"So, we're going to re-create that time-honored Morgan Valley tradition of not talking about things until they blow up in our faces? Because that's worked *so* well in the past."

He turned to face her, his expression guarded. "It was only a kiss."

"I know what it was, Danny. I was right there."

"The thing is." He shoved his hand in his pocket and kicked a loose piece of turf. "I don't know why I did it."

She studied him carefully. "I think we're working through things that we didn't get the chance to deal with when we were teenagers. Maybe things are going to get a little emotional sometimes."

He slowly raised his head to look at her, his gray eyes guarded. "Yeah . . . I guess I can go with that."

"It doesn't mean anything in the present," Faith said hastily. "I'm well aware that you're in a relationship."

"Who told you that?"

Jeez. Now he looked insulted.

"Um . . ."

"I'm not the kind of guy who goes around kissing other women when I'm in a relationship."

"You hardly kissed me," Faith pointed out. "And, it wasn't that kind of kiss anyway."

"Yeah, well, *we* both know that, but everyone else in this damn valley seems determined to misinterpret everything we do together." He was definitely scowling now. "People ask me about you every single damn day."

"Which is weird because no one will utter your name in my presence," Faith retaliated.

He shot her a look. "Really? I'd take that."

"It's not fun, Danny. It makes me feel like I'm an outsider, and that whatever I do, I will never belong here again."

"That's hardly my fault."

Faith raised her chin. "Did I suggest that it was?"

"Nope." He sighed. "Maybe I should just stop talking?"

Faith caught a glimpse of Adam coming toward her and half turned away from Danny.

"Sounds like an excellent plan to me." She waved at Adam and walked away from Danny. "I'm going to check out the perimeter. Do you want to come with me?"

Chapter Eight

"There are no environmental factors that I can see up at the Millers'. It's always been an extremely well-run ranch."

Faith set her coffee down on the desk and faced Jenna and Dave, who were listening intently. They were having their weekly meeting before the clinic shut on Sunday, something she'd initiated to keep everyone up-to-date.

"The lab results should be back soon, and then we'll have a clearer idea of what we're dealing with."

"Okay." Dave nodded. "So, it's probably infectious. I haven't heard or seen any other outbreaks in the valley yet, and we pretty much cover all the ranches in the area."

"Which is good," Jenna added. "Morgan Ranch is all clear as well."

"Jeff Miller wants the answers right now and I can't blame him," Faith said. "Sometimes I wish I was like Dad and could just yell at him to settle down and let me do my job."

"You still wouldn't win," Dave pointed out. "Even Dad couldn't best Jeff."

"I thought Adam was running the place now?" Jenna looked from Dave to Faith.

"Technically he is, but Jeff likes to be kept informed." Faith took another slug of coffee. "Any other business we need to discuss?"

"Nothing from my end, and I do need to get going." Jenna stood up. "I've got to pick Maria up from Dr. Tio's. She's decided she wants to go into medicine and can't decide whether it's going to be human or animal."

"As long as she doesn't get confused which clinic she's in that's a great idea," Dave said.

"Okay, thanks, Jenna." Faith blew her cousin a kiss. "Tell my lovely niece we definitely need more veterinarians in the family and to forget that human medicine stuff."

Dave seemed inclined to linger, so Faith sat back down again.

"I like the idea of the small pet clinic in town," Dave said thoughtfully. "Although, it's not really my thing. People are more willing to part with cash for their pets."

"And ranchers are notoriously tightfisted," Faith agreed. "It would definitely help our balance sheets. I'll talk to the letting agents about finding space in the medical building, and we can go and take a look."

"Sounds good." Dave reached inside his jacket, took out a check, and waved it in the air. "I almost forgot. I got money out of the Morrisons."

"*What?*" Faith grinned at him. "That's a miracle."

"It's not the complete balance, but I refused to offer them any more credit unless they paid off some of their five-year bill."

"Good for you. Now tackle the Brysons."

"Are they still suing you?" Dave asked as he placed the check on Faith's desk.

"I haven't heard anything official." Faith took the check before it disappeared again. "You?"

"I haven't seen or heard from either of them all week. As I said, Doug barely manages to run the ranch. He certainly doesn't have the cash for stupid lawsuits."

"I feel like I should check in with them, but I don't relish being insulted again," Faith admitted.

"Then leave them to sulk," Dave said. "They'll be quick enough to come back if they need something."

Faith finished her coffee and shut down her laptop. She and Dave would cover emergencies until the clinic opened again on Monday morning, but hopefully they would be few and far between.

"Dad called me."

Faith looked up. "Did he now."

"He wouldn't tell me exactly what was going on, but he sure as hell was mad with you. What did you do?"

"Nothing that affects you or the business," Faith said firmly.

"Was it about Danny? Because he was asking me whether you'd been out to the Millers' place. I told him about the scours outbreak."

"I hope that shut him up."

"Not really." Dave sighed. "Look, he thinks Danny's got some weird kind of hold over you."

"I hope you didn't encourage him with that ridiculously stupid idea."

"I laughed my socks off and told him he was way off base." Dave was watching her carefully. "But you two do have something between you."

Faith glared at her brother. "Can we drop this?"

Dave held up his hands. "Sure, we can. I just wanted you to know what Dad was saying to me."

"And I appreciate that." Faith stood, gathered her stuff together, and came around the desk. "And, if he asks, I have no intention of apologizing for anything I said to him."

"Okay, got it." Dave also stood and looked down at her. "I'm not going to tell tales on you, Faith. What you choose to do with your time here is up to you."

"Like sneak around with Danny Miller?" Faith asked.

Dave grinned. "I think you did enough of that in high school."

"Jeff Miller didn't like his boys dating because it took them away from their chores at the ranch. Danny had to get real creative to see me sometimes." Faith smiled at the memories. "We used to meet up here on Sundays after church when I was checking the inpatients."

"Eew . . ." Dave looked around the room. "I really didn't need to know *that*."

Faith punched him gently on the shoulder as she went by him. "Welcome to my life living with you, Mr. Over-Sharer."

Her cell buzzed as she headed toward the exit and she took it out of her pocket. The text was from Red Ramirez.

Hey, we've got another sick calf. If you can swing by at some point and take a look, I'd appreciate it.

Faith quickly replied.

I can come right now.

She checked the time and called out to Dave.

"I've got to go up to the Ramirez place. Can you lock up?"

"Sure." Dave appeared at the doorway. "What's up?"

"Sick calf."

He grimaced. "Man, I hope it isn't scours."

Faith picked up her newly replenished medical bag. "Not half as much as I do."

"Maybe while you're up there you should arrange that date with Red."

Faith looked at her brother. "What are you? My mother or something?"

He shrugged. "Just trying to think of a way to get you away from Danny Miller."

"Dave, for the last time, there is nothing going on between me and Danny except some really important conversations. Conversations denied us by our parents when we really needed to hear from each other." Faith held his gaze. "If that upsets you, I'm sorry, but if I want to stay here, we have to sort this stuff out."

Dave held up his hands. "Okay, I hear you. I'll shut up."

"Thanks." Faith marched past him to the back door. "I'll let you know what's going on as soon as I have a diagnosis."

She headed out to her truck, dumped her bag on the passenger seat, and started the engine. What was it with everyone in her family cautioning her like she was still a teenager unable to regulate her own emotions? She and Danny were completely different people now who deserved the chance to make things right. What had happened between them had been life-changing and the ripples of that decision continued to this day.

As she drove down the county road and along to the northern end of Morgan Valley her annoyance dissipated slightly. She was still attracted to Danny. She'd almost kissed him earlier. So maybe Dave was noticing something she was refusing to see?

"Ridiculous." Faith said the word out loud. "Dave wouldn't notice if someone dropped a rock on his head."

She pulled up at the lower gate of the Ramirez Ranch and checked her cell for the code Red had left for her. When she pulled up outside the barn, Red was there waiting for her.

"Hey. Thanks for coming up here so fast." He came to take her bag.

"You caught me at a good time." Faith followed him into the newly restored barn. "What's going on?"

Red pointed to the corner of the barn. "This calf is seven days old. He suddenly got sick just like the other one."

Faith went into the penned-off area and quickly examined the calf. "Definitely dehydrated, but not critical."

"Yeah, we started giving fluids a few hours ago."

"Great. Keep it up." Faith hesitated. "Was this calf in the same field as the other one?"

"No, we've taken all our cattle out of there and we'll probably be ploughing it up and using it for something else for a while."

"I can give the calf some broad spectrum antibiotics if you'd like?"

"Is it really necessary?" Red grimaced. "I hate to be that guy, but finances are tight at the moment, and we've already lost one calf."

"It's not essential," Faith said. "But I like to make sure you have all the options. How are the rest of the herd?"

"All good so far."

"Then I'll just take a sample for analysis by the lab and take it from there, okay?"

"Sure." Red sighed. "This is just the last thing we need right now. We're barely making it as it is."

"I get that." Faith got to her feet and brushed the straw off her knees. "Hopefully this will just be another one-off."

She studied the calf. "This one looks way healthier, so I hope we'll get her through."

After running through the protocols for keeping any infection contained, Faith handed over some electrolyte samples from her bag, discussed homemade solutions involving pectin, baking soda, and beef consommé, and asked Red to call her if the calf got worse.

He escorted her back to her truck and set her bag on the passenger seat before closing the door.

"Thanks for coming by, Faith."

She smiled at him. He was about the same height as she was. "I know this isn't a good time for you, but I'd still like to have that drink with you sometime."

His face lit up. "You would? That's awesome." He grinned at her. "Let me concentrate on keeping this calf hydrated for the next day or so and, if it survives, we can go out to celebrate."

"Sure." She smiled back at him. "I'm looking forward to it."

"Dad?" Danny poked his head into the ranch office where his father was sitting at the desk staring into space. "Did you move the trailer?"

"Yup."

"Then where is it?"

Jeff looked irritated. "Where do you think it is?"

"If I knew that I wouldn't be asking, now would I?" Danny tried to keep his voice level.

"I took it out to help a friend the other day."

"Okay, but where did you leave it?"

"Halfway up the back driveway. I pulled off the road."

His father frowned. "Something broke. It was already past sundown and I didn't have time to work out what it was."

Danny was about to say that wasn't like his father when something stopped him.

"You feeling okay?" His father's failure to immediately shoot him down made Danny come right into the office. "Is everything all right?"

"Dr. Tio wants me to come in for some more tests to-morrow."

"Okay." Danny paused. "Do you need a ride into town, or do you want to go by yourself?"

Jeff's hand clenched into a fist. "I don't want to go at all."

"Why not?"

Jeff shrugged. "Because I hate being poked and prodded. If it's bad news, I'd rather not hear about it."

"What if it's good news?" Danny suggested.

"It's never good. Dr. Tio's always going off about some-thing I'm doing wrong." His father sighed. "I'm sick of it, Danny. I just want to be left in peace."

Danny considered his father for a long moment. "If I'd just said that to you, what would you tell me to do?"

Jeff scowled at him. "That's hardly the point, is it?"

Danny carried on. "You would've told me to stop feel-ing sorry for myself, grow a pair, and get down to the clinic before you hogtied me and took me yourself."

His father shifted uncomfortably in his chair. "It's not the same."

"Yes, it damn well is." Danny held his gaze. "Daisy's getting married in two weeks."

"So what?"

"Don't you want to walk her up the aisle?"

"Sure I do." Jeff looked indignant.

"Then get those tests done and I bet you'll be in great shape to do that," Danny said. "Daisy wants you to be there for her and I know you don't want to let her down."

"Okay! But what if that fool doctor says I'm dying?"

"Why would he say that?"

"Because I'm exhausted all the time, I can't sleep, and I miss your mother!"

Danny winced as his father's voice rose with each word.

"If she was here you probably wouldn't be feeling exhausted because she would've stopped you doing too much," Danny pointed out. "What the hell were you doing taking the trailer off the ranch all by yourself anyway?"

"Because I thought I was up to it! And you boys were all busy with the calves."

Danny paused. "Hang on—did you disinfect it before you used it again?"

His father shrugged. "I washed it down with the hose, but I didn't get any fancier than that."

"We've been transporting our calves and mothers in that trailer."

His father frowned. "So what?"

"We've currently got an outbreak of what looks like scours and you took the trailer to another ranch."

"Shit!" Jeff slammed his hand down on the desk. "I didn't think."

"Where did you go?" Danny was already turning toward the door.

"To help the Ramirez brothers. I was talking to Red in town the other day. He mentioned they didn't yet have a large trailer. I brought him back here with me and we took ours up to his place."

"I'll go talk to him." As he walked, Danny pulled out his cell phone and searched for Red Ramirez's number. He tried to call but wherever Red currently was there was no signal. Adam was out in the barn with Evan checking on the calves and Danny went to find him.

After sharing what had happened, Danny considered whether to ride over to the Ramirez place or drive. It was quicker cross-country, but the heat was already building in the cloudless blue sky.

"Take Spot," Adam said, his expression grim. "He needs a runout and he's big enough to get over those boundary fences if you need to."

"Okay." Danny quickly saddled up his brother's black-and-white paint horse, grabbed some water, and mounted up. "If you hear from Faith or Dave, let them know what went down, okay?"

"Will do." Adam shook his head. "How the hell could Dad have been so careless?"

"He's got a lot on his mind," Danny said diplomatically. "I bet he's beating himself up over what he did right now."

"I'll check in with him and make sure the trailer gets fixed and thoroughly disinfected." Adam nodded. "Now get going."

Normally Danny loved being on the back of a horse and out on the ranch connecting with his family's space, but now he was more concerned with getting to the Ramirez place as fast as possible. What he was going to say when he got there was debatable, but he had to let them know what was going on. The last thing the valley needed was a massive outbreak of scours because no one was talking to each other.

He increased his pace and Spot responded, gathering his powerful body for the jump over into the Gomez Ranch with ease. Danny was already sweating as the sun beat down on him, and he tried to focus on the quickest route through to the Ramirez place. He bent his head to avoid some low-hanging branches and suddenly emerged into the pastureland around the ranch buildings. There were a couple of trucks parked outside the barn, but that didn't necessarily mean anyone was home.

Two dogs started barking as he approached, and he waved at Red, who was now looking his way. It wasn't until he got a bit closer that he realized Faith was standing right next to him. He couldn't decide whether he was pleased to see her, so he didn't have to call, or worried about why she was there.

"Hey, Red, Faith." He pulled up his horse and looked down at Red. "Sorry for the unexpected arrival, but I couldn't get you on your cell."

Red grimaced. "I definitely need a new phone. What's up, Danny?"

Danny dismounted and Red showed him a shady place with access to water where he could safely leave Spot.

"I should be going," Faith said, her gaze already moving toward her truck.

"You might want to stay to hear what I've got to say first," Danny said, and turned back to Red. "My dad said he lent you our trailer."

"Yup." Red nodded. "It was very kind of him."

"The thing is—we've got a suspected outbreak of scours at our place. Dad didn't fully disinfect the trailer before he lent it to you." Danny paused. "I just wanted you to know in case you encounter any problems."

Red sighed. "We already have." He looked over at Faith. "Ask the vet."

Danny silently cursed. "What's going on?"

"Red has a calf with severe diarrhea and dehydration. We're currently giving it fluids and electrolytes," Faith said.

"Damn." Danny looked Red right in the eye. "I'm sorry. If it has anything to do with us, I can guarantee we'll pay for any damages."

"That's good of you." Red nodded. "I hate to be that person, but we're running low on cash and good vibes right now."

"I'm fairly confident the calf will recover," Faith said. "Red called me in early."

"Good." Danny nodded. "If you need any help, I can send Evan over."

"It's okay." Red nodded. "I think Beau and I can handle it. So far there's only one affected."

"Let's hope it stays that way," Danny said.

"Amen to that," Faith agreed. "I need to get this sample off to the lab. As soon as I get the results, we can compare them to the Miller Ranch ones."

"Makes sense." Danny tipped his Stetson to Faith. "Thanks."

"You're welcome." Faith turned to Red. "I'll call you about the other thing, okay?"

"Absolutely." Red's smile lit up his face. "I can't wait."

They both watched her drive away before Red turned to Danny. "Come and get something to drink before you go back. It's absolutely sweltering out here."

"Sure."

Danny followed Red into the welcoming shade of the old ranch house, pausing to take off his boots and wash up in the mudroom before proceeding to the kitchen, which still had a very 1960s vinyl vibe to it.

"Iced tea okay?" Red asked.

"Great." Danny accepted the tall glass and wandered over to check out the view from the window. "You've got a great view of the mountains up here."

"Yeah. Not sure if it makes it worth all the other shit." Red joined him. "I'd much rather have a view of Morgan Creek and all that water."

"I hear you." Danny nodded. "Still is pretty though."

When drought hit the upper valley things could get dicey real quick. It was one of the reasons why the original occupants of the valley had moved their town from Morganville down to Morgantown, which was closer to the creek. Fighting summer fires without a water source was also a major cause of worry for the ranchers in the outlying high valley.

He sipped his tea and enjoyed the condensation rolling down the glass over his fingers. "I'm really sorry about the calves, man. It's not like my dad to forget important stuff like that."

Red shrugged. "It was still kind of him to offer to help, and we're not even sure the calves were infected by you guys. It could still be something else."

"That's nice of you, but I sure as hell feel guilty."

"Don't." Red smiled. "And every cloud has a silver lining. Getting Faith up here to see the calves meant she remembered to reset our date."

"Cool," Danny said, and took a big slug of tea.

Red cleared his throat as if suddenly realizing who he was talking to. "But it's not like we're really dating or anything. We're just friends."

"Nothing to do with me." Danny finished his tea. "I'd

better be going. I don't want to leave Spot standing in that heat for too long."

He rinsed his glass in the sink and set it on the avocado-green countertop. "Thanks for the drink."

"You're welcome." Red headed out and Danny followed him.

"Let me know what's going on with the calves. If you need me or Evan to come over and help out just holler," Danny said as he tightened Spot's girth and mounted up.

"Will do. And thanks again for coming."

Danny nodded, turned Spot's head to the left, and set off back toward the copse of trees. He didn't need to rush back, being more interested in finding shade to keep Spot cool on the return trip. It also gave him time to consider his gut reaction to the idea of Faith dating Red. He didn't like it. Intellectually he knew Faith's choices had nothing to do with him, but at some level he still thought of her as his soulmate, which was stupid as hell.

It wasn't as if either of them had spent the last seventeen years pining for the other. He'd dated other women and he was fairly certain Faith had been in relationships, too. But her being here, in Morgan Valley, was stirring up all kinds of emotions in him that he thought he'd buried for good.

Danny sighed as he set a course for the next group of trees. Maybe he shouldn't have buried all that shit in the first place. He tried to imagine what his father would've done if Danny's seventeen-year-old self had asked to see a therapist. He'd been expected to forget what had happened, concentrate on his work at the ranch, and never ever discuss it with anyone. It was the Miller family way and it sucked. Not only had he been deprived of the chance to make life-impacting decisions with Faith about their son, but he'd also been denied any information about her condition. She could've died and he wouldn't have been there for her.

His hand tightened on the rein and Spot tossed his head in protest.

"Sorry, buddy." Danny loosened his grip. "Maybe once I let all this stuff out, I'll feel better."

But who could he talk to? The obvious person was Faith, but every time they got together his attraction for her got in the way and made him behave like a fool. Not that she seemed to mind . . . But then she'd always understood him better than he understood himself. She'd already made a distinction between him working through his reactions to all the new stuff he was finding out and how he might feel about her in the present. Because if he was honest with himself, he didn't really know her anymore, did he? She was frozen in time, his best friend, his first lover, and the mother of his child—a child he'd never even gotten to hold.

Danny set his jaw and lined Spot up to jump the boundary fence. He needed to get a grip. It wasn't like him not to know his own mind and his way forward. Faith was back to stay, and he was just going to have to find a way to live with it.

Chapter Nine

Faith got out of her truck and gathered herself before taking a deep breath and walking toward the Millers' house. She was almost at the side door when Danny came out and stopped right in her path.

"How's it going?"

She tried to smile. "I got the results back."

His face went blank. "Dad and Adam are in the barn."

They walked together in silence toward the barn where Faith could see Jeff gesticulating about something while Adam leaned up against the wall and occasionally nodded. Ben and Adam were built like linebackers whereas Danny was leaner like his father.

"Hi, Mr. Miller, Adam." Faith set her bag on the ground. "I got a call from the lab this morning with the test results."

"Well, go on, then." Jeff gestured impatiently. "Spit it out."

"You've got E. coli and cryptosporidium."

Danny whistled. "Damn."

"The E. coli is very common and is bacterial in nature so by itself it's more treatable. The cryptosporidium is a protozoan parasite. It adheres to the cells that line the small intestine and damages the microvilli," Faith said. "It's harder to treat, but at least we now know what we're dealing with. The antibiotics I suggested wouldn't have worked on crypto."

"Glad I saved my pennies, then," Jeff said. "And I still don't know where this infection came from." He looked around at his silent sons. "What the hell have you been doing to this place while I've been laid up?"

"Nothing you wouldn't have approved of." Adam obviously wasn't having it. "And you've hardly been absent. You've been micromanaging me from your bed since the day you came back from the hospital."

"Obviously not well enough," Jeff snapped, and turned to Faith. "What happens next?"

"We keep a very close eye on the rest of the herd and hope that the infection hasn't spread any further."

"Obviously," Jeff snorted.

Faith took a deep breath. "And I think we should let the other ranchers in Morgan Valley know what's going on."

Jeff looked at her for a very long moment, but she didn't look away.

"Sure, why not? Let them know how incompetent the Miller boys are."

"Dad." Adam frowned. "That's really not helpful."

Faith gestured at the remaining calves in the barn. "Keep giving these guys fluids and electrolytes until they fully recover and then place them in a separate field from the rest of the herd just as a precaution." She looked at Adam. "You've had a couple of days without any new cases, right?"

"Yup."

"That's good." She paused. "Are you one hundred percent

sure that this current group of infected calves weren't brought in from outside?"

"They are all ours," Jeff stated. "I don't hold with buying in unless I have to."

"Okay." Faith paused to think. "Were they at any time in a group by themselves?"

"Like a prayer group?" Evan, who had arrived while Faith was speaking, spoke up. "Or a band?"

Faith just managed not to roll her eyes. "I meant like all in one field."

Danny frowned. "We did round them up from a few different locations on the ranch to bring them closer to home. I'd have to go check the records to see who we fetched from where, but I can definitely do that."

"Danny and Daisy set up this really cool interactive site for monitoring where the cattle are in real time on the ranch. It makes rounding them up using GPS way easier," Evan said.

"That's an amazing idea," Faith agreed. "I wish more ranchers had access to that kind of technology."

Danny shrugged. "Chase Morgan did say he wanted to take a look at it. I just haven't gotten around to sharing it with him yet."

"You should." Faith picked up her bag again. "Is it okay if I check the calves now, Mr. Miller?"

"Go ahead." Jeff sat down on a hay bale. He looked exhausted. "I'm not going anywhere."

"As to everything else you've been doing regarding hygiene and maintaining secure boundaries around the infected area keep going. It's obviously working," Faith said. "If it's okay with you I'll let Red Ramirez know the results of the testing, and make sure he is observing the same strict safety protocols."

"Fine by me," Adam replied. "Has he had any more calves go down with this thing?"

"Not so far."

"Thank God," Jeff muttered. "I should never had lent him our trailer."

Danny pressed his hand to his father's shoulder. "You were trying to do a good thing, Dad. You weren't to know."

"Harrumph," Jeff muttered. "That boy's got enough problems without me adding to them." He looked over at Adam. "You'll compensate him for any losses."

Adam nodded. "Already on it."

Evan went off to do his daily check of the pregnant cows while Adam insisted on walking their father back to the ranch house. He only managed it by reminding Jeff that Leanne was due to call to let him know when she and Rae were arriving for the wedding.

"Shit," Danny breathed.

"What's wrong?" Faith looked over at him from her kneeling position beside one of the calves.

"Daisy's wedding. We can't hold it up here when we've got calf scours."

"I certainly wouldn't recommend it." Faith stood up. "Especially since half the guests will be other ranchers. You don't want them taking it home with them."

"The Morgans aren't going to want us up at their place either, are they?"

"Maybe somewhere in town will work?" Faith came toward him and stripped off her gloves. "The hotel or the community hall?"

"Both great suggestions." He grimaced. "Daisy isn't

going to be happy. She was really looking forward to being married at home."

"I'm sure she'll understand. She's a rancher's daughter."

"I guess." Danny sighed. "As I'm the one who thought of it, I suppose I should go tell her."

Faith patted his hand. "She'll be fine."

"Will you come with me?"

She blinked at him. "To talk to Daisy?"

"No, to the wedding."

She slowly withdrew her hand. "Danny . . ."

"I don't know what's going on in my head right now, Faith, but I need to spend time with you." He hesitated. "I think I need to work through what we missed."

She raised her gaze to meet his, her expression serious. "Okay. I guess I understand that."

"Then you'll come? It would be a great way for the whole valley to see that we don't have any bad blood between us."

"Yes, but only if Daisy is okay with it," Faith said.

"I'm sure she will be." He smiled down at her. "Thank you."

"For what?"

"Putting up with me right now."

She smiled back. "It's not exactly hard." It was her turn to pause. "I guess I need some kind of closure of my own, too."

"I'll talk to Daisy," Danny said. "And get back to you as soon as I can."

"Okay." She came out of the gate and shut it behind her. "Do you think you might find time to come over to my place one evening?"

Danny went still. "So Dave can try and thump me again?"

"Hopefully he's gotten over his macho streak by now," Faith said. "There's something I'd like to share with you, and I'd rather do it in private."

"Okay." Danny reviewed his extremely limited social calendar. "How about tonight around eight?"

"That'll be fine."

He was still pondering Faith's invitation as he drove down to town to pick up the promised feeding pouches from Fred at the feedstore. He'd told Adam and Evan about the problem with the wedding location. They'd both agreed that he should stop in at Daisy's flower shop, take her out to lunch, and deliver the bad news. Adam had offered to tell their father, so Danny didn't think he was getting the worst job.

He kept reminding himself that Faith was basically a stranger to him now, but it didn't seem to work. He'd known her for seventeen years, loved her for two of them, and still felt like they were on the same page. During those tumultuous teenage years had they helped form each other's characters? Were there elements of himself that he owed to her for good and bad? It was an intriguing question and one he didn't yet have an answer for.

The fact that she'd broken his heart and changed him didn't seem quite so important as the rest of it now. Knowing that she'd been as helpless as he was at a crucial point in their relationship had somehow healed some of his deeply held wounds. He still wished he'd been there. . . .

"Hey Danny, what's up?"

He abruptly looked out his truck window as Fred waved

at him from the front of the feedstore. He parked the truck, got out and headed toward the entrance.

"Hi, thanks for calling."

"No problem, son." Fred stepped into the store and Danny followed him. For some reason it always smelled of fertilizer, grain, and dirt with a hint of sunshine. "I kept half a dozen back for you."

"That's awesome." Danny considered the store owner. If he wanted to get word out to Morgan Valley, Fred was a good person to tell. "We've been dealing with a case of calf scours up at the ranch."

"Oh, man." Fred shook his head. "That's terrible."

"Yeah, so if you see any of the other ranchers in here, please feel free to drop a word in their ear. So far, the outbreak is contained, and we've had no new cases for the past few days, but it's better to be careful."

"I'll make sure people know." Fred nodded as he rang up the purchase. "And I hope you guys get through it without too many losses."

"Can't disagree with you about that." Danny paid the bill and picked up the paper bag. "If anyone has questions ask them to direct them to Adam or me, and definitely not Dad."

Fred chuckled. "As if I'd let any unsuspecting person talk to Jeff."

Danny had to smile. "And Faith McDonald is our veterinarian so she's happy to answer questions, too."

"She's a good 'un." Fred wiped down the countertop. "I remember seeing you two out and about when you were teenagers. Never seen such a lovey-dovey pair."

"Yeah, we were pretty intense back in the day," Danny agreed.

"Shame she stayed away so long." Fred walked with

him to the exit. "I always thought there was more to it than her just going away to college. She loved this place as much as you did."

Danny shrugged. "People change. She's back now."

Fred nudged him. "You should ask her out."

"You think?"

"Definitely." Fred paused. "When a woman looks at you like that, you know you've found your soulmate. I met Azalea when we were fourteen and I just knew she was the one." He chuckled. "Took her a while longer to decide the same thing, but I kept the faith. We've been married forty-five years now."

"That's awesome." Danny shouldered the bag. "Okay if I leave the truck here while I go and have lunch with Daisy?"

"Sure thing, son." Fred patted his shoulder. "Give her my best and tell her I'm looking forward to attending the wedding."

Danny put the bag in the back seat of his truck, locked up, and walked down the boardwalk toward Daisy's flower shop, which was squeezed in between the Red Dragon Bar and the sheriff's office.

"Just how many people have you invited to this wedding, Sis?" Danny asked as he went into the front of the shop. "Fred at the feed shop says he's coming."

Daisy immediately looked guilty. "It's not me, it's Jackson. You know what he's like. He just opens his mouth and invites everyone he meets."

"That does sound like him." Danny kissed her cheek. She was petite like their mother and had hints of red in her long hair. She'd also inherited their mother's business ability and was a software nerd who still commuted back to Silicon Valley when necessary. "Are you still okay for lunch?"

"Sure!" She stuck a note on the front door and locked it. "If anyone desperately needs flowers in the next hour, I'm sure they'll find me in Yvonne's."

Danny waited for her to find her purse and they exited into the parking lot behind the shop.

"Why do you want to have lunch with me anyway?" She looked up at him. "It's not like you to just drop in."

"I can be spontaneous," Danny objected.

"No, you can't. You're almost as organized as I am."

"True." Danny sighed as he opened the door into Yvonne's and stood back to let his sister go through. "Except I don't have your brains. I'm also not currently running a flower shop and an IT startup that might make me a multi-millionaire."

"You just got your degree," Daisy reminded him as she found a table and sat down opposite him. "That's awesome."

"Took me long enough." He checked out the specials on the board.

"But it's still an achievement." Daisy studied his face. "What are you going to do with all that knowledge? Do you plan to stay with Dad and Adam, or branch out on your own?"

"I haven't really thought about it," Danny said.

"I don't believe that for a minute. You've always planned out your life." Daisy sat back. "What's going on?"

"Maybe things have changed around here?" Danny countered. "Dad's sick, Adam's taking on more responsibility for the ranch, and Mom might be coming back for good."

"I know." Daisy sighed. "I still don't know how I feel about that."

Danny frowned. "She said she'd talked to everyone and we were all okay about it. Are you worried?"

"Only because we have a lot of lost time to make up and sometimes it's hard to let go of my past grudges against her."

"Which were mostly untrue," Danny reminded her. "Because Dad couldn't face what he'd done."

"I'm still mad at him, too, don't worry." Daisy smiled. "But I'll get through this. Maybe having Mom back will help me find the perfect balance."

"I wonder if Ellie will come with her and stay as well?" Danny asked. "It's weird to think we have a half sister we've never met."

"Almost as weird as Faith McDonald coming back after seventeen years away from the valley."

Danny gave her a look. "What's that got to do with anything?"

"You tell me." She met his indignant gaze. "I remember how badly her leaving affected you. I don't think you were even the same person afterward."

"That's one hell of an exaggeration." Danny folded his arms over his chest. "I was just a kid. I got over it."

"Sure you did." Daisy waggled her eyebrows at him. Hanging around with the way too honest Jackson had obviously done a number on her. "You *changed*, Danny. I was there. I saw it in real time."

"No one stays the same as they were at seventeen," Danny reminded her. "You were going to be a rodeo star, remember?"

"Until I fell off the back of my horse doing that handstand and ended up with a concussion." She grinned. "I always wonder if that shook up my brain and helped me develop my affinity for coding."

"Hi, guys!" Lizzie arrived at the table to take their order. "How's it going?" She turned to Daisy. "Yvonne says if you have a minute after your lunch can you pop in the back and talk to her about the wedding cake?"

"Will do." Daisy nodded. "I'll have the big California salad with the shrimp and a glass of iced tea, please."

"I'll have the same," Danny said. "Thanks."

"You're both welcome." Lizzie scribbled on her tablet. "I'll be right back with your drinks."

"Anyway." Daisy barely waited for Lizzie to turn her back before she started speaking again. "I'm guessing you've changed your mind and want to bring someone to the wedding, right? And I'm also going out on a limb here and assuming that person is Faith."

"We thought it might be a good way for the whole of Morgan Valley to see we're on good terms all in one hit," Danny said.

"I suppose that makes sense." Daisy regarded him skeptically.

"She's been getting a lot of pushback from people who think she somehow did me wrong and it's just not fair."

"She left you, Danny, and she never ever bothered to come back and explain herself."

"I appreciate the loyalty, Sis, but it really wasn't that simple. Since she's been back, we've had a chance to talk." He hesitated, aware that he didn't want to give too much away, but also that Daisy was his sister and that she deserved at least some of the truth. "I can't tell you the whole of it because it's not just my story to tell, but just know that both Faith and I were deliberately kept away from each other."

"By your parents?" Daisy grimaced. "Okay, I can totally see Dad doing something that stupid, but the McDonalds? They've always seemed so good with their kids."

"Which just goes to show that you can never tell what's going on behind closed doors. And, I guess they thought they had reason to interfere. We were only seventeen."

"You're way too nice, Danny." Daisy sat back. "You should tell them all to take a hike."

"Like that's going to have any effect on Dad." Danny attempted to set the conversation back on topic. "I did want to talk to you about the wedding, but not just about Faith."

"Okay." Daisy picked up the glass of iced tea Lizzie had just delivered to the table. "What else is there?"

"You know we've had an outbreak of scours up at the ranch?"

"Yup, what about it?"

"We just got the results back from the state lab. It's E. coli and cryptosporidium which is super infectious."

Daisy grimaced. She was enough of a rancher's daughter to know that was bad. "That sucks."

Danny let out his breath. "It also means we can't invite the entire valley up to the ranch for your wedding."

Daisy blinked at him and then slowly closed her mouth. When she remained silent, Danny kept talking.

"Adam and I were thinking you could hold it here in town instead. That maybe the hotel or the community hall could host it. We'll pay for any extra cost." He reached over and took her hand. "I'm really sorry about this, Daiz, I wish things could be different, but we can't be responsible for spreading scours around the entire valley."

"I understand." She swallowed hard and a single tear

slid down her cheek before she shot to her feet. "I . . . just need to talk to Jackson, okay?"

"Daisy—" Danny also rose, but she waved him away and rushed out of the coffee shop leaving him standing there feeling like the worst brother in the world. She was normally the unflappable one in the family and he hadn't expected her to react like that.

"What happened?" Lizzie appeared with their lunch and set it on the table. "Is Daisy okay?"

"We can't hold the wedding up at the ranch," Danny said. "We've got to work out why our calves are dying first."

"Okay." Lizzie nodded, her worried gaze fixed on the door Daisy had run out of. "That's horrible, but I can see why you wouldn't want the whole valley up there right now."

"We thought they could hold it here in town." Danny groaned. "I didn't realize Daisy would be so upset. I should've gotten some feedback and presented her with some definite alternatives before I dropped that on her."

"It might have helped." Lizzie looked sympathetic. "Is she coming back?"

"I don't know." Danny gestured helplessly at the food. "Maybe you could box it up while I try and get hold of her?"

"Will do." Lizzie set the plates back on the tray. "I'll check in with Adam and see if she's gone home."

"She's more likely to be on her way to Jackson's place."

"I guess." Lizzie bit her lip. "I'm sure she'll be fine about it."

"Sure didn't look that way." Danny got out his phone, texted Daisy, and sent a heads-up to Jackson. "Adam's going to kill me. I was supposed to have the easier job."

He sipped his drink and waited to see if Daisy or Jackson would respond to him. He had to believe they were more interested in talking to each other than to the bearer of bad news. Just as Lizzie set the to-go boxes on the table the door opened, and Daisy came back in holding Jackson's hand.

Danny instinctively stood as they approached the table.

"Hey, I'm really sorry—"

Daisy held up a finger. "It's okay. I just . . . needed a moment." She looked up at Jackson, who looked uncharacteristically solemn. "Jackson reminded me that it's the getting married that counts, not where the actual ceremony takes place." She drew a resolute breath. "We're going to talk to Mr. Hayes at the hotel and see if there is anything they can do for us. If that doesn't work, as you said there's always the community hall."

"I should've done that before I even spoke to you," Danny said. "I just dumped the whole problem right in your lap. I'm really sorry, Daiz."

"We're good." Jackson spoke up for the first time. "We'll make it work. I mean I don't care if I marry Daisy in a pitch-black cellar as long as we're married by the end of it."

"Hardly flattering, Jackson, but I know what you mean," Daisy murmured. She gestured at the table. "Can we sit down and start again, Danny? It was really rude of me to run out on you."

"I thought you were very restrained," Danny said even as he relaxed a little. "I was expecting a bridezilla."

"Like I'd be that person." Daisy sat down and Jackson brought a seat over to join her. "It's not exactly your fault we have calf scours at the ranch now, is it?"

"Well, it's definitely someone's fault," Jackson said. "It rarely just appears by itself."

Danny was used to Jackson's plain speaking, so he didn't allow it to faze him. "If we knew how the infection started and where it had come from, we'd be in a much better place to hold a wedding."

"There's nothing up at our place," Jackson added. "And yeah, I wouldn't appreciate it if I went to a wedding and brought home an unexpected infection with me either." He glanced down at Daisy. "I just wish it wasn't our wedding."

Danny nodded as Jackson opened one of the boxes.

"Is this our lunch? Thanks!"

"Well—" Danny glanced at Daisy, but she was still smiling up at Jackson. "Sure it is." He turned to look for Lizzie. "Can we have another salad when you're ready, please?"

After delivering the bad news to the Millers and Red Ramirez, and running the afternoon clinic, Faith finally got the opportunity to go home and grab something to eat for dinner. She was now leaving all the clothes and instruments she used at the infected ranches in a separate place from her usual gear. The fear of cross contamination was real. As she and Dave were the only people who had to travel between ranches the onus was on them to keep the infection away from everyone else. Luckily, when her father had built the new house, he'd added a large mudroom and separate bathroom at the back just for veterinary clinic use, which was proving really useful. He'd even installed a washing machine and dryer out there.

Faith had already changed into a completely new set of clothes before she stepped foot in the house. She checked her cell as she waited for the microwave to heat up her leftover pizza. There was nothing from Danny, whom she was still expecting around eight. There was, however, a text from her mom.

Call me right now, young lady. No excuses.

Faith repressed a sigh. She'd known her mom would get involved in the situation with her dad and that she'd have to deal with it. She checked the time in Scotland and clicked on her mom's number.

"Hello?"

"It's me, Mom. What's up?"

Faith retrieved the pizza from the microwave. There was the sound of a TV and then of a door shutting.

"Okay, your father can't hear us now. Why are you two fighting?"

"We're not. We just had a fundamental disagreement about how he handled the whole Danny and the baby thing." She took her pizza and sat up at the counter.

"He didn't make those decisions on his own. We were all involved."

"Danny wasn't."

"He was still a minor. Jeff didn't want him making any impetuous choices that might ruin his life." Her mom sighed. "I know you think we were highhanded, but we genuinely were terrified that you were going to die. We wanted to make sure that your child had the best chance in life with two parents who loved him."

Faith winced. "Like you think Danny and I hadn't talked about the baby? Or made plans together?"

"Oh honey . . ." Her mom sighed. "I'm so sorry."

"Thanks for that, at least." Faith took a bite of pizza she really didn't want.

"It's way easier to look back and admit that maybe we

made some mistakes, but at the time we thought we were doing the best for *all* of you."

Faith couldn't deny the sincerity in her mom's voice.

"I get that."

"Then will you at least talk to your father? He's so upset he doesn't even want to play golf."

"That bad, eh?"

"Yes, and you know how much he's dreamed about this trip." Her mom continued. "I don't expect you to apologize for what you said to him because you have a perfect right to be mad, but maybe just acknowledge that he thought he had your best interests at heart?"

Faith wasn't sure it felt right to have to make her father feel better for what had happened to her, but he wasn't a bad person. None of them were bad people. Just human. She couldn't change what had happened in the past, she'd confronted him about his behavior, and now maybe it was time to let it go.

"Okay."

"Oh, sweetie, that's wonderful! I'll just get him on the phone."

"Mom—" Faith wasn't sure she was ready to talk to him right now, but her mother obviously had other ideas.

"Faith?" Her father's gruff voice came on the line.

"Hi, Dad."

"I'm sorry I lost my temper with you, sweetheart."

"I get that you were just trying to do your best for me," Faith said.

There was a pause before he spoke again. Faith wondered if her mom was coaching him through the call. "Thanks for saying that."

"You're welcome." That was as far as Faith was willing

to go right now. "Now, go and play golf and have a great vacation."

"Will do." This time there was a definite pause and the sound of muted discussion. "Faith, before you get off the line, there's something you should see in my office. Check the right-hand drawer of my desk, the bottom one, and look for a red leather folder with your name on it." Her dad cleared his throat. "I should've given them to you years ago, but I didn't want to upset you."

Chapter Ten

"Hello?" Danny let himself in through the mudroom and took off his boots and hat. The smell of pizza hung in the air but other than that the house was quiet. "Faith?"

"Come on through."

He made his way into the kitchen, checking carefully that Dave wasn't going to pop out and punch him again. Faith was sitting at the counter with a half-eaten piece of pizza in front of her.

"Hey. Sorry I'm early. I snuck out before Dad noticed and wanted to know where I was going."

Even as he said the words Danny realized how lame it was for a guy who was over thirty to be worried about what his dad thought. He moved closer and then paused.

"Is this a bad time?"

Faith hastily scrubbed at her eyes. "No, it's just that I talked to my parents, and—" She gestured helplessly in front of her. "I wasn't expecting . . ."

Danny was already reaching for her when she started talking again.

"I asked you to come over because I wanted to show

you the pictures Dad took of Marcus after he was born. The ones you never received."

Danny's hand dropped to his side. "You still have them?"

"I carried them around with me for years until I started to worry they were going to fade away." She swallowed hard and pushed a tattered envelope toward him. "Here you go."

Danny perched on one of the stools and slowly took out the three small photographs. He reminded himself to breathe as he scrutinized each picture.

"He's beautiful." Danny cleared his throat. "Man . . ."

Faith nodded. "He weighed about six pounds, which isn't that big, but I wasn't at full term when they did the caesarian."

Danny traced a finger over the tiny scrunched-up face. From the state of the photo he obviously wasn't the first person to do so. A rush of love for this tiny unknown human being he and Faith had created together threatened to overwhelm him, which was ridiculous.

"Thank you." He lifted his gaze to meet hers. "This means a lot to me."

She nodded and offered him a watery smile. "I just wish you'd received my original letter."

"If I'd seen him then," Danny said slowly, "I would've come to Vegas, taken him home, and dared anyone to try to stop me."

She leaned in; her body aligned with his as they both gazed down at the picture of their son.

"About five minutes after that picture was taken all hell broke loose, and I ended up in a medically induced coma," Faith said. "I didn't see him again."

Danny wrapped his arm around her shoulders. "That sucks."

"Tell me about it." She sighed. "I talked to my dad today."

"I guess it didn't go well?" Danny asked, aware of the catch in her voice.

"We kind of made up." She paused and he was aware of her whole body stiffening as though whatever she was going to say next was going to be hard. "He told me to go and look in his desk." She tapped the red leather folder in front of her. "I found this."

With a shuddering breath she opened it and Danny went still.

"Is that . . . *Marcus*?"

She nodded. "Apparently his new parents sent regular pictures of him for the first couple of years. I obviously had no idea because Dad chose not to share them with me until now."

Danny was hardly listening as he sifted through the pile of photographs and notes. Marcus sitting up for the first time, walking, sitting on the back of a horse . . .

"Damn." Danny's throat closed up and he pushed away from the counter. He had to get away, had to deal with this somehow, had to—

"Where are you going?" Faith watched Danny march out of the kitchen, her mouth hanging open. "Are you okay?"

She was now speaking to herself as the door banged shut behind him. Was he leaving? Had she done something wrong?

She waited a couple of minutes and then got down from

her stool and followed him outside. It was cool with a cold wind blowing off the Sierra foothills that tempered the high heat of the day. The pine trees around the house were roaring and sighing like high tide at the beach and it was difficult to see. She almost fell over him as he'd slid down the side of the house, his head in his hands.

"Danny."

She crouched beside him and put a tentative hand on his shoulder. He turned his face away but not before she'd seen the tears on his cheeks.

"It's okay." She wrapped her arms around his rigid shoulders. "It's *okay*."

His reply was muffled against her shoulder, but she kept holding him until his arms came up and held her back. It wasn't until she settled against him that she realized she'd been wanting someone, wanting *Danny* to comfort her like this for years.

He pulled her close until she was basically sitting on his lap as the trees swayed and murmured around them and the moon appeared through the clouds. For the first time in forever, Faith finally felt at peace even as her heart broke right alongside Danny's.

He'd never been a great talker and she had no problem merely being in the moment for him, being *there*.

"Sorry," he eventually said.

She kissed his ear. "Nothing to be sorry about. I'm a wreck, too."

"I just lost it."

She concentrated on breathing him in, not quite sure where the pine scent of the trees and his shower gel diverged, but quite willing to stay there until she worked it out.

"It was the shock."

"I know." She didn't want to move—hadn't felt so safe with anyone since they'd been together in their teens.

"I mean, like, I've imagined what he looks like a million times but actually seeing him?" He shuddered. "It just hit me hard."

"He looks like you," Faith said.

"With your dark blue eyes." He finally raised his head and leaned back against the wall of the house as Faith settled against his shoulder. "My dad doesn't think Miller men should cry."

"Your dad is an idiot," Faith said succinctly.

"True. Why do I still care what he thinks? I'm almost thirty-five. It's pathetic."

"He's hard to ignore, especially when you live in the same house."

"Which is also ridiculous. I should've moved out years ago," Danny said.

"Hard to run a ranch from town," Faith said.

"Adam's doing it."

"So I heard." Faith shivered slightly as the wind kicked up a notch.

"I just see those pictures of Marcus looking so damn happy and well cared for, and part of me is like, that's wonderful, and the rest of me is like, *I* should have been there. *I* should've been the one making him happy," Danny said. "And then I realize that I'm talking like this has just happened and we weren't two scared seventeen-year-old kids with no money, nowhere to go, and parents who would've been absolutely horrified if we'd admitted you were pregnant."

"They were horrified," Faith agreed. She looked him in the eye. "And if Marcus came and told me he'd done the same thing right now I'd be freaking out, too, wouldn't you?"

Danny sighed. "I'd sure be disappointed." He slid his hand around the back of her neck. "We'd already decided that if we couldn't make a go of it, we were going to have him adopted, so I'm not sure why I'm getting bent out of shape about it now."

"He did look happy," Faith said. "But I still wish—"

Danny angled his head and kissed her, stopping her words. She didn't have to think about whether to kiss him back and opened her mouth to him. With a groan he delved deep and she clung to his shoulders. He tasted the same, but the body beneath his clothes was now fully formed and honed with the strength of hard work into something far more potent.

Eventually he drew back and looked down at her, his expression careful.

"Do we mark this down to closure or is it something else?"

"I don't know," Faith said honestly. "I just need—"

This time she was the one who leaned into him and took his mouth. His arm locked around her hips bringing her astride his lap, making her aware of the hard ridge trapped behind the fly of his jeans. She rocked against him aware in some part of her brain that she was not thinking straight but was too into what was happening to care. She might care later, she tended to overanalyze everything, but not now, not now.

She slid her hand into the collar of his shirt and explored his collarbone and his shoulder as his fingers curved around her breast. God, she wanted this . . . needed this.

* * *

A sweep of light monetarily dazzled Danny's eyes as a truck pulled into the parking space in front of the house.

"Oh shit!" Faith squeaked. "That's probably Dave!"

Danny hastily removed his hands and groaned as she climbed off his lap, her knee almost catching him right in the nuts. Footsteps crunched on the gravel as they scrambled to their feet.

"What the hell are you two doing?" Dave asked.

"Uh . . ." Danny looked at Faith and she looked back at him. "Searching for my contact lens?"

"Yeah, right." Dave didn't look convinced. "I hope you're not messing around with my sister, Miller. You know what happened last time."

"Dave, why don't you go inside, and Danny and I will follow you in," Faith said. "There's still stuff we need to talk about."

"Outside against the wall?" Dave asked. "Looking like you've been making out?"

As they walked toward the house, Faith self-consciously patted her hair, which was sticking up on end, and Danny did up a couple of buttons on his shirt that had somehow come undone.

"Hey." Danny caught her elbow. "I can just go if you'd rather."

She glared at him. "No, you damn well will not go! I haven't finished talking to you yet."

He smiled slowly. "Talking? That's what the kids are calling it now?"

"Yes." She gestured at the door and shoved him toward it. "Go in."

The first thing Danny saw when he reentered the kitchen were the photos spread out on the countertop.

Unfortunately, Dave had already seen them too and stopped to check them out.

"Is this your kid?" Dave swung around toward Faith.

"Yes," Faith said. "I talked to Dad earlier. He told me to go and look for this folder in his desk. I was just sharing the pictures with Danny."

Dave frowned, his gaze drifting back to the photos. "Dad didn't give them to you at the time? That's kind of mean. I can see why you and lover boy might have gotten upset about that."

"It was a little overwhelming," Danny spoke up, and came to stand beside Faith. "We had no idea his adopted parents had kept in touch."

"I thought California adoptions were all closed back then," Dave said as he helped himself to coffee.

"I'm not sure," Faith said. "I wasn't in any fit state to ask about the technical details at the time. I wish I had."

"Your parents probably know. Maybe you could take it up with them," Danny suggested.

"Yeah, because that kid is going to be eighteen soon, and he might want to find out who his real parents are." Dave sipped his coffee. "I know I'd want to find them."

Danny and Faith stared at Dave in mutual horror.

"I never thought of that," Danny said. "I suppose it depends on whether the adoption records are sealed or not." He gestured at the photos. "I mean, it looks like he's having an amazing life, why would he care where he came from?"

And what would he think when he found out that his parents had been two seventeen-year-old kids from some Podunk town in Northern California and that his father still lived at home and had only just got his degree?

"I definitely need to talk to Dad again." Faith gathered up the photos and placed them in the file.

Dave refilled his coffee and ambled toward the door. "I'll be in my room if you need me to get rid of Miller at any point, Sis."

Danny barely managed not to roll his eyes as Dave left. Somehow, being left alone with Faith after everything that had just gone down was kind of scary. He'd kissed her, she'd kissed him back, and if Dave hadn't arrived, he wouldn't have stopped before he'd gotten her into bed. He glanced over, noting the red patch on her throat where his teeth had grazed her skin, and got hard all over again.

"Should I be apologizing?" The words came out of his mouth before he could stop them.

"For kissing me?" She was nothing if not direct. "I kissed you back."

"We were both . . . somewhat emotional."

"We've still got a lot going on between us." Faith smoothed a hand over the folder. "It's hardly surprising if we find comfort in each other while we're working through all this stuff."

"Comfort." Danny considered that word. It definitely sounded like she was relegating their kisses to the past. But she had a date coming up with Red Ramirez so maybe she was simply making her priorities clear. "Yeah, nothing to worry about then."

He found his keys, which he'd somehow left on the countertop. "I should go."

"Okay." She definitely wasn't meeting his eyes right now, which told him everything he needed to know. "I really appreciate you coming by."

"Sure." He found a smile somewhere. Wasn't this always

how it had been between him and Faith? Her giving the orders and him going tamely home to his dad? She was on the verge of a new relationship. The last thing she needed was her old boyfriend messing things up for her, or thinking he was somehow important. "Thanks for sharing the pictures. That meant a lot."

"Oh!" She finally looked up at him. "You should take some."

Danny stared at the red folder. "How about you pick me out a couple that you don't want and hand them over when you're good and ready?"

"Danny . . ."

He couldn't look at their son again. He just couldn't. He set his Stetson on his head and turned toward the door. "Good night, Faith. Thanks for everything."

Even after the drive home where he'd at least gotten control of his unruly body he was still unsettled. He walked into the kitchen to find Evan and his father sitting at the table.

"Where did you go?" his father demanded.

"Out." Danny noticed the hot chocolate jar was on the counter and started making himself a drink.

"That's not an answer."

"I'm almost thirty-five, Dad. I think that's all the answer you should get."

"You still live in my house, Son, and while you do, I have a perfect right to your time. If I don't know where you are, you aren't working."

"I do my work." Danny met his father's gaze. "My evenings are my own."

"Not when we have sick calves."

Danny looked at Evan. "We have more?"

"Nah, Dad's just scaremongering to make you feel guilty. You know how he is." Evan set his mug down on the table. "Everything's fine. The calves are all getting stronger and we have no new cases of scours."

"No thanks to you," his father muttered.

"I did my part." Danny leaned back against the counter-top and stared at his father. "We all did."

"Mom called. She'll be back with Ellie three days before the wedding." Evan made a valiant effort to change the subject, which for once, Danny appreciated. "I can't wait to meet her."

"Yeah, that's going to be wild." Danny took his lead. "From the photos she looks like a taller version of Mom and Daisy."

"I can't believe your mother went and had a child with that man," their father muttered.

"What business is it of yours?" Danny asked. "You divorced her, she married him, and from what she says he made her very happy."

"She should've been here."

"Except you ran her off." After talking to Daisy earlier, Danny wasn't having his father's revisionist version of history. "You had a fricking bonfire in the yard of all her stuff."

"That might have been a mistake."

"Yah think?" Evan asked, and rolled his eyes. "You left your kids without a mother because you've got a terrible temper and an inability to forgive."

"I've forgiven her now!" his father protested.

"No, she forgave *you* and you should be groveling at

her feet in thanks," Evan said. "She's a goddammed saint to even put up with you."

"That's true. She is." Jeff nodded.

Danny and Evan stared at their father until he frowned. "What?"

"He just admitted it," Evan said to Danny in awed tones. "Like right out in the open and I didn't have my phone to record this monumental moment and send it to Mom."

"I've been thinking about a lot of things since my heart attack," Jeff said. "There's nothing quite like the imminent ending of your life to shake you up."

"Next he'll be apologizing to his kids," Evan said to Danny in awed tones. "For working us like dogs."

"Not happening." Their dad shook his head. "Hard work never hurt anyone, but I did make some terrible mistakes with your mother."

Evan stood and patted his father on the shoulder. "It's good you're thinking like this, Dad. It shows that growth is possible even when you're old and crabby as hell. I'm proud of you."

Even as Jeff growled something uncomplimentary under his breath, Evan winked at Danny and walked out of the kitchen.

"It's okay, Dad. Evan's always super annoying."

"I'm well aware of that." Jeff was still glaring after his son. "That boy has no respect for anyone."

Danny went to sit in the chair Evan had vacated.

"Did Adam tell you about Daisy's wedding being moved to town?"

"Yup, he mentioned it. I can see the need, but I still don't like it."

"Daisy texted me to say that she and Jackson talked to

Tom Hayes at the hotel. He thinks he can help them out, which is great."

"Tom's a good guy." His father finished his drink. "I'm off to bed. Will you lock up? Kaiden's staying at the Garcias' and everyone else is already in."

"Will do." Danny hesitated. "There is just one more thing. . . ."

"What now?"

"How would you feel if I built myself a place to live up here?" Danny asked.

"Like your own house?"

"Yeah." Danny waited for the explosion, but it didn't come.

"It's far cheaper for you to live in this house, but if you're determined to do it, I'd rather you stayed on our land than rush off somewhere else."

"Okay, then."

His father picked up his mug. "Talk to Adam and your mother about it."

"Will do. Thanks."

Jeff got slowly to his feet, making Danny aware of just how frail he was, and then hesitated. "You thinking about getting hitched?"

"Why would you say that?"

Jeff shrugged. "Seems as good a reason as any to move out."

"Like who would marry me?" Danny chuckled.

"Faith McDonald?"

Danny blinked at him. "Come again?"

"Son, I've known you all your life and the last time you looked this happy was when you were with Faith. I'm guessing that even after all this time she's still the one for you."

"Bull crap," Danny said firmly. "I just want my own space."

"Sure, you keep telling yourself that." Jeff went toward the door. "Sleep tight."

Chapter Eleven

"Thanks for coming, everyone." Faith smiled brightly at the ranchers who had assembled in the town community hall. They were a rowdy bunch and it had taken her fifteen minutes to get them to all stop talking long enough to let her speak. "Dave and I really appreciate it."

When the clinic phones had rung off the hook as rumors spread about the scours outbreak, she and Dave had decided to hold a meeting to address the problem and reassure the rest of the local ranchers. From what she could tell, almost everyone had turned up, which was encouraging.

"We wanted to keep you up-to-date about the current scours outbreak. So far, we've seen the same symptoms on the Miller and Ramirez Ranches. State testing discovered both E. coli and cryptosporidium." She checked her notes. "Two calves have died and around eight were infected. Neither ranch has had any further incidences and both of them are following all the necessary health regulations and restrictions to keep the infections contained."

Jackson Lymond raised his hand. "That's it?"

Faith frowned. "What do you mean?"

"With all due respect, and apologies to the Millers and Ramirezes, but that's not a huge outbreak."

"It's not huge because both ranches acted responsibly, contained the problem, and contacted us for help," Faith countered.

"I think what Jackson's trying to say is are you *sure* that's it?" Cauy, Jackson's much quieter brother, spoke up. "Can you connect the two outbreaks and the source?"

"We can definitely connect the two outbreaks through a shared cattle trailer." Faith hesitated. "We're still not sure we've found the source of the problem, which is why we're reaching out to you guys."

Dave came to stand beside her. "We'd like you to keep an eye out in the valley." He looked around the hall. "There are a few ranches not represented here: Rio Martinez's, Doug Bryson's, and the Perez place, to name a few. Is anyone willing to let them know what's going on?"

Adam Miller raised his hand. "I can talk to Ben at the Perez Ranch."

"I'll speak to Rio," Ry Morgan added.

"And I suppose I can go speak to the Brysons." Danny made a face.

"Doug's been sick," Ry said. "I saw him at the pharmacy when I went to get Avery's meds. He said he and Sue Ellen had some kind of stomach bug."

"Which explains why he isn't here," Danny commented before returning his gaze to Faith's. "I'll check up on him first thing tomorrow."

She smiled, aware that he was looking his usual calm self and not like a man who had kissed her like a fool a few nights ago. But he'd made it clear that his reactions were ignited by their shared past and had nothing to do with the present. And she agreed with that. They needed each other's help through their emotional journey. She wasn't going to spoil it by overanalyzing everything, which was hard because that was part of her DNA, and one of the reasons she'd become a vet.

"And, if you think of anyone we've missed, and can let them know what's going on, that would be great." Faith pointed at the table in front of her. "If you're interested in the latest research about managing a scours outbreak, I printed out some copies to share. Please help yourselves. And if you have other questions please come up and ask."

By the time the hall cleared out, Faith had repeated herself at least twenty times, promised more copies of the research, and managed not to get offended by some of the older ranchers patting her on the head and then repeating their questions to Dave. Her cell buzzed and she took it out of her pocket.

"Hey, Brandon! How's things?"

"Good this end. I'm just checking in. You've been gone a month and you haven't called. Callie and I were getting worried."

Faith sat on the corner of the table. "I'm sorry, I've been so busy settling in I forgot to call."

"I suppose that's good." Brandon chuckled. "Business must be booming out there in the sticks."

"We're the only veterinarians in the valley, so yeah." A movement behind her brought her attention back to the hall. "Can I call you back? I'm in the middle of something."

"Sure!"

"Thanks, Brandon." Faith was still smiling as she finished the call and looked up to see Danny standing beside her.

"Sorry, did you want something, Danny? I was just talking to one of my old partners in Humboldt."

"Another vet?" Danny asked.

"Yup, we set up the practice together when we got married."

"You were married?" He went still.

"Yes, but not for long. Two years after we opened, we added a third vet to our staff and Brandon fell in love with her," Faith said lightly. "Things were a bit intense for a while, but we all get on great now."

"Wait—he cheated on you with another employee?" Danny frowned.

"Trust me, our marriage was already in big trouble before she came on board. Callie's arrival just confirmed we'd made a mistake."

"You sure she didn't make it worse?"

"No, because if we'd truly been in love, I don't believe anyone would have been *able* to come between us." She met his gaze. "I married Brandon for all the wrong reasons and working together, when I was in charge of all the financial decisions, just exacerbated our fundamentally different approaches to life. We argued all the time, we could hardly bear to be in the same space, and that made conditions at work untenable. He got together with Callie after our divorce and I was really okay with that."

"Is that why you finally decided to come home?" Danny asked.

"It might have been part of the reason, but it certainly wasn't the deciding factor." Faith picked up her tablet and empty paper file. She certainly wasn't going to get into the rest of it with Danny of all people. "Brandon and I divorced three years ago. He's been married to Callie for the last two and a half. I even went to their wedding."

She headed toward the door, wondering where Dave had gone.

"I can't believe you're okay about all that." Danny followed her.

She shrugged. "Not much I can do about it now, is there?"

"I suppose not."

"You sound almost disappointed." Faith looked over her shoulder at him.

He shrugged. "Not disappointed, just surprised."

"Why?"

"Because the Faith I knew was incredibly loyal and valued her friendships deeply, and would've been really hurt by that kind of betrayal."

"Maybe that Faith didn't exist after what happened between us."

"So, it's my fault?"

"That's some giant leap." Faith stopped walking. "Maybe everything isn't about you, Danny. What would you like me to say? That I was devastated? That I thought I'd failed at life?" Faith held his gaze. "I had to move forward. I had to make the best of a bad situation."

"Doesn't mean it didn't hurt you, though."

She raised her chin. "I can assure you that I'm completely over it."

He sighed. "You're way better at this stuff than I'll ever be."

"Maybe that's because after I almost died, I promised myself that I wouldn't waste any more of my life regretting what happened in the past. That I'd allow myself to grieve and then I'd move on."

His slow smile warmed her heart. "Much easier to say than to actually do."

"Not for me." She turned back to the door. "Are you good to go? I've got to lock up and get the key back to the church."

"Sure! I just wanted to check in with you about the wedding next weekend. Daisy's fine with you coming with me."

"Great. Dave's also been invited so we can meet you at the ceremony." Faith snapped the lights off and locked the door, but Danny was still lingering. "Is there something else?"

"I thought I'd walk you back to your truck." He shrugged. "Just making sure you're safe out in the wild streets of Morgantown."

She glanced around the empty sidewalks. "That's really sweet of you, but I'm meeting someone at the Red Dragon."

"I'll walk you there, and I'll take the key back."

"There's no need."

"Humor me."

She sighed and set off down the street, Danny by her side. Even though it was past eight it was still hot and humid. She could feel the heat radiating through the soles of her boots. Eventually, after delivering the key, she paused at the crosswalk on the corner opposite the bright neon lights of the bar.

"I think I'm good from here."

"You meeting Red?"

"Yes." She looked up at him.

He smiled and tipped his hat to her, a challenge in his gaze. "Give him my best."

"I will."

Faith stepped off the curb and went toward the bar. She might have kissed Danny, but they'd both agreed that had nothing to do with the present, so he had no right to make her feel guilty about anything. So why did she feel guilty? Hadn't she just airily told him that she never looked back or felt bad about what happened in the past? The problem was that Danny assumed he knew her and that she hadn't changed, which wasn't the case.

Except he did know her in ways no one else had ever come close to. . . .

She pushed open the door and immediately saw Red sitting up at the bar joking with Nancy. He wore a green shirt, blue Wranglers, and a white straw cowboy hat and fitted in perfectly with the rest of the clientele. She walked through the crowded tables, noting half the ranchers who'd attended her meeting had decided to stay in town and have a drink together. She smiled and nodded to anyone who called out to her and eventually ended up beside Red, who got off his barstool to smile at her.

"Hey! You made it. Sorry I couldn't get to the meeting. I had to wait for Beau to get back from Bridgeport with the truck."

"It's all good. I just brought everyone up-to-date with the scours outbreak, which you knew about already." She smiled. "It took a while to answer all the questions." She looked around the crowded bar. "Has anyone said anything to you?"

"Anything bad? Nope, just a lot of sympathy, actually." Red pulled out another barstool and patted the seat. "Why don't you hop up here, and what can I get you to drink?"

"A beer will be fine. Hey, Nancy." She smiled at the bartender.

"Hey, Faith. You coming to Daisy's wedding next weekend?"

"Yes, I am." Faith took the bottle from Nancy and declined a glass. "It will be nice to see everyone gathered in one place."

"And get the grilling and gossiping over with," Nancy joked.

"It hasn't been easy," Faith said, sighing. "Someone in Morgan Valley really hates my guts."

"That'll be Sue Ellen Bryson." Nancy nodded. "She holds you personally responsible for Danny Miller never asking her out in the last twenty years. And Doug's not a big fan of yours, either. He was in here last week with his crew complaining about you killing two of his calves."

Red, who'd been listening intently, frowned and leaned toward Faith as Nancy turned away to serve another customer.

"Doug's blaming you for what exactly?"

"Some of his cows were on Miller land. Doug refused to come and get them so Jeff Miller called me in to ask whether it would be okay to move them. I said it would. Sue Ellen and Doug decided I was the devil incarnate all over again and threatened to sue me when the calves died."

"Doug's not good with his livestock."

"So I hear. As I'm not allowed on their property I couldn't say."

Red swallowed some beer. "He's a fool."

"Can't disagree with that." Faith grinned at him.

"I gather you and Danny Miller were once an item, then?" Red said casually.

"A long time ago when we were at school, but you know how places like this are—people never forget anything."

He hesitated. "If you don't mind me asking. What happened between you?"

Faith shrugged. "I went off to college and Danny stayed here. That's about it."

"Rumor has it you ran off with a rodeo star."

"I wish it had been that exciting." Faith drank some cold beer. "We just wanted different things and neither of us wanted a long-distance relationship, so that was that."

"Sounds like Sue Ellen and Doug need to let it go," Red commented as he signaled to Nancy for two more beers.

"You think?" Faith asked.

"I know what it's like when the whole town starts gossiping about your family," Red said. "That's one of the reasons Beau and I decided to move out here." He hesitated. "He was having some problems settling down after three tours in Afghanistan."

Faith considered Red's usually silent brother anew. "Well, thank him for his service from me, won't you?"

"I'll try. He doesn't really want to talk about it."

The flash of worry on Red's normally smiling face made Faith reach across and pat his hand.

"I can only imagine. Sam Morgan runs camps and classes up at their place for kids and wounded vets. I wonder if Beau would talk to someone who'd been through it herself?"

"Maybe." Red didn't sound convinced and then he grinned. "Wow, look at us clearing the air on our first date."

Faith went to answer, and he held up a finger.

"I know it's not really a date, but a guy can hope." He

studied his beer with unnecessary attention. "I'm going to guess that you've got stuff to sort out with Danny Miller before you're ready for another relationship."

"Why would you say that?"

"I dunno, just something about the vibe between the two of you. Beau noticed it as well." He looked up at her, his brown gaze clear. "It's okay. I can wait."

"Right now, I'm more worried about sorting the veterinary clinic out and getting it running efficiently than my personal life. It's going to take time to get it to where I think it should be." Faith knew she was avoiding the question. "And dragging Dave and the rest of the team into the twenty-first century is a full-time job."

Red chuckled, displaying his dimples. "I bet." He gestured toward the diner. "Now that we've got all that out of the way, do you want to get something to eat? I'm starving."

As Danny drove up toward the Bryson place the next morning his mind kept returning to his conversation with Faith. Was she really that different? Was he hanging on to and judging a completely different image of her from the past and not allowing that she might have changed and grown? He wasn't the same anymore—the fallout from his teens had changed him considerably, and Faith had almost died. What did that do to a person? Even his dad was rethinking his life after his heart attack.

And then she'd casually let on that she'd married and divorced one of her veterinary partners—like it was no big deal. Danny wasn't buying that. Whatever she said about how much she'd changed that had to have hurt, especially for someone as competitive as Faith. But maybe she had learned to move past huge obstacles and he just hadn't.

The fact that she'd continued working alongside her ex and his new love for years afterward indicated that she either had nerves of steel or really had gotten over it.

Danny sighed as he slowed the truck and approached Bryson Ranch. To his surprise the gate was locked, meaning he couldn't drive in and park alongside the house and barn. He got out into the cloudless menace of the bright sunny sky and shaded his eyes.

"Hello?" he shouted. "Anyone home?"

Just as he was about to get back into his truck to enjoy the miracle of air-conditioning someone came out of the house. He squinted into the sun as he recognized Sue Ellen.

"Hey, how's it going?" Danny called out. Sue Ellen looked like she'd fallen out of bed on the wrong side. Her skin was pale, and she hardly seemed to have the energy to stand upright.

"What do you want?"

"I just came by to pass on some information from the veterinary clinic." Danny held up the information sheet Faith had put together about the current scours outbreak and protective measures each ranch could take. "Have you got a minute?"

"We're both sick. Go away."

Danny frowned. "Anything I can help you with?"

"No! Go away!" She brought up her hand and Danny took an instinctive step back as he looked down the barrel of a gun. "And tell Faith McDonald where she can stuff her stupid advice."

Danny held up both his hands. "Take it easy, Sue Ellen, I'm just trying to be neighborly." He slowly bent down and slid the paper under the locked gate. "I'll leave this here for you. If you have any questions, I suggest you talk to Dave."

Sue Ellen brought the gun down to her side as if she could no longer hold it steady. "Get out of here, okay? Leave us alone. We'll be fine without any charity from you or the rest of the town."

Danny considered arguing, but from the set of her jaw and his knowledge of her stubborn nature, he knew it would be pointless.

"Okay, I'm going. But if things get bad and you can't look after the ranch, feel free to pick up the phone."

Sue Ellen didn't even bother to answer him and turned around. The slam of the door shutting behind her sounded loud in the silence. Danny frowned. Where were the dogs that usually ran free in the yard? Were they stuck inside or caged up in the barn?

He reminded himself that it was none of his business and got back in the truck, only pausing to wipe the sweat from his brow before he headed back home. Sue Ellen and Doug had always been prickly neighbors, so he wasn't surprised they'd chosen to barricade themselves in rather than reach out for help, but it still bothered him. It was calving season and if both Brysons were sick, who was taking care of the herd?

He was still pondering the problem when he got home and found his auntie Rae's car parked up in front of the house. In all the goings-on with Faith, the calves, and the Brysons he'd forgotten his aunt and mother were due to arrive today. He went in through the mudroom taking care to thoroughly wash up and remove his boots before going into the main house. Long before he reached the kitchen, he'd already started to smile at the chattering voices and laughter wafting down the hallway.

"Hey." He went in and spotted his mother and Daisy making coffee while his dad sat at the table talking to Rae and another red-headed woman.

"Danny!" Auntie Rae stood up and opened her arms. "My little treasure."

He went willingly into her embrace. After his mother's departure, Jeff had drafted his sister in to take care of his kids and in many ways, Rae felt more like his mother than Leanne ever would.

"Have you met Ellie?"

He turned to the young woman sitting beside his aunt who smiled shyly up at him. She had their mother's red hair and a fair sprinkling of freckles on her fair skin.

"Hi?"

He offered her his hand. "It's good to finally meet you. I'm Danny, your fourth oldest half brother and definitely the best of the bunch."

She grinned. "Funnily enough that's just what Kaiden said."

"He would, but he's such a liar." Danny liked her immediately. "He's definitely the jokester of the family so don't believe a word he says." He glanced around the kitchen and lowered his voice. "This must all be a bit overwhelming for you."

"No, it's amazing. I've been wanting to meet you all since Mom told me that I had a ready-made family in California." Ellie mock frowned. "She made me finish high school and start college before she decided it was a good idea for me to come out here."

Danny sat down next to her at the table. "She was probably trying to make sure she could handle being around us again before she dropped you in it."

"So she said." Ellie sighed. "Everyone has been really nice."

Danny glanced uncertainly over at his father, who was smiling benignly at his ex-wife—a sight not often seen. "I guess Mom told you about our dad's bad temper?"

"She did, but he's been incredibly sweet to me." Ellie hesitated. "She told me everything. It must have been really hard to lose your mom like that."

"We were lucky we had Rae to fill in, but it wasn't quite the same," Danny acknowledged possibly for the first time ever. "Rae's amazing."

"I met her in New York a few times when she came to visit Mom, but she never told me about Mom's other family. She'd been sworn to secrecy."

"But you know now, and here you are, all ready to celebrate a family wedding."

For the second time, Ellie looked hesitant. "I haven't met Daisy yet. Do you think she'll be okay with me being here?"

Danny frowned. "I can't see why not."

"Mom said Daisy took her leaving the hardest because she was the youngest, and not to expect her to instantly like me," Ellie continued. "I get that, I really do, but I am worried that she won't want me here and I don't want to upset her before her wedding."

Danny considered that. "Daisy's a really good person. If she hadn't wanted you to come, she would've said it straight out."

"I hope you're right." Ellie didn't look convinced. "Mom said everyone's coming here for a big family dinner tonight, so I suppose I'll find out soon enough."

"Yeah." Danny stood up. "Which means I'd better go and say hi to Mom and get myself washed up before Adam starts cooking up a storm."

Much later, he and Rae decided to unload the dishwasher for the second time before they turned in. Danny was still buzzing from the sight of the whole family around the dining table—something that rarely happened anymore what with Ben and Silver often in LA, Kaiden at the Garcias', and Adam commuting back and forth to town to be with Lizzie and Roman. He'd sat there and let the roar of conversation—in jokes and catching up on everybody's news—wash over him. Daisy had welcomed Ellie like a new sister and immediately encouraged her to gang up on her brothers. Whatever Daisy still felt about their mother, she wasn't the kind of person to let that influence how she would treat her half sister.

"So, what's up with you?" Rae asked as she stacked the still-warm plates and handed them over to the much taller Danny to put away.

"Nothing much." Danny took the next pile and placed them neatly beside the first.

"Jeff said Faith McDonald finally came home."

"Yeah." Danny shut the cupboard and started sorting the silverware.

"He also said that's been tough for you."

"Dad did?" Danny smiled. "I've no idea why. Faith and I are cool."

Rae set down the dishcloth and gave him a skeptical

look. "Danny, this is your auntie Rae you're talking to. I was there when everything happened, remember?"

"Did you know that Dad and the McDonalds deliberately prevented me from staying with Faith when she had the baby?"

"Yes," she sighed. "I told them they were making a terrible mistake and that you deserved to know what was going on with Faith, *and* the baby. But you know what Jeff's like. He wouldn't listen to a word I said. The McDonalds were so worried about Faith surviving that I didn't have the heart to keep going on at them."

"It's nice to know someone was on my side back then." Danny shut the last drawer with something of a bang. "At the time I thought Faith didn't want anything to do with me. Of course, she thought I blamed *her* and wanted nothing to do with any of it."

"I'm sorry, love." Rae smoothed a hand over his back. "I wish I'd been more forceful. At one point I thought about getting in my car and driving you there myself, but Jeff told me not to interfere."

"It's okay. As I said, Faith and I have had a chance to talk things through and work out our misunderstandings. It's really helped." Danny smiled as Rae sat down and took the seat next to her. "She said she sent me some photos of Marcus just after he was born. I never got them and never replied to her, so she thought I wasn't interested."

"If I'd seen them come in our mail, I would've given them to you," Rae said.

"I gather it was her dad who stopped the letter going out. But as I said, we're at peace with what happened now, and we've forgiven each other."

Rae's eyes filled with tears. "I offered to give you and Faith a home here—swore to Jeff that I'd help with the baby, but they wouldn't let me. The McDonalds wanted Faith to go to college and move on with her life as planned."

Danny took her hand, aware of emotions he thought he'd finally conquered rising up again. "That was really kind of you."

"You told me that was what you wanted. A family of your own. I didn't realize you were actually talking about you and Faith at the time, but I should've guessed when I saw the state of you later." She met his gaze. "Do you remember that?"

"Yeah, I think we were right here in this kitchen talking just like we are now." Danny swallowed hard. "Maybe I was being stupid, or naïve thinking I could've been a father at that point in my life but even then, I figured I couldn't be worse than Dad."

Rae squeezed his fingers. "You would've been great. You always had the most patience with Daisy. I always thought you'd be the first to get married and start a family."

"I'm not sure that'll ever happen now," Danny admitted. "After everything that went down with Faith, I guess I thought I'd blown my chance, and I didn't deserve another one."

"That's just silly," Rae said fondly. "You just haven't met the right girl yet."

"I've tried. I haven't been sitting here sulking for the last seventeen years."

"I know that." Rae made a dismissive gesture. "You'll find someone. Look at all your brothers! Ben's married to a movie star, Daisy's marrying Jackson on Saturday, Adam reunited with Lizzie, and even Kaiden's settled down."

"I know that last one's a real kicker," Danny said, smiling. "I mean, who on earth would take *Kaiden* on?"

"I think Julia Garcia is up to the task," Rae said. "Now we just need to find the right woman for you."

Danny rose to his feet and dropped a kiss on the top of his aunt's head. "Thanks for the pep talk. I think I needed it."

"You're welcome, honey." She smiled up at him. "Maybe you'll meet someone nice at the wedding?"

"Seeing as Jackson has invited the entire world, you may be right. 'Night, Rae."

Danny blew his aunt a kiss and went down the hallway to his bedroom at the back of the house, his smile fading as he walked. He went into the bathroom he still shared with Evan and stared at himself in the mirror. He wasn't bad looking, he earned a living wage and would soon have his own place to live in; so what was stopping him committing to a relationship? The answer he'd avoided facing for seventeen years stared him in the face. He'd never really gotten over Faith McDonald.

But now, when he and Faith had finally put the past to bed, was he finally ready to move on?

Chapter Twelve

"Faith?"

Faith set her bag back down on the corner of the cluttered desk at the clinic and put her phone to her ear. "Hey, what's up, Danny?"

"I had some free time last night, so I checked on where those cows had been before we brought them into the field closer to the house."

"I'm surprised you had any time considering your mom and auntie Rae are visiting."

Danny chuckled. "They're mainly busy with Daisy stuff and Dad's not the kind to let us slack off work even right before a wedding."

"Anything interesting about the cows?"

"Well, yeah. They were all up in the top field by the Bryson boundary."

Faith's mind immediately leapt ahead a few steps. "Where the calves were born?"

"Yeah, the same ones we took down to the Bryson place in our cattle trailer the week before, which I guess might be where the infection came from. I can't believe I didn't make the connection sooner."

"Neither can I." Faith groaned. "I'll have to see if Dave can get out there and ask if they need any help."

"I stopped by the other day and Sue Ellen wouldn't even let me near the house or barn. She literally pointed a gun at me, said they were sick, and to keep away. I doubt she'll be letting Dave in."

"We can't force them to see us and until we test, we can't confirm whether they are the source of the outbreak," Faith said. "And unless the county declares some kind of health emergency, we can't get them in there either."

"Damn." Danny sighed. "I'd go out there again myself, but with the wedding rehearsal coming up and all that other stuff I don't want to risk bringing infection back home or into town."

"I'm sure it can wait a few days," Faith said. "I'll ask Dave to look in there today while he's out at the Ramirez place. If it's that bad you'd assume Doug would welcome some help."

She wasn't sure about that, but she didn't want Danny thinking he had to be responsible for everything that went on in the valley. If Doug stayed where he was and didn't interact with anyone else, the chances of further infections were limited. Even Doug knew what to do if a calf got scours.

"Speaking of the Ramirez place, how did your date with Red go?" Danny asked.

"Great, thanks!" Faith made a face at the phone even though she knew Danny couldn't see her. "Hey, I need to get going, how are your calves doing?"

"Starting to thrive. It's amazing how fast they shrug off these things once they set their minds to it." He paused. "I'll see you Saturday, yeah?"

"Absolutely," Faith said, glad that he'd let it go. "Bye, Danny, have a great rest of your day."

She was just about to put her phone away when her mom's number flashed up.

"Hey, Mom."

"Hi!" Her mom waved as she switched to FaceTime. "How's it going?" She was wearing a McDonald tartan sweater with a pink blouse underneath and her hair was pulled back into a neat bun.

"All good here. We've got the Miller wedding coming up on Saturday."

"Are you going?"

"Yes, Danny asked me." Faith hid a smile.

Her mom's horrified expression was priceless. "Danny Miller?"

"The one and only."

"Why?"

Faith shrugged. "Because it's a good way for the whole valley to see that we're cool with each other. I'm tired of all the suspicious looks and chat behind my back. Did you know half the town thinks I ran away with a rodeo star?"

"I did know that, but I let it go because I thought it was as good a reason as any to be going along with at the time."

Faith sighed. "Thanks, Mom. Anyway, how's things with you?"

"Your dad's golfing again today and then we're getting on a train and traveling down to London to see the sights before heading over to Paris."

"Nice. Can I ask you something?"

Her mom looked wary. "About what?"

"The adoption. Was it sealed? Is there any chance Marcus could find out who we are when he turns eighteen next year?"

"I . . . don't know, Faith. I'll have to ask your father when he gets back."

"I'd appreciate it if you could, Mom. Danny and I want to be prepared this time."

"It might take me a while to get back to you, sweetie, what with all the traveling we'll be doing."

"There's no rush," Faith said. "It's not like he's going to turn up and surprise us any day now."

"I certainly hope not," her mom said briskly. "Give my love to Daisy and Jackson, won't you? We'll bring them something back from Europe for their wedding present."

"They'll love that. Bye, Mom."

Faith ended the call and picked up her bag. She wasn't sure whether her mom had been trying to hide something, or if she was just getting paranoid, but something had seemed off. Was there a way to look up an adoption in California without invading someone's privacy? She didn't know, but she was fairly certain she'd be finding out in the next day or two.

After pausing at the front desk to check in with Blanche, she headed out to her truck. Dave was already out and about so she'd text him about the Bryson situation before she went into town. She'd made an appointment to check out some retail space in the new medical building by the gas station for the potential small pet clinic. She knew she was being slightly optimistic about the chance of opening it before she got the clinic running more profitably, but it would be good to get a sense of where she was financially and explore the possibilities.

Dave liked the idea as long as he wasn't expected to run it, which hadn't exactly been a surprise. Despite everything going on with Danny, the clinic, and the scours outbreak, Faith found herself appreciating the valley anew as she drove down the narrow county road. The sky was an endless untroubled blue, the grass golden and way too inclined to catch fire, and the pine and eucalyptus trees smelled wonderful.

It felt like home.

She parked up behind Dr. Tio's medical center and went to stand in the shade of the building while she sent a text to the Realtor she was meeting. Dave had also texted her about checking in on the Brysons and would let her know what was going on. She looked up as the back door to the clinic opened and Sue Ellen Bryson came out with one of the nurses.

"If he's that bad, Sue Ellen, you'll either have to bring him in yourself, or ask Dr. Tio to visit him up at your place."

"We can't afford that!" Sue Ellen snapped. "Why can't you just fill a prescription?"

"Because he might not have the same thing as you do." Jackie was nothing if not patient. "We can't prescribe without seeing him."

Sue Ellen marched over to her truck and Jackie turned back toward the clinic, her expression frustrated. She put on a smile when she saw Faith in the shadow of the building.

"Hey! I didn't see you there."

"Sue Ellen giving you problems?" Faith asked. She'd treated Jackie's pet dog two weeks previously and had liked her immediately.

"When doesn't she?" Jackie winced. "Sorry, I shouldn't have said that, but she's been extremely unpleasant this morning."

Faith hesitated. "I know this isn't my business but as a fellow professional you might want to warn Dr. Tio that the Brysons may have an outbreak of calf scours up at their place, which can also infect humans."

"Okay, is that bad?" Jackie asked.

"Why don't you let Dr. Tio know. If he wants to call me about it, I'd be happy to chat." Faith paused. "And you might want to do an extra special cleanup of where Sue Ellen was in the clinic."

"Man, I've already put someone else in that room." Jackie ran toward the door and tapped in the security code. "Thanks, Faith. I'll get Dr. Tio to call you as soon as possible."

Faith turned to see a smartly dressed woman approaching with a cell phone and folder in her hand.

"Are you Faith McDonald? I'm Lyndsey Callahan."

"Yes, I am." Faith shook her proffered hand. "It's good to meet you."

An hour later, Faith said goodbye to Lyndsey and decided to go to Yvonne's to grab a bite to eat. She had a lot to think about, and food and good coffee would definitely help her come to some preliminary decisions. Yvonne also had good Internet, so she'd get out her laptop and check out the California adoption system. Faith paused as she went to open the door. Marcus had been born in Vegas. Did that make a difference? Had he been adopted in that state? Why had she assumed he'd come back to California?

"Hey!" Lizzie called out to her as she finally went into the café. "What's up?"

Despite Lizzie being Adam's significant other she'd been nothing but sweet to Faith, but that seemed to be her way. For someone who'd gone through such a lot she was amazingly tolerant of other people's mistakes. Faith found her easy to like and hoped that once things settled down with Danny, they could be friends. She missed her girl-friends in Humboldt. Communicating by text and video wasn't the same as actually seeing them.

Faith sat at a small table for two squeezed against the wall. Yvonne had expanded the café into the shop next door, but it was still always busy.

"Hi, Lizzie. Can I start with some coffee?"

"Sure." Lizzie handed over a menu. "Just in case you want an early lunch."

"I'm definitely thinking about it."

Lizzie laughed as she went to get Faith's drink. "That's how we do it. We lure you in with coffee and then you never leave."

"Death by cake sounds fine to me."

One good thing about having such an active job was that Faith burned up a lot of calories and definitely needed her strength to deal with large animals on a daily basis. She set up her laptop and typed in a basic question about adop-tion, and immediately fell down a rabbit hole of informa-tion and links.

By the time Lizzie came back with her coffee, Faith had taken out her notebook and started scribbling notes.

"Tricky case?" Lizzie asked as she carefully set the coffee and a glass of water as far away from Faith's laptop as possible.

"Kind of." Faith picked up the menu again. "Can I have the vegetable omelet with the salsa and avocado on the side?"

"Sure thing. Do you want toast as well?"

"Yes, please, white is fine."

"Got it."

Faith ate the omelet while she read until she had at least a basic understanding of the process in California. On impulse, she got out her phone and sent a text to Danny.

Are you by any chance in town right now?

Nope

Okay, so can you come and see me at home this evening?

There was a much longer delay before he replied this time.

You sure that's a good idea?

Faith snorted.

Conceited much?

I can't because of the wedding thing.

Oh right!! I forgot about that. No worries, it will keep.

Now I am worried . . .

Faith smiled as she imagined Danny saying that to her face.

Don't be. I sometimes forget that everything doesn't have to be solved immediately or on my timeline. ☺ This will give me more time to research and present you with the full picture anyway. I'll see you Saturday. X

Even as she clicked send, she regretted the kiss at the end, but it was too late to do anything about it now. Even though she'd only been back a few weeks, she still felt that connection with Danny so strongly. Which was why she wasn't ready to start anything with Red Ramirez and even he knew it, which was rare for a man. But Danny was the past, not the future. Getting along with him, being prepared for anything that happened because they'd had a child together was great, but there didn't have to be anything else between them but friendship.

Did there?

"Faith?"

She looked up to see Dave staring at her.

"Hey!" She pushed out the other chair. "Sit down and I'll buy you some lunch."

He grinned at her. "That's the best invitation I've had all day." He gestured at her laptop. "You're usually the one bugging me to shut down all my electrical devices when we're eating."

"Doesn't count when you're on your own." Faith immediately closed the lid of her laptop and put it back in her bag. "But I'm done now anyway."

"Red sends big smoochy kisses."

"Sure he does." Faith wasn't buying it. "How are his calves?"

"Doing great." Dave took a sip of her water. "I went to the Brysons', and everything was locked down like you said. Neither Bryson would come out and talk to me."

"Dammit," Faith said. "Is there anyone in this town the Brysons trust?"

"Maybe Pastor Mike?"

"Did you see any of their cattle on the way up there?"

"Nope, there were some cows behind the barn and house, but I couldn't get a good look at them. I didn't see any calves."

"I really want to get in there and see what's going on,"

Faith said. "I feel bad that I didn't make that connection between the calves born in the Millers' field and the darn cattle trailer sooner."

"Don't beat yourself up, Sis. We've all had a lot on our minds this last couple of weeks, what with the scours outbreak and the regular calving season." Dave helped himself to her coffee. "I could ask Jenna to go out there. Sue Ellen has always gotten along well with her."

"Jenna!" Faith took out her cell. "That's who I need to talk to!"

"Okay, calm down, Sis, she'll be at our place this evening for dinner and we can ask her then." Dave picked up the menu. "Now, seeing as you're paying, what's the most expensive thing on the menu?"

"I hear you're bringing Faith with you to the wedding."

Danny looked down at his mom, who was sitting beside him in the pew while Daisy and Jackson played out their wedding with the pastor. It was taking way longer than Danny had anticipated because what was there to practice? A quick walk up the aisle, the selection of some music, and maybe a sermon, and you were done. Except, according to Silver, that wasn't the way things happened these days, so they all had to sit there until they got it right.

"Yeah. We thought it would be a good way to stop all the gossip once and for all."

"Rae says you went out with Faith at high school and then when she went to college she never came back."

"That's right."

Danny returned his gaze to the front of the church where Jackson was still yapping about something to Silver, who'd decided to organize everyone. If he ever got married, he was going the courthouse route. He'd never liked being the center of attention.

"You know what small towns are like, Mom," Danny added. "Everyone decided she must have done me wrong and some of them haven't been very nice to her since she came back."

Leanne's smile was crooked. "Having been in a similar position, I have a lot of sympathy for her."

"I bet."

"Are you glad she's come home?"

"Yeah, I guess so. I would've hated to think she couldn't come back because of me."

His mom patted his arm. "I'm glad to hear you say that. It reminds me that you're nothing like your father."

"He's come around."

"Somewhat." Leanne sighed. "We lost a lot of years though."

"You got Ellie." Danny indicated his half sister, who was talking away to Kaiden like they'd known each other forever.

"But I lost all of you."

Danny thought about how he'd lost Faith *and* the baby. "Maybe you just can't have everything you want in life."

"Which doesn't mean you should stop trying."

Danny frowned. "Are you talking specifically to me or just making general remarks?"

His mom smiled sweetly up at him. "I suppose it depends if something I said got to you, doesn't it?" She rose to her feet. "Excuse me, I've got to go and try out for mother of the bride. Although I really think Rae should be doing it seeing as she brought Daisy up."

Danny stayed where he was and watched the proceedings, aware that he was always the one sitting back, the one not participating. In a big noisy family, not everyone could be a shining star, and he wasn't the kind of person to scream and shout to get attention. But when had it become a habit? To stand outside and not participate? When had he decided to opt out and why?

As soon as she heard Jenna's truck pull up outside the house, Faith ran into the mudroom to intercept her guest before Dave saw her.

"Hey!"

Jenna paused in the outer doorway and dramatically clutched at her chest. "Hey yourself, you scared the crap out of me."

"Sorry, I just wanted to ask you something before we got into things with Dave."

"Okay." Now Jenna looked wary.

"It's about the adoption thing. You said you'd looked for your parents?"

"Yes, I did."

"In California?"

Jenna nodded. "It wasn't that hard. I knew their names and where they'd lived when I was born. My adoptive parents never kept that from me, so it was a good place to start."

"You didn't have to formally petition the courts or anything?"

"No, because they'd agreed to share information." Jenna paused. "Have you decided to try and find Marcus?"

"We're more concerned about whether he can find us when he's eighteen," Faith confided.

"If you're going through official channels, he'd have to be twenty-one to request that information in California."

"Which is something of a relief," Faith said. "I don't even know if he was adopted in California. I kind of just assumed he would've been."

"Did you sign a consent to contact form at any point?"

Faith frowned. "I don't think I was ever given that option. I was in a medically induced coma at the time."

"Well, if you didn't consent to be found, the state won't release those details to anyone, so you should be fine."

"Okay." Faith nodded. "And if Marcus does try and find us, you're saying he's got to be twenty-one, which gives Danny and me a chance to get our shit together."

Jenna grinned. "I like the way you think."

"Unless his adoptive parents know who we are and tell him anyway."

Jenna patted Faith's shoulder. "I think you'll handle it. You and Danny are two of the calmest and most sensible people I know."

"As you're married to BB Morgan that isn't the greatest recommendation in the world," Faith joked. "Keeping up with him must be an adventure in itself."

"It is and I love him for it," Jenna said as they went through to the big kitchen where Dave was setting the table. "Which is just as well, seeing as we're going to have a baby."

"*What?*" Dave looked up. "Like BB's going to be a dad again?" He came over to Jenna and gave her a big hug. "Congratulations, kiddo. I can't wait to be an honorary uncle."

Jenna turned to Faith. "I wanted to tell you both early so that we could make plans for my maternity leave and covering Morgan Ranch while I'm home with the baby at the end of the year."

"We can definitely do that." Faith nodded. "Hopefully

by then we'll have a new vet on the team, and it'll be a breeze."

Dave went to get some beer out of the backup refrigerator in the garage to drink to the baby's health as Faith checked on the food. She'd left a pot roast in the slow cooker when she'd left that morning, which had been simmering all day and now smelled fantastic.

"Anything you can't eat now, Jenna?" Faith asked as she stirred the pot, breaking up the meat.

"So far so good. I haven't even had any morning sickness." Jenna perched on one of the kitchen stools. "You okay about this, Faith?"

"Taking over your Morgan Ranch role? I'm sure it will be fine." Faith set the lid back on the pot and checked the potatoes baking in the oven.

"No, I meant about the whole baby thing." Jenna grimaced. "I just realized you might think I was totally being insensitive—especially after what we were just talking about."

"Not at all!" Faith hastened to reassure her cousin. "What happened to me was so long ago I can't relate it to the here and now. I'm just so excited for you."

"That's really good of you," Jenna said in a rush. "Because the last thing I would ever want to do was make you feel bad."

"It's really okay." Faith met Jenna's eyes. "I mean it."

"You're okay that we get extra work while Jenna gets to sit around gestating?" Dave reentered the room and the conversation.

Faith rolled her eyes at her cousin. "And Dave wonders why he doesn't have a girlfriend, Jenna."

"Because of my sense of humor?" Dave offered them both a beer from their father's private stash. "You're not the first person to say that. Maybe I don't want a girlfriend anyway."

"Really? How long is it since you actually went out with someone?" Faith took the beer, but Jenna declined, her concerned gaze still on Dave.

Dave held up his beer and Faith did the same. "Congrats, Jenna."

"Thank you." Jenna blushed. "I'm kind of excited myself."

Chapter Thirteen

Because cows didn't care whether your sister was getting married, the night before the ceremony Danny was out in the cowshed with Evan at three in the morning supervising the birth of twins. By the time he got back to the house, everyone else was up and rushing around in a panic he wanted no part of. He excused himself to his aunt and went to take a much-needed shower. His right shoulder was aching like the devil from pulling on the ropes, but he ignored the pain and focused on the list of tasks he'd been given the night before. The main one was keeping an eye on his dad and making sure he got to the ceremony on time, and in good order.

As Danny toweled off and shaved, he mentally reviewed the timeline and realized he'd better get cracking. On exiting the bathroom, he discovered someone had been in and laid his ironed and pressed shirt on his bed alongside his best white Stetson and khakis. Daisy hadn't wanted a too formal look at the wedding, which suited Danny just fine. Even when he'd left the barn at eight the sky was a clear cloudless blue and it was already warming up. By eleven it was going to be heading toward ninety degrees and maybe more. In town, it would be worse.

A knock on his door had him checking he was decent as his brother Kaiden looked in.

"You're on Dad duty, right?"

"Yup. I promise I'll get him there just in time to walk Daisy up the aisle and before he tries to insult any of the guests."

"Good on ya." Kaiden nodded. "I'm going to pick up Julia and Juan. I'm also taking Ellie. I'll see you there."

"Okay."

Evan had already disappeared down to town muttering about helping out at the hotel. Everyone else had significant others to pick up or bring with them to the church. Danny had already agreed to meet Faith at the ceremony, and they weren't really a couple anyway. He thought about that as he got dressed and the house grew quiet around him. Evan would eventually find someone to love; he just wasn't the kind of guy to live his life alone. Would one day it just be him and his dad staring at each other across the table? But his mom was moving back to Morgantown, so even Jeff would have someone. . . .

Danny threw off his depressing thoughts, buttoned his shirt, put on his best cowboy boots, and headed into the kitchen. His dad was sitting at the table drumming his fingers against the wood.

"We'll be late."

Danny checked the time. "We're fine. Have you got everything you need?"

"Yes, and Rae has checked me over like a schoolkid more times than I can count." His father levered himself to his feet. "Let's get going. I don't want to be late walking my only daughter up the aisle."

* * *

Faith checked her appearance in the mirror in the hotel bedroom set aside for wedding guests, glad that she'd decided on something long and floaty to combat the heat that was already building up outside. The small church was only a few yards up the street, but it would still be sweltering just walking there. Her layered chiffon dress with its blue pattern and the contrasting silk shawl arranged over her shoulders should provide just the right amount of coverage. Her dark hair wasn't long enough to put up, so she'd compromised with a cornflower blue slide on one side.

She was just about to put her cell into her small purse when it buzzed. With a grimace she accepted the call.

"God, I'm so sorry, Brandon. I completely forgot to call you back."

"I guess you really are busy." Her ex-husband paused. "I wouldn't normally be bugging you like this, but we really wanted to let you know before you heard it from any other source."

"Okay." Faith frowned at her reflection in the mirror. "What's up?"

"Two things. Callie's pregnant and we're separating."

Faith came to a dead stop. "*What?*"

"You know how I feel about kids, Faith. Callie knew, we discussed it before we got married, and she let this happen."

"Accidents happen, Brandon. You know that and it takes two to create a child," Faith said evenly.

"She obviously came off birth control and didn't tell me." He snatched a harried breath. "I guess she *thought* that if she just got pregnant it would be a sign, and that I'd come around to the idea."

"Have you actually talked to her about this?"

"No, I just . . . couldn't deal with it. I moved back into the apartment above the clinic. I've been there ever since. Callie's taken a week off, so I haven't had to see her at work, either."

Faith considered what to say, aware that she didn't want to get dragged into the middle of someone else's marriage.

"I think you should sit down with a third party and at least talk to her."

Brandon groaned. "I feel so . . . trapped right now. I loved her and she did this to me, knowing all the shit you and I had been through, stuff I *confided* in her."

"I'm really sorry, Brandon." Faith let out a breath. "I hope you can work things out together, okay?"

"Faith—would you call her for me?"

Faith pressed her fist against her chest. "Brandon . . . that's—"

"I know! But what else can I do?"

"Goodbye, Brandon."

Even as he continued pleading with her, she ended the call and dropped her phone into her purse. She was only aware that she was shaking when she walked toward the door. Unaccustomed anger blossomed in her chest. How *dare* he call her, after everything, and ask her to make things right for him. It was totally unacceptable, and *totally* like him.

"Are you okay, Faith?"

She looked over to the bottom of the staircase where Tucker Hayes, the oldest son and assistant manager of the historic hotel, was eying her with some concern.

"I'm fine." She found a smile somewhere. "Am I too

early to go to the church, or is there somewhere I'm supposed to wait here?"

"You're good to go." Tucker smiled at her. "And if you want to avoid the worst of the heat, I'd say the sooner the better."

She stepped out onto the raised walkway and put her sunglasses on. She had to slow down to accommodate the height of her heels, which were very different from her usual work boots. She also needed a moment to compose herself before she stepped into the church. The whole valley was going to be there and if she looked upset, they'd all notice and probably assume the worst.

It was a relief to walk into the shade at the rear of the church and be greeted by Silver Meadows, Ben's movie star wife, who handed her an order of service and pinned a small white flower to the front of her dress.

"Hi, Faith, you look lovely! Danny said to tell you he'd be along as soon as he's gotten Jeff settled, and to save him a seat in the second row on the bride's side."

"Will do," Faith said.

At least Danny wasn't around to witness her current state. He still knew her well enough to be asking all the right questions, and she really didn't want to examine exactly *why* she was feeling the way she was right now with anyone. She forced her attention back to the occasion at hand, taking in the beautifully arranged flowers and the almost full seats because when two Morgan Valley families married into each other, everyone had some connection with the happy couple.

She smiled at everyone who smiled at her, and even made small talk while her mind hummed with Brandon's news. Dave stood up to wave at her from his position beside Dr. Tio and his grandmother on Jackson's side of the church as the sweet sound of harp music filtered through the quiet chatter. She noticed Red Ramirez at the back chatting with one of the Morgans, his dimpled smile flashing out as he nodded. There was a stir at the rear of the church as Cauy escorted his and Jackson's mother, who now lived in Florida, to her seat at the front of the church. There was a redheaded young woman seated beside Leanne Miller whom Faith didn't recognize, but who somehow seemed to fit right in with the rest of the family.

A familiar face turned around from the row in front.

"Faith? How are you?"

"Rae, I'm doing good, how are you?" Faith asked. Danny loved his auntie Rae and she had always been kind to Faith back in the day. "Are you excited to see Daisy getting married?"

"I absolutely am. She's like a daughter to me," Rae said. "And I know Leanne won't mind me saying that."

"Saying what?"

Danny's mother also turned around, her expression amused.

"Hi," Faith said. "I haven't seen you for about twenty years, but you haven't changed a bit."

"Hi, Faith." Leanne leaned closer. "I guess I should thank you for taking some of the heat off me in the valley, but I wouldn't wish this bunch of gossips on anyone. We should talk." She touched the shoulder of the young woman beside her. "Have you met my youngest daughter, Ellie? She's currently at NYU studying architecture."

"No, but it's a pleasure." Faith shook Ellie's proffered hand.

It also gave Faith proof that Leanne hadn't let her divorce

from Jeff stop her from getting on with her life, something she desperately needed to remember.

"If you'll excuse me, I must go over and say hello to Jackson's mother." Leanne stood up. "She's all on her own today, and, as Cauy's acting as best man, and Amy couldn't get away from her job, she'd probably appreciate some company."

"I'll come with you," Ellie offered. "I'd be happy to sit with her through the ceremony."

"She's such a sweetheart," Rae said as Ellie and Leanne quickly crossed the aisle to the groom's side. "Leanne didn't tell her she had five half brothers and a sister until after her second husband died. That must have been quite a conversation."

"I bet," Faith replied, her gaze drawn to the rear of the church where she could see a gaggle of Miller-sized men and Jackson in his full United States Air Force dress uniform. "She looks a lot like Leanne."

"And Ben." Rae smiled. "I'm glad Danny invited you to be his date for the wedding."

"It's no big deal." Faith shrugged. "We're just trying to make sure everyone in Morgan Valley knows we're getting along just fine."

"Well, of course you are," Rae said. "You were perfect together."

Luckily, Faith didn't have to answer that because Jackson strode up the aisle with his brother Cauy. He was yapping about something and Cauy was definitely arguing with him, but what else was new? Whenever Faith went out to Lymond Ranch there were always major differences of opinion, but somehow everything still got done.

Jackson paused to give his mom and Leanne a hug and then went to stand at the front of the church. He looked great in his uniform and quite unlike his normal self. He fidgeted, chatted away with Cauy, and glanced back down the aisle every ten seconds.

Eventually, the harpist struck a loud chord, and everyone stopped talking long enough for her to launch into a processional tune that meant the bride was just about to show up. Faith stood with everyone else and craned her neck to watch Jeff slowly walk Daisy up the aisle. She wore a knee-length cream lace dress that looked vintage and a short veil with the same lace design under a crown of fresh flowers. She'd left her long hair down and looked absolutely beautiful.

"Hey," Danny whispered in her ear making her jump.

"Your sister looks amazing," Faith whispered back.

"Yeah, I think I might lose it any second now."

Faith looked up at him and realized he wasn't joking. The expression in his eyes made her want to cry, too. Heck, she needed to cry so why not let it out?

She swallowed hard as Daisy reached the front. Jackson finally stopped fretting, went quiet, and stared at her open-mouthed. He took her hand like it was made of precious china and turned to face the pastor.

As she listened to the familiar words of the marriage ceremony, Faith's fingers brushed against Danny's and he folded his hand over hers. They stayed like that until the pastor invited everyone to sit down while he gave his sermon.

The rest of the ceremony passed in something of a daze as Faith's mind buzzed with the ramifications of Brandon's phone call and his expectation that she would be willing to call the woman who had replaced her, and act as her ex's explainer-in-chief.

"You good?" Danny asked.

Faith jumped as she realized everyone was on the move following the newly married couple down the aisle.

"Yes! Sure! Do you need to be somewhere else right now? Because that's okay."

"Not right now." Danny's brows drew together. "Shall we walk back to the hotel? I might need to be in some photos but other than that I'd rather be talking to you."

"I have no idea why," Faith said as she followed him out of the church where they'd just missed an honor guard of Jackson's USAF friends.

"Faith." Danny gently took her elbow and drew her out of the heat into the shade. "Are you okay?"

She took a calming breath. "I'm sorry, I'll be fine."

"That's not what I asked you."

"And I don't believe I gave you the right to ask me about *anything*, okay?"

He immediately let go of her arm. "You're right. I'm sorry." He looked toward the hotel. "Shall we get inside before we roast?"

She was back to being prickly again. Danny smiled automatically for yet another picture even as his mind was taken up with his earlier encounter with Faith. Past experience meant she was upset about something and mad at him for noticing. She'd always had this weird belief that if she didn't acknowledge the hurt, it would somehow go away.

He'd wanted to tell her how beautiful she looked in her blue dress, but she hadn't given him the chance. What had happened before the ceremony to upset her? Had someone made an unpleasant comment about her return to Morgan Valley?

"Danny!" His mom nudged him. "Move out, you're not in this one."

He moved over to the sidelines as Daisy had her picture taken with Rae and Leanne, her two moms as she'd taken to calling them. He admired her ability to roll with the times because at one point she'd been adamant that she never wanted to see Leanne again. Aware that he was still supposed to be keeping an eye on his dad, he searched around and found his father sitting down chatting with Roy, the Morgan Ranch manager, and Juan Garcia. His father was being remarkably well behaved, but Daisy was his favorite child and he was probably unwilling to spoil her big day. Danny's attention moved to tracking Faith. He was relieved to see she was standing with Dave and Nancy, who was one of the bridesmaids and was not on her own.

"Last family picture!" the photographer called out. "Daisy's siblings."

"Okay, let's go." Kaiden nudged Danny forward. "Come on, Ellie. You're in this one."

Danny smiled one last time and then was released. Tucker Hayes had given them keys to half a dozen rooms in the hotel so that the guests could deal with their children, take a nap, or get changed for the evening event. Danny had left his well-worn-in boots in one of the bedrooms in case he wanted to dance, along with a jacket if the weather took a turn for the worst.

He guessed Daisy and Jackson would be a while as the hotel waiters started circling with appetizers and cold drinks. He hated fiddly food. Where were you supposed to put it while you were standing up, holding a glass, and trying to talk to people? He took a glass of mimosa, glad of something cool to drink, swiped another off the tray, and headed over to Faith.

"Here you go." He handed her the glass. "It's still hot even in here."

She eyed the glass suspiciously. "What's in it?"

"Arsenic?"

He was pleased to see her smile. "Rather too obvious if I drop dead at your feet and not in line with our mission to make everyone think we're getting along famously."

"All good points. It's a fancy mimosa, champagne, orange juice and passion fruit." He gestured over toward his brother Ben and his wife. "That's what you get when a famous movie star organizes the catering."

"Top-level stuff." Faith took a sip. "It's really nice."

"I know."

"Is Daisy's dress vintage?"

"Does that mean old?" Danny asked.

"Yes." She smiled again.

"She borrowed the dress from Rae and the veil is a Miller family heirloom. Rae had the lace on her dress made to match it when she got married."

"How lovely." Faith hesitated. "Was Leanne okay with that?"

"Why wouldn't she be? She's always the first to acknowledge that Rae brought Daisy up."

"Your mom was very nice to me."

"She's a good person." Danny nodded. "Do you want to check out the seating plan before we go in so we can avoid the last-minute scramble?"

"That's such a Danny thing to say."

Danny set his hand in the small of her back and started making his way across the crowded room toward the big double doors that led to the dining area.

"So much for a small wedding," Danny commented.

"This is small?"

"That's what Daisy wanted. Jackson apparently had other ideas. He's never met a stranger."

"It's nice to see all the familiar faces," Faith said. "Everyone's been really kind to me so far."

"Good, because I wouldn't want to have to start anything at my own sister's wedding."

"Like you'd do that," Faith scoffed.

"Okay, well, maybe I'd get Ben and Adam on it seeing as they're built like linebackers, and I bet Dad can start the ball rolling."

By the time they stopped by the seating arrangement board Faith was smiling far more naturally. If no one had been unpleasant to her, then what had set her off earlier?

"Any news from the Brysons?" Danny asked.

"Nope. Dave tried to get in, but Sue Ellen wouldn't even speak to him. We were going to ask Jenna, but—" She stopped. "Well, it didn't seem like a great idea if Sue Ellen's waving a gun around."

"I could ask Pastor Mike," Danny offered.

"I suppose even Sue Ellen might pause before she shot him," Faith said. "If they are the center of the scours outbreak then it would set my mind at rest about it spreading any further."

So, nothing was wrong with the Brysons and from Faith's relaxed demeanor the scours outbreak was under control in the rest of the valley.

"Are your parents still enjoying Scotland?"

Faith looked up at him. "Why all the questions?"

He shrugged. "I'm just making conversation. That's what you're supposed to do at weddings."

She turned to check the seating. "I'm next to you."

"Yeah, that's the plan, remember?"

"Right up front and center." Faith stepped back from

the board. "Are you sure you wouldn't rather be sitting with—"

"Hi, Danny!"

He looked past Faith and saw Sonali beaming at him. She wore a vivid orange and yellow silk sari and had piled her long black hair up on top of her head.

"Hi!" He gestured at her dress. "You look amazing."

"Thank you. It's my party dress." She rearranged the silk folds that went over her shoulder and down her back. "Not very suitable for helping out in the kitchen, but I wasn't really supposed to be in there. Are you having a good time? Daisy looks beautiful and so happy."

"She does."

"I only came out to get a quick look at her." Sonali glanced over at the door into the kitchen. "I helped with some of the advanced catering. I have to get back to check everything's going to plan."

"I bet it's going to taste awesome."

"I hope so! I'm trying to impress Mr. Hayes." Sonali crossed her fingers. "He's on the lookout for a new chef."

"I'll put in a good word for you," Danny offered.

She gave him a high five and then hurried toward the kitchen as Danny turned back to Faith.

"Sorry about that."

But he found he was talking to empty air.

Faith carefully reapplied her lipstick in the quietness of the ladies' restroom. Whatever Danny said about not being interested in Sonali, Sonali was certainly interested in him, and why wouldn't she be? Danny was good-looking, kind, and had a calm personality that made you want to lean on him. He was also aware that something was up with her and, if she'd had her way, she would currently be trying to keep her distance from him. But the wedding made that impossible. The last thing she needed was the whole valley thinking she and Danny hated each other.

The door into the restroom opened and Faith looked up to see Sonali coming in, her expression distraught.

"Are you okay?" Faith asked tentatively.

"Yes, I'm fine!" Sonali dabbed at the corner of her eye. "I'm just . . . tired of dealing with Morgan Valley men."

"I know the feeling." Faith hesitated. "But I can tell you that Danny is a really good man."

"I know." Sonali mustered a smile. "He's the best. But let's be honest here, he can't see anyone but you. I never stood a chance." She darted past Faith into one of the stalls. "Excuse me."

Faith left the restroom and spotted Dave talking animatedly to Dr. Tio. She considered going over and interrupting them, but they looked like they were having such a good time she didn't want to be a downer.

"I swear this is the last time I'll ever agree to be a bridesmaid for anyone." Nancy grabbed hold of Faith's shoulder, gathered her skirts in one hand, and took off her shoes. "My feet are killing me."

"Did you bring flats?" Faith asked.

"Yeah, they're upstairs in the bridal suite. I was hoping to get through the reception before I changed out of these, but I don't think I'm going to make it." Nancy glanced over at the dining area. "Do you think I've got time to put them on before we go in?"

"I would think so," Faith said. "Daisy and Jackson are nowhere in sight."

Nancy grinned. "Did you know that Jackson went to Daisy's shop to buy flowers before he asked me out and, after I turned him down flat, he went back to Daisy and asked her out instead?"

Faith couldn't help but laugh. "And she said *yes*?"

"Nope, she told him to take a hike. He had to work very hard to get back into her good graces I can tell you that." Nancy handed Faith her flowers. "Hold on to these and tell Daisy I'll be back in a minute."

Faith was still smiling as Nancy hiked up her skirts and headed up the main staircase.

"Ah, there you are," Danny said from behind her. "I wondered where you'd gotten to. Tucker says we'll be ready to go in five minutes."

"Good, because I'm starving." Faith reminded herself to radiate positivity and good humor. "I bet Silver picked something awesome for the entrée."

"From what Sonali said, it's going to be great."

"She's working here today?" Faith asked. "Is that why you didn't bring her as your guest?"

Danny's smile dimmed. "One, I didn't ask her, and two, she's not officially working, but she can't stay out of the kitchen because she wants it all to be perfect." He paused. "Is there a reason why you're constantly trying to set me up with Sonali?"

"She does seem great and she really likes you."

"She *is* great, but she's not what I want."

Faith looked up at him. "What do you want, Danny?"

He grinned. "I wish I knew." His gaze caught on hers. "Sometimes I think you ruined me for any other woman."

Just as she started to reply, Tucker Hayes banged the dinner gong.

"The bride and groom, everyone! Please follow them into the dining room, thank you."

Chapter Fourteen

Danny was still wondering why he'd said such a stupid thing to Faith when his father stood up to give his wedding speech. They'd all told him that he didn't have to do one if he didn't want to, but he'd written something out and even printed it before anyone had a chance to go over it. The food had been absolutely delicious, and Danny had taken the opportunity to eat rather than talk as had Faith. He wished he'd taken a moment to corner his dad and demand to read the speech. . . .

Even as the room went quiet, Danny tensed and idly worked out how many seconds it would take him to leap the table and take his father out if he started to say anything inflammatory. Ben caught his eye and nodded slightly as if he'd come to the same conclusion.

"Thank you all for coming." Jeff looked out at the room. "I didn't expect to see the whole valley here, but it's okay because Silver and Ben offered to pay for the food."

There was a slight ripple of laughter, even though Danny was fairly certain his dad had simply been speaking the truth.

"Daisy's a good girl who's held her own against her

brothers and gone on to become not only an accomplished florist, but a Silicon Valley entrepreneur—something I was originally against, but she's made it work."

Danny glanced over at the table near the back where a huddle of obvious techies was clustered together waving at Daisy, who grinned.

"Along the way she met up with Jackson, who had the kind of father most folks in Morgan Valley tried to avoid, but Jackson isn't like him. He served his country and he and his brother are on their way to making Lymond Ranch a fine and prosperous place."

He paused as people clapped and whistled.

"But Daisy also had to deal with having me for a father and, well, I screwed things up pretty badly back in the day." Jeff looked over at Leanne and Rae. "I pushed my wife away and expected my sister to bring up my kids. I regret that now, and I want to thank them both for turning up here and for still supporting me and Daisy."

Danny let out a tentative breath, aware that his hand had fisted on the tablecloth as his father raised his glass.

"Here's to Daisy and Jackson. Let's hope they don't make the same mistakes their stupid fathers made and that they enjoy a long and happy life together."

He sat down and Daisy kissed his cheek to much applause. A quick check on the members of his family made Danny realize that everyone was as surprised by their father's speech as he was.

The best man stood up and Danny drank a huge slug of champagne.

"Are you okay?" Faith asked.

"Yeah, that was just . . . a surprise. I was thinking we were going to get a list of grievances against every rancher in the valley and instead he was . . . okay."

"He was more than okay," Faith said. "He owned up to his past mistakes, thanked the people who had supported him, and wished his only daughter a long and happy life. It was quite inspiring."

"Yeah, that's what I meant."

"People can change, Danny," Faith said gently.

"Yeah." He rose abruptly to his feet. "Will you excuse me a minute?"

He went into the hotel lobby and then out through the kitchens to the small bricked-in yard at the back, which had once fronted the livery stables and local brothel that had been incorporated into the existing hotel. For the first time in his life he wished he'd taken up smoking because he needed a moment to unwind and process his chaotic thoughts. He leaned up against the wall and stared up at the darkening sky. He'd lost track of time being stuck in the hotel all day.

Maybe he was the problem. Maybe he didn't want to change because he liked things the way they were. Wasn't it easier like this? Not dealing with all the emotional shit? But seeing Daisy's face and hearing his father admit to his mistakes meant that things were changing around him whether he liked it or not. . . .

By the time Danny returned, the tables had been cleared and the DJ was setting up while everyone had more coffee or lined up at the bar. The rest of the speeches had been delightful, including Jackson's make-it-up-as-he-went-along free fall and Daisy's more thought-out comments. Cauy had been his usual quiet self and kept his speech to the bare minimum, which Faith had appreciated.

She'd helped herself to coffee when she spotted Danny coming back in and immediately went over to him.

"Are you okay?"

"Yeah, sorry about that." His smile didn't quite reach his eyes. "I guess my dad's speech affected me more than I expected."

"That's okay." She patted his arm. "Do you want some coffee?"

"Thanks, I'll get some in a minute. I need to check in with my dad first."

"He's sitting by the fireplace with your mom and Rae waiting for Daisy to be ready for their dance."

"Dad's dancing?" Danny's eyebrows shot up. "He hates dancing."

"Apparently. Nancy says he might even have been practicing," Faith joked, aware that she really wanted to get rid of that desolate look in his eyes. Just as he always seemed to know when she was upset, she knew the same about him.

Daisy appeared in the doorway, Jackson by her side, and made her way over to her father. Faith noticed she'd changed out her heels for tennis shoes and thoroughly approved. She was beginning to wish she'd brought some herself.

"Here goes," she murmured to Danny. "You're about to see your dad dance for the first time ever."

It was sweet to watch Daisy smile up at her father and count his steps for him as they executed a formal if slow waltz around the room before Daisy beckoned for everyone to join them. Faith grabbed Danny's hand and pulled him close. As his arms closed around her, she let out a wobbly sigh. What with Brandon's antics and her ongoing conversations with her parents it was nice to simply be held.

"Let's have another slow one for you lovebirds and then we'll speed things up," the DJ called out.

The music changed to a very familiar Daniel Bedingfield song and Danny stiffened in her arms.

"Wow," she murmured. "Out of all the songs in the world to choose from, why did they choose 'If You're Not the One,' which was basically our song?"

"Jackson's our age. Maybe he picked it?" Danny suggested. "If you don't want to dance, we can—"

She dug her fingers into his shoulder. "Don't you dare move."

With a sigh, he gathered her close again and within seconds was singing the lyrics in her ear as their bodies moved slowly together around the room in perfect harmony. She'd never felt so safe in her life.

"Danny."

"Hmm?"

"I really want to kiss you," Faith whispered.

"It's just the song talking, hon."

"No." She raised her head to look at him properly. "It isn't."

He stared down at her and then nodded. "Okay."

He took her hand and walked her right out of the room, through the lobby, and up the back stairs to the first landing. There was a bunch of old-fashioned room keys on the small table and he grabbed one and kept on climbing the stairs until they reached the third floor of the building.

After unlocking the door, he drew her inside and re-locked it, leaving the key in the door. Faith recognized the room, which had once belonged to her friend Avery Hayes before she married Ry Morgan and moved up to the ranch.

"This okay with you?" Danny asked. "I didn't want anyone—"

She stopped his words with her mouth and with a stifled sound, his arms closed around her. He kissed her with such heat that she moaned his name. His hands came up to frame her face and he drew back a scant inch.

"You want this? Because once I start kissing you, I don't think I'm going to want to stop until I've got you naked and under me in that bed."

"I'm good with that," Faith said breathlessly.

"You're sure?"

"Danny—" She leaned in and bit his lower lip. "Just don't talk."

"But—"

She stepped away from him and, still holding his gaze, pulled her dress right over her head, leaving her in a cute matching bra and panties set that she kept for best. She carefully laid the dress over the back of a chair and advanced toward her suddenly dumbstruck cowboy.

"We're going to have to be quick and make sure our clothes aren't rumpled."

"Yeah." As if in a trance, he started unbuttoning his crisp green shirt without taking his eyes off her. "You look fantastic."

She plucked at his belt buckle, eased the buckle free, and slid the leather out of the keepers. "So do you."

"Don't stop," he murmured as she tackled the button of his pants and he ripped his shirt free. "Don't ever stop."

Two minutes later, she was pressed against his naked chest as he kissed her with such intensity that her knees went weak. Her hands were equally busy roaming over his perfect ass and the muscled line of his shoulders and upper arms. He backed up to the side of the bed and sat down, bringing her astride him. They both gasped as the silk of her panties grazed the hardness barely contained in his boxers.

"We need a condom," Danny murmured as he kissed her neck, making her writhe against him.

"We don't," Faith said. "I'm good."

He grinned at her. "You know that's how we ended up in all that trouble in the first place, okay? Humor me." He gestured at the internal door. "Tucker keeps them stocked in the hotel bathrooms."

"And you know that how?" Faith inquired as she scrambled off his lap and headed toward the bathroom.

"None of your business."

She returned with the foil packet in her fingers and waited as Danny checked the expiration date before climbing back on the bed and slowly unclipping her bra.

"Man . . ." he breathed, his gaze now fixed on her breasts. "You're so beautiful." He cupped her mound, his fingers seeking out the intimate places where she was already wet and wanting him. She leaned into him as he slid his thumb over her swollen bud and slipped two fingers deep inside her.

"Hurry," she urged him, reaching out to trace a line down from his chest to the tight muscles of his stomach and then lower to slip under the band of his tight black boxers. He groaned as his hips instinctively rolled forward.

"Give me a second and I'm all yours." He pushed his boxers down, scooted back on the bed until he was against the headboard, and rolled on the condom. "Come here."

Faith gladly obliged, gasping with pleasure as her naked breasts brushed against the hair on his chest and his callused hands grabbed her hips.

"I should take more care—" Danny murmured. "I want—"

"Next time." Faith raised herself over him and sank down, making them both catch their breaths. "This is . . . perfect."

"God, yeah." Danny claimed her mouth again as she rose and fell over him, his fingertips gently on her hip as his thumb continued to rub her bud until she came so suddenly, she bit his shoulder.

His grip tightened as he fought not to come with her. The scent and feel of him was so familiar and yet so different that she didn't know what to do with all the sensations. He growled as he claimed her mouth again and rolled her onto her back, his narrowed gray eyes glinting down at her with feral possession.

"Now it's my turn."

She smiled up at him. "Then make it quick. We've got a wedding to get back to."

"Quick I can do because I don't have much choice right now." His answering smile was crooked as he drew back his hips and thrust deep. "I've got this."

Danny came hard dropping all his weight on Faith as he lost his bearings and floundered in a sea of lush sensations. With a groan he rolled away, one hand coming up to cover his eyes.

"Sorry about that. I'm usually better at this than my teenage self."

She touched his shoulder. "Nothing to be sorry about."

"Do you want to use the bathroom first?" Danny offered.

"No, you go ahead. I need a minute." She smiled back at him, her mouth as lush from his kisses as her skin was flushed from their lovemaking. "That was wonderful."

Danny cleaned up in record speed and came back into the bedroom to find Faith gathering clothes. She held up his boxers.

"You'll probably need these."

"Darn straight."

"Although I have to say that covering up that body of yours is a sin."

Danny mock frowned as his dick responded way too favorably to her comment. "Don't get me all excited again or we'll never leave this room."

She cast a wistful glance at the door. "That sounds kind of nice right now."

He took a step toward her. "Then, let's do it. Let's stay here. No one will notice I'm not around."

She moved past him to the bathroom. "Yes, they will. It's your sister's wedding. Of course you'll be missed."

Danny doubted that, seeing as everyone else was too involved in their relationships to notice what he was up to, but the last thing he wanted was to upset Faith right now. He put on his boxers, retrieved one of his socks from under the bed, and slowly got dressed again, hating every second of it. All he wanted to do was take Faith in his arms, stay naked, and take a nap together in between the crisply starched sheets of the hotel bed.

Their timing sucked.

Again.

He walked over to the mirror to check out his appearance. Inside he was burning up with lust and need but he looked his usual calm self. And, even as he waited for Faith to reappear little doubts started to trash his mellow. What the hell had they done?

"No need to look so horrified." Faith spoke from behind

him, her reflection over his left shoulder. "If you think you made a mistake just let it out."

He swung around. "I didn't say that."

"I saw your face." She'd reapplied her makeup and looked absolutely beautiful, but somehow more remote. "I know you, Danny Miller. Jumping into bed with someone is so not you."

"You're not 'someone,' you're *Faith*." He met her gaze. "And this goes both ways. If you want to pick a fight with me then go ahead."

She bit her lip but didn't look away. "Maybe we should both just stop talking right now? We don't have the time to sort this out properly. I really don't want to spoil your sister's wedding."

"Okay." Danny nodded as his happiness took a nose-dive. "Can I just ask one thing?"

She regarded him carefully, her head on one side. "Okay, shoot."

"What upset you earlier?"

She sighed. "Brandon called. He and Callie are splitting up, and he wanted me to talk to her."

"That's all kinds of screwed up." Danny frowned. "Like, what's it got to do with you?"

"Everything, apparently." She shrugged like it wasn't important, but he wasn't fooled. "I didn't give him an answer. I just ended the call, but as you might imagine it kind of threw me for a loop."

"Enough of a loop to get back into bed with me?" The words were out before Danny could stop them.

Faith raised her chin and walked over to the door. "As I said, maybe this isn't the time to do this. How about I go down and you wait five minutes and then follow me?

God knows, we wouldn't want anyone to know we'd been together."

Danny watched her leave and then let out a stream of quiet curse words while he berated himself for being an idiot. She'd kept her calm with him, but he knew at some instinctual level he'd hurt her, and that in the middle of a wedding he had no way of sorting it out. Was he jealous of Brandon? A man who apparently still occupied Faith's thoughts enough to make her seek out the comfort of her old flame's arms. Was that all he was? Some kind of security blanket?

"Jeez, Danny." He addressed his reflection before shoving his hand through his hair. "Nice going, you fool."

Faith reached the first landing and then forced herself to slow down. She should take her own advice and not put too much store in what Danny had said in the aftermath of an unexpected sexual encounter. It was way too easy to misunderstand each other and she'd had enough of that. There were things they needed to talk about and here and now was not the best place for them to get into it.

She slowed her steps and walked down onto the main landing, which overlooked the doors into the dining area, the reception rooms, and the hotel lobby. Music still boomed from the dance floor and a constant stream of people gravitated between the bar, the restrooms, and the supper buffet, which was currently being laid out.

Even as she went to descend the stairs a flash of motion near the door into the staff area of the hotel caught her attention. From her elevated position she could clearly see Dave and Dr. Tio kind of dancing together, their faces alight with laughter. Somewhere in Faith's head a penny dropped with a resounding clunk. Maybe Dave didn't want a girlfriend for a very good reason.

She continued down the stairs, pausing at the bar to pick up a glass of iced water, and went toward the supper room. Through the doorway she noticed the dance floor was full of real-time cowboys strutting their stuff in a line dance, hats on, fingers in their belts whooping to "Achy Breaky Heart." In the snug opposite the bar a group of old timers including Jeff Miller and Ruth Morgan were swapping stories and amicably arguing about valley stuff.

Her parents would've loved it. Faith found herself smiling. She loved it; the sense of home was palpable.

"Hey."

She looked up to see Evan Miller at her side. He didn't look very happy.

"Are you having a good time?" Faith asked politely.

"Have you seen Danny?"

"Not recently, why?" Faith hoped she wasn't blushing.

"Weird, because I saw the two of you creeping up the back stairs together a while ago."

"What's it got to do with you?" Faith wasn't into playing games with anyone called Miller right now.

"I don't want him getting hurt again." Evidently Evan wasn't playing either. "When you left last time you nearly destroyed him."

"Surely that's between Danny and me?"

"He deserves to be happy and hanging around waiting for you to come home hasn't been good for him."

Faith stiffened. "I never asked him to wait for me."

"Oh, that's right! You never even bothered to talk to him again, did you?" Evan wasn't letting up. "It's not that I don't like you, Faith, it's just that if you get my brother's hopes up and then run out on him again, I'm not going to let you forget it."

Faith made herself meet Evan's gaze. "All I can say is that I have no intention of hurting your brother. But maybe you should be talking to him. I'm not the only person in this relationship, Evan."

"Oh, don't worry, I'll remind him," Evan said grimly. "He's my favorite brother. I'm not going to allow him to fall in love again with someone who doesn't reciprocate."

"That's really not up to you," Faith said. "We can't always control whom we love, and we certainly can't make those kinds of decisions for others."

Evan nodded and turned on his heel leaving Faith feeling like she really wanted to find Danny, go back upstairs, and hide under the blankets like they'd done when they were teenagers.

After a quick glance around, she went through the front lobby and out onto the wooden verandah that fronted onto Main Street. It was still hot, and she didn't need to wrap up. The air was heavy, and rumbles of thunder echoed among the peaks of the distant Sierra Nevadas. She took a seat on one of the cast-iron benches that faced out over the street and briefly closed her eyes.

"Hey." Nancy slipped into the seat beside her. They'd fallen back into their earlier relationship much more easily than Faith had anticipated. "What the hell was Evan Miller lecturing you about?"

"Messing with his brother again?" Faith was too tired to pretend that everything was okay. She'd already told Nancy the basics about her relationship with Brandon and her divorce and wasn't averse to discussing the Millers. "That if I hurt Danny's feelings Evan would never let me forget it."

Nancy snorted. "What a big man."

"I get that he's worried about his brother, but how come I'm the one who has to make everything right?" Faith asked.

"Because you're the woman," Nancy said. "Evan seems to have forgotten that his bro is quite capable of making up his own mind about stuff. Danny might be sweet, but he's definitely no pushover. In fact, I bet if you told Danny what Evan said to you, he'd be pissed as hell."

"I'm not telling Danny anything." Faith sighed. "The last thing I need is to set them against each other. I'm already tired of being enemy number one in Morgan Valley. I wish none of this had ever happened."

Nancy settled back against the seat, her shoulder comfortably against Faith's, and looked up at the stars. "Why did you leave, then?"

"I was pregnant. I nearly died having the baby."

"Ah . . ." Nancy nodded. "Makes total sense now. I guess you had the baby adopted?"

"Yes."

"Did Danny know?"

"Some of it, although our parents went all Romeo and Juliet and decided to keep us apart. Part of the deal was me not coming back here to screw up his life anymore, so we only got a chance to talk it through last month when I came back for good."

Nancy whistled. "That's a lot of shit to deal with."

"Tell me about it," Faith said. "I just wish everyone would keep their noses out of our business and let us deal with it in our own way. The Brysons hate me, half the valley thinks I ran off with a rodeo cowboy, and the other half keep asking me when my dad's coming back so they can consult a real vet."

Nancy made a stifled noise and Faith turned to look at her.

"Are you laughing?"

"Yup."

Faith sat back and found herself laughing as well. It was way better than the alternative.

"So is Danny better than he was when you were teens?" Nancy asked idly.

"Better at what?"

"You know." Nancy nudged her in the ribs. "I saw you heading upstairs with him."

"God, did everyone see us? We might as well have sold tickets!" Faith threw up her hands. "We should've stayed up there all night and enjoyed ourselves."

"Well?" Nancy prompted her.

"None of your business," Faith retorted.

"If you're going to claim the Fifth, you'd better cover up that bite mark on your neck," Nancy commented. "Not sure you can do much about that 'I just got laid' look on your face, though."

Faith slapped a hand over her throat. "I should've stayed home and let Danny bring Sonali."

"Sonali isn't really into Danny," Nancy said very definitely. Faith remembered they worked together at the Red Dragon, so Nancy should know. "She's got her eye on someone else."

"Not from where I'm standing. She'd be perfect for him."

"Except he's not interested."

"That's what Danny keeps telling me, but she sure wasn't happy with me earlier." Faith groaned. "Like I need another enemy in Morgan Valley."

"If Sonali's mad at you, it's probably because of Red Ramirez," Nancy said thoughtfully.

"*What?*" Faith sat up straight.

"She's definitely keen on him, but she's playing so hard to get that the poor guy is totally oblivious," Nancy said. "I think she was flirting with Danny to make Red jealous, but of course it went right over his head. Think about it from Sonali's point of view, Faith. You waltz back into town and take out her two top choices."

"No wonder she doesn't like me," Faith said glumly.

"You can't help being a femme fatale, babe." Nancy patted Faith's hand. "Stay here, I'm going to get us some wine."

Chapter Fifteen

When Danny's alarm went off at five a.m. the morning after the wedding he winced as the sound hurt his head. He wasn't normally much of a drinker, but in an effort to keep away from Faith he'd hung around with a group of ranchers who were intent on dancing until the music stopped and drinking the bar dry. Evan had been by his side all night so they'd helped each other home after making sure the rest of the family could handle their dad.

He opened his eyes into the predawn darkness and tried to remember which parts of the day had been real and which the product of his dreams. He'd definitely made love with Faith; he couldn't forget that—and then argued with her until she'd walked away and not come near him for the rest of the night. He'd seen her sitting out on the porch with Nancy, both of them cradling large wineglasses in their hands, and had decided to leave well alone. If she didn't want to go home with Dave, Nancy definitely had space to put her up at the Red Dragon.

The thing was—had what happened with Faith been the natural end of something? Or was it a beginning? And how did he begin to ask that question when he didn't know what answer he wanted to hear even from himself? They were different people now, but somehow, they still connected at a deep level. Did a shared painful experience bond you with someone for life, or was there something more?

He reached for his phone, blinking at the brightness of the screen, and checked his messages. There was nothing from Faith, but Daisy had sent an emoji-filled text thanking them all for making her wedding so perfect. She and Jackson were off to Napa Valley on a wine-tasting tour for part one of their honeymoon as Daisy had to get back to work.

Using his thumb, he sent a text to Faith.

Hope you got home safely, let me know when you want to talk.

Even as he hit send, he hoped she didn't keep her phone right next to her bed because she probably wouldn't appreciate being woken up at the ass crack of dawn by his text. With a yawn, he got out of bed, staggered next door into the shower, and then pulled on whatever random items of clothing came out of the drawer first. Even in the height of the summer the mornings could still start off cold in the shadows of the towering Sierras.

He banged on Evan's door as he went past and continued on into the kitchen where he brewed himself a quick cup of coffee. He'd come back in for a proper breakfast after he'd finished his chores. There was still no sign of his dad or Evan, and Adam had stayed with Lizzie, so he guessed the load was all on him. With a sigh, he took his coffee through the mudroom, stepped into his work boots, and went outside into the crisp cut air.

He started by checking out the chickens, topping up their feed and letting them out to do their free-range thing for the day. Gathering the eggs would have to wait until his headache subsided. His dad wouldn't appreciate it if he came back in with an omelet. It was cold enough for his breath to condense as he stomped over to the barn, which was at least warmer than the outside. There were ten horses to turn out, which, if no one else bothered to turn up would take him hours.

Danny silently cursed as he unlocked the feed room and several horses poked their heads out of their stalls in anticipation of their next meal. He really should've taken some painkillers for his headache. He checked the wall cupboard where there was a medical kit and discovered some ibuprofen, which he chased down with his coffee. If he built his own house, he'd have to get up even earlier to get back to the ranch to help out.

It would still be worth it, Danny told himself as he unlocked the feed barrel and dug the scoop in. Not having to look at his father's face every morning was a big plus. He started with the first stall on the left, which contained Adam's huge black-and-white horse, Spot, and worked his way down the line. By the time he heard someone whistling as they entered the barn, he'd forgotten about being cold and had worked up a sweat.

He stuck his head out and saw Evan petting his horse like he had all the time in the world.

"Hey. You're late. Get a move on."

"I'm just coming, Bro." Evan gave his horse one last pat. "Not sure why you're mad. It looks like you've got everything in hand."

"No thanks to you," Danny said as he locked the stall door behind him. "Start on the right, okay?"

"Sure." Evan strolled leisurely toward the feed room. "How's your head this morning?"

"Not great." Danny followed his brother into the room. "How's yours?"

"I don't get hangovers." Evan smirked.

"You will." Danny handed his brother a bucket. "How about you get on with the feeding while I take the ones who are finished outside?"

"Any new calves this morning?" Evan asked.

"I haven't had a chance to check yet," Danny confessed. "I'll look in when I'm out there."

"Cool."

They worked together to get the horses fed, watered, and let out to graze and then started mucking out the empty stalls. It was hard work, but Danny was so used to it that he just got on and allowed his thoughts to roam free. Not that his thoughts were very comforting this particular morning. He'd slept with Faith again and introduced a whole ton of complications into their new relationship.

He wheeled a barrow of still-steaming manure around to the back of the barn. It had all happened so fast. The stupid song, Faith melting into his arms, and the need to be with her and comfort her overcoming his common sense. But when had he ever had any sense with Faith? She'd always been the one person in his life whom he couldn't say no to.

"Did you enjoy the wedding?"

He looked up when he reentered the barn as Evan spoke to him.

"It was great."

"Things went okay with Faith?"

Danny set the wheelbarrow down. "Yeah, they did, although I'm not sure what that has to do with you."

Evan shrugged. "Didn't look like it. You ended up drunk and hanging out with me, remember?"

"We did enough to silence the gossips."

"You think?"

Danny turned to face his brother. "If you've got something to say why don't you just spit it out?"

"I saw you going upstairs with her."

"So what?"

"You didn't come down for almost half an hour." Evan held his gaze. "She's not . . . good for you, Bro. She's using you—"

Danny held up a finger. "Stop right there. You know nothing about my relationship with Faith, and you don't really know her at all so keep your opinions to yourself."

"Bullshit! I'm your brother! I've watched you sit back for the past seventeen years and let life pass you by just because she walked out on you," Evan said. "And, as soon as she returns, you run straight back into her arms like an obedient puppy?"

"It's not like that," Danny defended himself.

"It damn well is, and maybe it's time I pointed it out to you seeing as no one else has the guts to do it."

"You're saying the whole family thinks the same thing?" Danny asked incredulously.

"The whole *family*? The whole damn *valley* knows what she's doing to you, Danny!" Evan flung out his hand. "They're all worried."

"Because they think I'm too spineless to make my own decisions? That I'll allow myself to be led around by the horns?" Danny shook his head. "Well, thanks for that at least. It's good to know what everyone really thinks about me."

"I didn't mean that." Evan took a step toward him. "Don't—"

Danny turned toward the exit. "I'm done for the day. Have a good one."

"Danny—"

He flung up his hand as he marched back to the house. He rarely got angry, but today he was shaking with it.

When he reached the kitchen his father and auntie Rae were sitting at the table talking quietly to each other. His father immediately frowned.

"Why are you in so early? Have you finished up in the barn?"

"Evan arrived late so I've left him to finish up." Danny helped himself to more coffee and stared at the pile of bacon and waffles his aunt had left warming on the stove.

"Would you like some eggs?" Rae asked. "I can make you some."

"I'm good." Danny wished he didn't have to sit down with his father but knew that if he attempted to leave Jeff would want to know why.

"I talked to Mom yesterday. She's willing to front me the money to get my house started." Danny sipped his coffee.

"That's great!" Rae smiled at him. "It's about time you had your own place."

"I never did," his father said. "I lived here with my father until he died."

"But you were inheriting the ranch." Danny drank his coffee too fast and almost scalded his throat. "I'm not."

His father frowned. "What's up with you this morning?"

"Just the usual shit, Dad. That I'm almost thirty-five and I still live at home and work for you."

"That's how family ranches operate. What's wrong with that?"

"Nothing." Danny shook the maple syrup bottle so hard it came out all over his fingers.

"Is everything okay, Danny?" Rae asked softly. "Are you upset about Daisy leaving?"

"Nope." Danny cut into his bacon and waffles and chewed for as long as he could to avoid having to look up.

"Then did something happen with Faith?" Rae hadn't brought up five kids without learning to be both perceptive and relentless.

Danny set his jaw. "Faith and I are fine. Why the hell is everyone so obsessed with us?"

"Maybe because you were looking like a besotted calf at her all yesterday," his dad commented. "I mean, she's a great-looking woman and a damned fine vet, but she gave you your marching orders seventeen years ago." He chuckled. "I suppose you're just a glutton for punishment."

"Is that what you all think?" Danny looked from his dad to his aunt. "That I'm kind of some stupid pushover?"

"No, of *course* not, Danny," Rae spoke before his father could get in there. "And, I don't agree with you at all, Jeff. I think Faith is just as keen on Danny as he is on her."

"Ha!" Jeff smacked the table with his hand and roared with laughter. "Why the heck would she be interested in *him*?"

Danny picked up his plate. "How about I leave you two to discuss my nonexistent love life while I get on?"

Rae jumped up and followed him into the kitchen while his father sat there still chuckling to himself.

"She does like you, Danny. I can sense it."

He scraped the rest of his breakfast into the pig bin. "It doesn't matter."

"Why not?"

"Because Dad's right. She's moved on and done stuff while I've sat around and achieved nothing."

"You just got your degree! That's hardly nothing." Rae's cheeks flushed as she defended him from himself. "You're smart, loyal, patient, and kind. A lot of women would *love* to have a man like that in their lives."

He bent to kiss her cheek. "Thank you."

"I mean it." She held his gaze. "Don't you go putting yourself down now, you hear me? If Faith is half the girl she once was, she'll work out you're the right guy for her all over again."

As Rae sat back down again to continue arguing with her brother, Danny helped himself to more coffee. He was just about to go back outside when his phone rang. Thinking it might be Faith he picked up.

"Danny?" someone whispered.

"Yeah?" It definitely wasn't Faith. "Who's this?"

"Please, can you help me, I don't know what to do anymore. . . ."

He checked the display. "Sue Ellen?"

"*Please . . .*"

The call cut off leaving him staring at the screen. He pocketed his phone and turned to his dad.

"I just got a weird call from the Brysons. If you need me, I'll be at their place."

"What about your job here?" his father called out as he strode toward the door. "I don't pay you to work somewhere else!"

Ignoring his dad, Danny picked up his truck keys in the mudroom and went out. The sun had crested the high mountains, but the foothills were still in shadow making patches of light and dark on the road as he drove along. The lower gate of the Bryson place was secured by a looped chain and easy to get through. Danny shut the gate after he'd gone through and continued along to the ranch house.

This time the top gate was open, so he pulled up in front of the eerily quiet barn. As soon as he stepped out of the truck, he sensed something was wrong. The smell of death was hard to miss and unfortunately familiar on a ranch, but not usually so blatant.

"Sue Ellen?" he called out, the sound bouncing back off the stone-walled house. "It's Danny."

"Here!"

There was a faint reply from behind the barn, so he went toward it, the smell growing stronger.

"*Shit.*" Danny breathed out hard as he stared at the almost biblical disaster in front of him. "What the hell's been going on?"

Cows and calves lay everywhere, and some of them weren't moving. Sue Ellen sat on the ground with her back against the wall, a calf's head propped up on her knee as she tried to feed it from a bottle. Her eyes were closed, and she looked exhausted.

"Sue Ellen." Danny went over to her and she blearily opened her eyes.

"I can't do it anymore. They just keep dying, and Doug's so sick he can't get out of bed."

Danny looked around at the discarded plastic pouches, boxes of baking soda, pectin, dextrose, and beef consommé. It dawned on him that the day he'd seen Sue Ellen in Maureen's she'd been gathering supplies to treat the calves, not making preserves. No wonder she'd gotten so defensive with him.

He hunkered down beside her and checked the calf, which was barely alive.

"You can't do this alone." He took out his cell. "I'm going to call Dr. Tio and ask him to come out here and take care of you and Doug. Then I'm going to help set things right, okay?"

"Thank you," she whispered as tears flowed down her cheeks. "I knew you'd come."

Danny patted her shoulder and walked back toward his truck, his mind racing as he considered what the hell to do next. This wasn't a one-man job but asking any of the other ranchers to help out might spread the infection. He called Dr. Tio's office and was put through directly to the doctor, who promised to come out immediately and take care of the human part of the problem. Danny gave him specific instructions about where to park and what to wear before he came into the ranch, which were well received.

His next call was to the veterinarian's clinic. He asked to speak to Dave, but neither of the McDonalds were there yet so he left an urgent message on Dave's cell phone. The last thing Sue Ellen needed to see as she was hopefully taken to hospital was Faith turning up.

His cell rang immediately, and he took the call.

"Danny? Tio says you've got a problem up at the Brysons'."

"A massive problem. I'd say at least half if not more of their herd is down with scours. It's like a slaughterhouse up here."

"Damn," Dave said. "We'll be with you as soon as possible, okay?"

"I'd sure appreciate it."

"We're on our way."

Danny grabbed the two blankets he kept in the back of his truck for his dogs and took them to Sue Ellen. He folded one up behind her head and draped the other over her lap. She hardly stirred, her complexion ashen even as she shivered with fever.

"Dr. Tio will be here in ten minutes," Danny murmured. "Hang in there, honey."

He knew he needed to check on Doug, but he was reluctant to go into the ranch house without permission. But Dr. Tio needed to know what he was about to deal with. Danny rose to his feet and set off toward the dilapidated building. He paused at the open back door and peered into the darkness.

"Doug?"

There was no answer, so he stepped inside where the smell of rotting food hit him squarely in the face. The kitchen was a mess of unwashed dishes, containers full of what he assumed was homemade hydration fluids for the calves, and empty open cupboards. He'd been in the house several times before and knew his way around well enough to locate Doug's bedroom. The door was open giving Danny a view of Doug with a bucket beside his bed. The smell was bad. Danny clamped his lips together as he approached the bed.

"Doug."

There was no response. Danny carefully gripped Doug's wrist and tried to find a pulse. It took him a while because his own heart was beating so loudly. He heard the sound of a vehicle outside and made his way back to the front of the house, breathing deeply as he hit the fresh air.

Dr. Tio and Dave emerged from the medical vehicle, and both of them suited up before approaching him.

"Thanks for coming so fast." Even though Danny had been expecting Dave to arrive with Faith he was too pleased to see him to ask what was going on. "Doug's in there. He's barely got a pulse. Sue Ellen's propped up against the rear of the barn surrounded by dead and dying calves."

Dave winced. "Wow, sounds like the beginning of a horror movie."

"It looks like one, too," Danny said.

"I've already called for an ambulance from Bridgeport. By the time it gets here I hope to have made Sue Ellen and Doug more comfortable." Dr. Tio sighed. "I asked Sue Ellen to bring Doug in to see me last week, but she refused. When I offered to come out here, she said I wasn't welcome." He gazed around the stricken farm. "Now I see why, but I feel bad that I didn't press the issue."

"It's not your fault," Dave said. "You can't make stubborn people like the Brysons do anything they don't want to do."

"True," Danny agreed, although he was feeling pretty guilty himself. He turned to the doctor. "Can I leave you to deal with the Brysons while I take Dave to see the cattle?"

"Absolutely." Dr. Tio retrieved his large medical bag from Dave. "I'll start with Doug."

An hour later, both the Brysons had been taken away in the ambulance suffering from dehydration and exhaustion brought on by contracting the human version of scours. Sue Ellen was conscious enough for Danny to ask her permission to take care of the herd while she was away. Dr. Tio left to write up his notes leaving Dave with Danny.

While Dave did a preliminary assessment of the state of the cattle, Danny fed the ravenous dogs, and checked in on the horses in the barn. There were only four and there was no sign of the usual crew of workers most ranches relied on to get stuff done. He guessed they might have walked out when the Brysons failed to deal with the scours outbreak. No rumors had reached him of discontented ranch hands, which was unusual in such a small place, but he had been pretty tied up with Faith and the scours infection at home. He fed the horses and let them out to graze while he mucked out the stalls and replenished their water and hay.

There was precious little hay or feed left in the barn, yet another indication that dealing with the scours had consumed Doug and Sue Ellen's attention. When Danny called Fred at the Feed and Grain store, he confirmed that the ranch was in arrears paying its bills but, after listening to Danny's plea, agreed to send some sustenance for the livestock. Danny wasn't sure how he was going to get the stuff up to the ranch yet, because he was still in the early planning stages of managing the outbreak, but he'd find a way.

Danny's phone buzzed and he took it out to see a text from his dad.

WHEN ARE YOU COMING HOME?

His dad always texted in caps, which was an assault on the eyes. Unwilling to start typing long explanations his father probably wouldn't even read, Danny called him.

"What?"

"Hey, I'm still at the Brysons'. Sue Ellen and Doug are

both sick and have been taken to Bridgeport. Almost their entire herd is infected with scours. Dave and I are trying to make sense of it right now."

Danny tensed as he waited for his father to explode.

"Okay."

"That's all you've got?" Danny asked.

"Yup. Nothing wrong with helping out a neighbor, even one as incompetent as Doug. Don't bring it home and keep me informed."

His father ended the call, leaving Danny staring at his phone. His dad might be a giant pain in the ass, but sometimes his heart was in the right place.

He heard the sound of an approaching truck and turned to face the driveway wondering if some of the work crew were finally going to show up. It wasn't the Bryson workforce but a familiar veterinary vehicle.

"Hey." Faith got out and immediately started suiting up. "I've got the supplies from Fred. I also brought a load of electrolyte and rehydration treatments for the calves."

"Dave's here."

She straightened up from stepping into her boots. "He *is*?"

"Don't you guys talk to each other in the mornings?" Danny asked.

"I didn't go home. I stayed with Nancy. Blanche called me from the clinic and relayed your message because she couldn't get hold of Dave."

"He turned up with Dr. Tio."

"Oh." Faith busied herself buttoning up her top. "Are Sue Ellen and Doug okay?"

"They're not good." Danny gestured at the house. "Doug was seriously dehydrated and running a fever and Sue Ellen had all of that and exhaustion from trying to home treat the

calves. They've gone to Bridgeport Hospital." He grimaced.
"I wish I'd insisted she let me in last week. If only I'd
known . . ."

"You shouldn't blame yourself, Danny. Doug's been in
this business his whole life and he knows how dangerous
a scours outbreak can be. He shouldn't have tried to con-
ceal it. If anyone is at fault, it's probably me for stopping
them seeking professional advice," Faith added.

"That's also a crock, you definitely aren't to blame."

She smiled at him and he noticed the dark shadows
under her eyes.

"You okay?"

She considered him, her head to one side. "I think I
should be asking you the same question."

He gently touched his forehead. "I have the headache
from hell."

"So do I." She winced and put her sunglasses on.
"Nancy is a terrible enabler." She picked up her bag. "The
back seat is full of stuff; do you want to help bring it into
the barn?"

Faith gasped as she rounded the corner and looked out
over the Brysons' paddock. There were cows and calves
crowded in everywhere.

"Yeah," Danny spoke from behind her. "It's that bad."

"Why did they put them all in one space?" Faith asked.
"It's like asking for trouble."

"I suspect their crew left and they decided to gather as
many of the cows together as they could so they could get
to them more easily."

She spotted Dave moving through the field, his gaze

focused downward as he stopped to check each calf and mother.

"What triage system are you using for treatment?"

"You'll have to ask Dave. I'm just the fetcher and carrier around here." Danny whistled. Dave looked up and came toward them his usual cheerful expression absent.

"This is a nightmare. I'm tagging symptom-free calves with green, possible cases with yellow, red for definite, and black for dead."

"Okay, what do you want me to do?" Faith asked.

"Deal with the reds and yellows while I continue to sort them out?" Dave looked over at Danny. "Could you set up separate treatment stations in the barn, or out here?"

"Sure." Danny nodded. "The barn isn't big enough to take many. I'll rig up some overhead tarps to protect you and the calves from the sun. And I'll deal with the dead as well."

"Thank you." Faith turned to Danny. "That would make our work so much easier."

He nodded and walked back toward his truck.

"Despite everything, I'm glad he's here," Dave said. "He gets shit done, and man, there is a lot of shit." He let out a breath. "Do you want to start making up some fluids while Danny sets us up? I think we're going to need them."

The barn had a good water supply, and Faith was able to mix up gallons of hydration for the calves. By the time she emerged back into the light, Danny had spread tarps on the ground, formed two distinct paddocks, and rigged up overhead shade. She stayed in the shadow of the barn and watched him work, his movements sure and deft as he hammered in the last of the posts. As if he sensed her gaze on him, he looked up.

"This okay?"

"Perfect." She went toward him. He was already sweating through his denim shirt and had unbuttoned it to display the T-shirt beneath. "I really appreciate all your hard work."

"Just helping out a neighbor." He shrugged. "Do you want me to help you move the calves in?"

"Yes, please. I doubt I can do it myself," Faith said.

He grinned and she was struck anew by the strength of his features and how rarely he smiled like his teenage self.

"I bet you can do anything you put your mind to, Faith," he said softly.

She instinctively reached out to him, her gloved hand wrapping around his wrist. "Look, I know we still have a lot to talk about, but I really appreciate you setting that aside so that we can handle this disaster like adults."

He dropped his gaze to her hand. "The thing is—I'm not setting anything aside. This is all part of it, you know?"

"I don't understand."

This time his smile was sweeter but tinged with something sad. "Yeah, I'm beginning to see that." He eased free of her grip. "Shall we get on? It's getting hot out there."

By the time Dave finished his initial survey the results were grim. Over half the calves were already dead, only a handful were well, and the rest would require full-time care around the clock.

Dave drew Faith into the barn to talk.

"I know this is bad, but we can't both stay here. Jenna's doing her best, but she can't cover the whole valley all by herself."

"I know," Faith said. "And you're scheduled for two days of surgery at the clinic starting tomorrow, so you should go back. I'll call you if I need anything, okay?"

Dave frowned. "Are you sure you'll be okay dealing with lover boy all by yourself?"

"Number one, don't call him that, and two, yes, of course I will. We get on just fine and we work together really well."

"Okay." Dave wasn't one to labor a point. "I'll get going. I've taken all the necessary samples for the state testing lab and I'll ask them to prioritize the results. Call me if you need anything at all."

"Oh, I will," Faith said. "We're going to need a lot more feeding pouches, fluids, and electrolytes."

"I'll get on that." Dave paused. "How many do you think we're going to be able to save?"

Faith grimaced. "Not many. My main concern right now is trying to keep the healthy calves safe while we contain the outbreak."

"This'll break Doug," Dave said. "Both financially and mentally."

Faith reluctantly nodded. "Is anyone keeping the Brysons up-to-date with what's going on here?"

"Tio's offered to tell them, but he's concerned that the thought of the McDonalds traipsing over their property might stress them out, and he doesn't want that right now. They're already worrying about how to pay their medical bills let alone anything from us."

"Understandably." Faith paused. "How long are they going to be away?"

"At least a couple of days, but I can get Tio to recommend they stay away for longer if you like?"

"I think that would be best." Faith nodded. "I'd like to have things in some kind of order before they return."

Dave looked out over the improvised shelters. "Good luck with that."

"I thought I'd tidy up the house as well."

"Sue Ellen won't appreciate you going through her stuff."

Faith shrugged. "If Sue Ellen comes out of the hospital and attempts to eat in that kitchen, she'd be straight back in. I'm not talking like a home makeover, just some basic hygiene."

"You do what makes you happy, Sis, but don't expect any thanks for it." Dave patted her shoulder. "I'll just go and say goodbye to Danny and then I'll be off."

Chapter Sixteen

"I'm fine, Dad," Danny repeated. "It's really bad up here so I'm staying put." He glanced out of the kitchen window at the darkening sky. "I can bunk down in my truck or in the barn, I don't want to bring anything home."

"Okay." There was a pause as if his father was talking to someone else. "Rae says she'll drop some hot food off for you."

"That would be great." Danny smiled for the first time in hours. "Tell her to leave it outside the gate. I'll come and pick it up when she's safely on her way home."

"Will do. Evan wants to know if you want him to come over and help."

"Nah, we're good." Danny could do without seeing Evan's face for a day or so.

"Who's we?"

"The McDonalds."

"Ah, makes sense. Hang in there, Son. Everyone sends their love."

Danny pictured his family in the kitchen getting ready to serve dinner, Adam was probably cooking with Rae and Leanne, and everyone else would be chatting as they set the table and put out the beverages. The contrast between the brightness at the center of his family life and the desolation up at the Brysons' couldn't have been clearer. Sure, they drove him mad, interfered in his life way too often, and loved to tell him where he was going wrong, but he wouldn't trade that for anything.

"Hey."

He looked up to see Faith in the kitchen doorway. She looked even more exhausted than he did.

"Hey yourself." He indicated the coffeepot. "I made a fresh brew. Would you like some?"

She came into the kitchen and looked around. "Did you clean up?"

"Yeah, I couldn't stand looking at it anymore."

"Whenever did you find the time? You've been working all day."

"I was desperate for coffee, but when I saw the state of the place, I knew I'd have to hose everything down before I touched a thing." He indicated the plastic mug in his hand. "This is from my truck. I've got another one right here."

He switched on the lights and handed her the mug of coffee. "I literally made up a bleach and boiling water solution and cleaned every surface and the floor. I ran the dishwasher at max all day and double cleaned everything that came out of it."

"It looks about a million times better," Faith said as she gulped down her drink. "Even the bleach smells better than outside."

Danny shuddered. "Yeah, that wasn't fun."

She smiled at him. "But we're definitely winning now."

"Good to hear." He hesitated. "You can go home for a while if you like. I can keep an eye on everything tonight."

She frowned. "You don't need to do that, Danny."

"I've already told my dad I'm staying put. Rae's bringing me some dinner and my favorite pillow so I'm all set. Any news on the Brysons?"

"They are both on the mend but will be kept in the hospital overnight for observation." She paused. "You can't take on the burden all by yourself—it's too much."

"If I can't cope, I'll definitely be calling you, don't worry," Danny tried to reassure her. "It's not exactly difficult."

"But you won't get a wink of sleep."

"You'd be surprised. I can sleep anywhere." He gestured at the door. "Go home, take a shower, and come back later if you want. I'll be here."

She regarded him steadily, set her mug in the sink, and came over to his side.

"What?" Danny asked. He was way too aware of her proximity and that despite the mud on her clothes she still smelled sweet to him.

She cupped his bristled chin. "You really are a wonderful person."

"I'm really not," he countered.

"I couldn't have got through this day without you, so stop talking, and accept a compliment, okay?"

He had to smile. "Thank you and right back at you. We make a good team."

"We always did." She paused. "About what happened yesterday—"

"I thought we weren't going to talk about that right now," Danny reminded her.

"I just wanted you to know that I don't regret a thing."

"Neither do I."

Their gazes met and clashed. Danny stepped out of

her caress before he made the mistake of leaning into it instead. The Brysons' kitchen was not the place where he was going to kiss Faith McDonald again, especially when they were both exhausted and covered in cow shit.

"Would you like more coffee?" Danny asked.

"No, I guess I should be on my way." Faith smothered a yawn. "I need to talk to Jenna and Dave about how the clinic is running, and make some provisional plans for to-morrow."

"Sounds good." Danny ran the water into the now sparkling sink and washed out her mug. "I'll call if I get overwhelmed."

"You do that." She patted his shoulder and turned toward the door, her gaze moving to the window. "Are you expect-ing anyone? Someone is flashing their lights at the gate."

"That'll be Rae with my dinner." Danny set the mug down. "I'll walk you out."

As Faith drove back home, her stomach grumbling all the way, she thought about Danny—the way he'd stepped up to help the Brysons. The massive amount of hard physical work he'd put in to set up the treatment centers and get rid of the dead calves. And he'd done it without a word of complaint and a willingness to listen that in-spired confidence. He might not have left Morgan Valley, but he'd become a strong, competent man whom others could rely on.

She hadn't wanted to leave him there alone.

She wanted to sit down beside him at the table and just talk about everyday stuff because she knew he'd be inter-ested in what mattered to her. Just being with him made her calmer. She paused to get out of the truck to unchain the lower gate and drive through. But what did *he* want? She still wasn't sure, and until she sorted out the current mess with Brandon, she wasn't in a good emotional position to press Danny on anything.

Thinking of Brandon, she checked her cell and saw he'd both called and texted her again. There was also a missed call from Callie, which made her want to throw her phone out the window. She stuffed her cell back into her pocket and focused on driving safely home. The lights were already on when she drew up and Dave's truck along with another car were parked in the drive.

She went in through the mudroom and spent a while hosing off and disinfecting her boots, sticking all her clothing into the washing machine on sterilize mode, and taking a long shower. By the time she emerged, fragrant smells were coming from the kitchen making her stomach growl even more.

"Hey," Dave called out to her from his position at the stove. "Tio wanted to give you an update on the Brysons so I asked him to stay for dinner, is that okay?"

"Fine with me." Faith smiled at the doctor, who was sitting up at the countertop using his laptop. "Hey, Doc. How are the Brysons doing?"

"Physically much better." Tio frowned. "But Doug's refusing to come back to the ranch. He says he can't handle it anymore. I told him to take a couple of weeks off and revisit the decision after he's spoken to his sister."

"Good advice." Faith helped herself to a beer from the refrigerator. "Once we get this scours outbreak contained and the ranch back up to speed, he might change his mind."

"I hope so." Tio didn't look convinced. "I think some of it is that he's ashamed of letting things get so out of hand. He's worried that everyone in the valley is going to make his life hell if he does come back."

"As long as we can keep him away from Jeff Miller, I think he's good," Dave said as he offered Tio another beer. "How's it going up there anyway?"

"It's okay. We're now able to focus on getting fluids into the calves that still stand a chance of making it, which is progress. Danny's been a saint."

"Yeah?" Dave stirred one of the pots. "Well, he owes you."

"He doesn't, and he's helping the Brysons, not me."

"Faith, are you really that dumb?" Dave turned to face her. "He's doing all this for *you*."

Faith met his gaze. "Can you just drop this right now? We have a guest."

Tio politely cleared his throat. "I can go home right now if you need some space, guys."

"No, don't do that," Faith said. "We're good, aren't we, Dave?"

Her brother heaved an exaggerated sigh. "Sure, but you're still an ass."

"Takes one to know one," Faith said. "Now, can I help you with dinner?"

"Nah, I'm good. You're okay with chicken Alfredo, right?"

"You made it yourself?" Faith went to get glasses and silverware out of the cupboards.

"Yeah, of course!" Dave looked insulted. "I can cook, you know; I just don't like doing it." He glanced over at Tio. "I got this recipe from Tio's grandmother. She made it for dinner a couple of weeks ago, and I loved it."

"I can't wait," Faith said. "Any news from the parents?"

"They're settled in London for a few days. Dad said not to worry about calling him because they're super busy."

Faith had an inkling as to why her father might not want to talk to her, but she wasn't going to discuss it in front of Dr. Tio. Her dad hated being questioned and asking for information about the adoption was never going to sit well with him. In fact, with the Callie and Brandon stuff, and the scours outbreak, she was more than willing to give him a break right now.

After a surprisingly great meal from Dave and good dinner table conversation with Dr. Tio where they all got to dish in a most unprofessional manner on their favorite and not so favorite Morgan Valley patients, both human and animal, Faith went to catch up on her paperwork. She was pretty sure that her assumption about Dave and Tio being a couple was correct, but she'd wait for her brother to let her know if and when he was ready.

She sat behind her father's oak desk and enjoyed the silence around her before opening up her laptop. Brandon had sent her an e-mail as well. . . . With a soft curse she got out her phone and reluctantly read through his texts, which were a jumble of apologies and pleas for her to still talk to Callie. She checked Callie's text, which only said "call me" and realized she had no intention of doing that either.

One of the reasons she'd decided to take up her parents' offer to move home had been an increasing sense that she needed to get away from her ex. Nothing that had happened since had caused her to doubt that decision. She shuddered imagining what it would be like if she was still at the old clinic while Brandon and Callie were going through a divorce. . . .

Luckily, because she'd been stuck at the Brysons' all

day, she didn't have too much paperwork to turn in. She reviewed some blood tests, wrote some follow-up notes for the staff, and was done by ten. She also had a text from Red Ramirez to say his calves were doing great and he owed her a drink.

Her gaze dropped to the file of pictures her father had concealed from her in his desk for years. She took them out, her smile deepening as she looked at the incredibly happy expression on her son's face. Whatever had happened before his birth or just after it, knowing Marcus was loved made sense of everything.

She sorted out the photos into several piles and put half of them away in the folder again. It wasn't that late, and a full moon meant driving over to the Brysons' would be a piece of cake. She went back into the kitchen where the lights had been dimmed and made a flask full of hot chocolate, nabbed some brownies she'd bought at Yvonne's, and left a note for Dave on the countertop.

Gone back to the Brysons'. Will check in if any problems.

She gathered up a new set of supplies in the mudroom, stepped into clean coveralls and socks, and carried her second-best pair of recently disinfected rubber boots over to her truck. Dr. Tio's car had gone and Dave had parked in the open garage giving her plenty of space to turn. The fact that she wanted to get back to Danny no longer surprised her, but the why eluded her. Was Dave right? Was Danny doing this for her? And, if so, what did that mean?

She concentrated on keeping her truck within the narrow lane of the unlit county road and turned into the Brysons'. There was a single light in the kitchen of the ranch house, but the barn was well lit. She assumed Danny had no more desire to spend time in the Brysons' sad kitchen than she did and headed for the barn. She found him propped up against the wall in a homemade bed of hay bales, his pillow behind his head and his sleeping bag over the prickly straw. He was frowning down at his phone as he played some kind of game.

"Hey," she called out softly. "I'm back."

"I heard your truck."

"Cool." She went toward him. "Room for one more?"

"Sure, climb on board." He patted the space next to him, his attention still on the screen. "Just let me kill this boss and I'll give you an update."

There wasn't much space, which meant she had to get real close.

"Did you eat already?" Danny asked. "Because Rae brought enough to feed a family of six."

"Dave cooked dinner for me and Dr. Tio."

"Dave did?" Danny grinned. "He must have been pleased to see you."

"I don't think that was it," Faith said diplomatically. "Dr. Tio said that the Brysons aren't planning on coming back anytime soon if at all. Doug's thinking of giving up."

"Wow, that's a huge decision. His family have been there for at least three generations. I hope he sleeps on it for a few weeks."

"Dr. Tio told him the same thing." Faith sighed. "Apparently Doug's embarrassed about what people might think of him."

"Well, he's right about that," Danny said. "He couldn't have handled things more badly if he'd tried."

Faith reminded herself that there was a little bit of Jeff Miller in all his children, even the sweetest ones, and that loyalty to the land, the ranch, and the family was bred into their bones. Doug's decision to give up would not sit well with any of the Millers, including Danny.

"He'll need to sort that out with Sue Ellen. I can't see her up and leaving the valley anytime soon," Faith said. "She loves this place."

"But it would be hard for her to run it on her own. Even with Doug on board it was a struggle."

"Maybe you could run it with her?" Faith suggested.

"Right." Danny rolled his eyes as he stood up. "She'll never forgive me for seeing her at her worst, you know that."

"Where are you going?" Faith asked.

"To check the calves. Do you want to come?" He turned to look at her. "Isn't that why you came back?"

"Of course." Faith scrambled to join him. "How are things?"

"Stable. Which considering what we found today is as good as it's going to get right now." He handed her a large flashlight. "Let's start with the mild cases."

By the time they returned to the barn, Faith was feeling a lot better about the state of the remaining calves. Danny had kept all the survivors alive. The longer they stuck around the better their chances of recovery. They washed up in the tack room and Faith returned to her truck to bag up her coveralls and boots and change into her backup clothes. She also took the opportunity to put the envelope of photos on Danny's passenger seat.

Danny was waiting for her at the barn door, the soft lamplight illuminating his frame. With a resolute breath she picked up the box of brownies and travel mug and marched toward him.

"You up for brownies and hot chocolate?"

He took a moment to answer her. "Sure, if you don't have to get back."

"Nothing to get back for. Dave doesn't need tucking in

every night anymore—just when there's a thunderstorm, or when he finds a spider in his bed."

Danny chuckled and stepped aside and into the barn. "Then come on in."

She followed him back to his makeshift bed and paused. "I've got my sleeping bag in the back of the truck. I'll go and get it."

"No pillow?"

Faith went and got her sleeping bag and an old blanket she folded up to put behind her head. "That's better." She arranged the bag next to Danny's.

"I could add a few more bales if you like."

"No, I think we're good." She slipped off her shoes and got in beside him. "This is cozy."

He dropped an arm over her shoulders. "I was going to say just like old times, but I don't think we ever slept together in a real bed, did we?"

Faith smiled. "Plenty of barns and the back seat of your truck, but no beds. The fear of being discovered by our parents meant we did a lot of skulking around."

His work-roughened fingers caressed her upper arm. "I'm not sure I could make out in the back of a car these days without having to call the fire department to cut me out."

She poked him in the ribs. "You're not that old."

"Sometimes I feel like I'm a hundred years old, and other days like I haven't changed from when I was a kid."

"You've changed."

"Ya think?" he sighed. "Evan keeps telling me I'm stuck seventeen years ago."

"Evan should keep his opinions to himself," Faith said tartly.

"Like he'd ever do that. He's always putting his foot in

his mouth." He paused. "And, I have changed because I know that the Danny I am now would never have allowed what happened back when you had the baby. I would've fought harder, stood my ground, and found out everything I needed to know before stating my case."

"We were both blindsided by what happened," Faith said. "And there is an argument to be made that what happened to us *then,* helped make us the people we are now."

"I can't disagree with that."

Silence fell between them for the first time and Faith hurried to fill it.

"Can you open the brownies and get us some hot chocolate while I quickly write up a few notes about the calves?" She reached over to her bag. "I have my laptop right here."

"I can do that."

The sweet scent of chocolate soon overrode the smell of dried hay as Danny set out their supper. Faith typed as quickly as she could, stopping occasionally for mouthfuls of hot chocolate and brownie.

"I think that's done." She sent the e-mail to the clinic and directly to Dave just to make sure. "While I've got my laptop open would you like to know about adoptions in California?"

"Wow, you have been busy," Danny said as he set his mug on the floor beside the stacked bales.

"I thought it was important to know the basics," Faith said. "The good news is that if Marcus was adopted in California, he can't look for us until he's twenty-one. Even if he does look, he can't access much information about us unless we specifically agreed that he could before the adoption."

"I don't remember being asked my opinion on that." Danny frowned.

"Neither do I, so for the moment, let's assume that no permission was given, which means that the most he can get if he applies is non-identifying background information."

"Which means what exactly?"

Faith fired up her notes. "Our ages and education, medical history if known and circumstances of the adoption." She looked over at him. "I guess the caseworker who originally deals with the adoption takes notes and that's what is handed over to the adoptee with some details obscured. Obviously, I have no idea what any of those original notes said."

"I assume your parents dealt with it?" Danny asked.

"I guess so. I've been trying to talk to my dad about it, but he's not playing ball."

"It would be nice to know what it said, although as we were seventeen-year-old ranch kids there probably wasn't much information." He half smiled. "I can't decide if I'm glad he can't find out about us or sad."

"He could still try," Faith added. "As an adult he could petition a court and show," she read from her notes, "a good and compelling cause to disclose his original birth certificate, which shows our names and where he was born."

"Like what would that be?"

"I'm not sure—emergency medical reasons maybe?" She wrinkled her nose. "I still think we're pretty safe."

He leaned back against the wall and looked out into the darkness. "What about us?"

"What do you mean?"

"If we wanted to find out about him. Could we do that?"

"I'm . . . not sure." Faith hesitated. "Why would we want to do that?"

Danny shrugged. "To make sure he was doing okay?

That he was happy?" He turned to her. "Haven't you ever wondered about that?"

"Of *course* I have, but I decided that if I wanted to remain sane, I'd have to assume the best things in the world for him and stop obsessing over something I couldn't control."

"That's so you."

Faith paused. "Why does that sound like a criticism?"

He held up a hand. "It wasn't meant to be. I just . . . admire your ability to compartmentalize. It's a skill I've never mastered."

She folded her arms over her chest. "Great, but it still sounds like a criticism."

He leaned in and gently elbowed her in the ribs. "You're puffing up like my dad's best cockerel."

She poked him back and thirty seconds later found herself flat on her back with him straddling her hips.

"I always forget how strong you are," she said breathlessly.

"Your mistake." His smile was hard to resist. "Although you're no weakling yourself."

"I have to say that right now, I'm feeling a bit helpless." She slowly bit down on her lip. "Like I can't move or anything."

He transferred his two-handed grip on her wrists into one and drew them over her head. "I know this is a barn, and we've kind of agreed that we're too old for barns, but seeing as our own beds aren't available right now, would you still be interested?"

"In what?" Faith asked.

"This." He bent his head and kissed along the line of her jawbone to her mouth, feathering his tongue along the seam of her lips.

She responded to him so naturally that she didn't even have to think about it.

"Wait." Danny raised his head. "We shouldn't be doing this again."

"You started it," Faith reminded him.

"Yeah, so let's talk this through." He took a deep breath. "What are we doing here, Faith?"

"I would've thought it was obvious."

"Okay, so let me put it another way. *Should* we be doing this?"

"I don't have a problem with it," Faith said. "Do you?" The struggle between his desire to continue and his attempt to rationalize the unexplainable was clear on his face. "We're both adults, we're single, and we want each other. What's wrong with that?"

"Because it's not that simple, is it?" Danny said. "We have a history together. Last night . . . we could kind of agree that we were swept away in the moment, but here and now?" He looked right into her eyes. "We're making a conscious decision."

"To have sex?"

He nodded.

"What do you want me to say, Danny?"

His smile was crooked. "I suppose I'm asking what you want from me. Is this just about sex? Like we hook up when we get horny and that's the end of it? Or is this something more?"

Faith sighed. "I don't know. Thinking like that? About *all* of it right now? It frightens me. I guess I just want us to have the here and now because we *can*."

He considered her for so long that she almost forgot how to breathe.

"Like take it day by day and see how it goes?"

"Yes." Faith made herself look at him. "But I totally understand if that doesn't work for you. We can still be friends."

"I'm not sure about that." Danny ran his fingers along her jawline making her shiver. "I still want you."

"And I want you."

His smile was back. "Is it really that simple?"

"Maybe," Faith said. "There are so many complications in my life right now that having this—with you—seems like the best thing ever."

"Then how about we just go with that for now?" He lowered his head and kissed her slowly, his fingers sliding into her hair holding her just where he wanted her. "Having time with you, being with you seems right to me, too."

Danny continued to kiss his way down Faith's neck until he reached her shoulders where he gently grazed his teeth against her skin. She arched against him, the hard tips of her breasts rubbing against his chest, driving him wild. But he was determined to take his time tonight and prove that he'd learned some new stuff since his teen years.

"May I?" he murmured as his fingers brushed the hem of her long-sleeved T-shirt.

"Please." She lifted her arms to help him take the garment over her head. His brain almost exploded when he realized she had no bra on under the shirt.

"Nice." He cupped her breast and lowered his head to caress her nipple with his tongue. "I love a woman who smells like lemon disinfectant."

Her chuckle made him smile against her skin and allow his hand to drop to the curve of her hip where he spread his fingers wide.

"How about taking these sweatpants off?" Danny kissed her belly button. "They're just getting in my way."

"What about you taking some clothes off first?" Faith asked.

"After you." He waited as she undid the drawstring of the pants and scooted out of them. "I have plans."

"Really?"

He enjoyed the catch in her breath as he kissed her hipbone.

"Oh, yeah." He settled himself more comfortably between her legs and twirled his tongue over the tiny bow at the front of her panties. Her hips lifted toward his mouth and he wanted to cheer. He eased a finger under the cotton and breathed in hard. "You're wet for me."

"Well, duh." Her fingers flicked his hair and then settled on his scalp.

"I was thinking I'd have to spend a long, long time and a lot of my attention getting you like that," he murmured.

"You can always improve on perfection."

He paused to look up at her. "Yeah, I guess I can." He took off her panties and pressed a lavish kiss to her mound. "Let's see if I can stop you talking and start screaming, but not too loud because we don't want to scare the calves."

Chapter Seventeen

Faith woke up to the birds singing and the sun shining in her eyes, her cheek pressed against Danny's shirt as he lay on his back beside her. After he'd taken his damned time making her beg, he'd finally relented, stripped off, and made slow sweet love to her. Eventually, they'd ventured into the Brysons' mudroom to share the old shower and made more coffee and hydrating solution in the kitchen. They'd gotten up every two hours to check the calves and fallen asleep fully dressed inside their zipped-together sleeping bags.

Despite the prickly nature of their bed and her awareness that she definitely had a crick in her neck, Faith had never felt more content. Being here—in this moment with Danny—was somehow everything she needed right now. She firmly squashed down any desire to think further than that, which really wasn't like her. But they'd agreed to take things as they came and for the first time in her life she was going to try and do just that. Didn't they deserve some time together after everything that had been stolen from them?

"Morning, Danny! I brought you some breakfast!" The

slight gasp that followed Rae's greeting was followed by a chuckle. "Oh, *my*."

"Hey, Rae," Danny spoke up as Faith pretended to still be asleep. "Didn't I ask you to stay behind the gate because of the risk of infection?"

"I've got my boots on." Rae pointed down at her feet. "Jeff says I'll be fine."

She busied herself setting a tablecloth over one of the stacked bales. "I've brought enough for two, so don't you worry, Faith, dear."

"Faith? What the hell?" Dave's voice carried even farther than Rae's, turning Faith's morning rapidly into soap opera territory. "Why are you in bed with Danny Miller?"

Despite her desire to hide under the covers until everyone went away Danny gently set her aside and sat up. "There's no need to lose your shit, Dave. We're fully clothed."

"So what?"

"And we've been up to tend the calves every two hours, which hardly left us any time for hanging-from-the-rooftops monkey sex."

Rae chuckled. "Dave, for goodness' sake leave them be. They must be exhausted."

"I bet they are," Dave muttered under his breath and he glared at Faith like some old maiden aunt. His gaze strayed to the food Rae was putting out on the table. "Hey, you made waffles?"

Faith finally sat up. "They're not for you, Dave. How about you go and check out the calves while Danny and I eat something?"

With one last wistful glance back at the food, Dave went out into the paddock leaving relative peace behind him. Rae smiled at Faith.

"Come and sit down, dear. You must be starving."

Faith didn't dare look at Danny as he joined her.

"This is very kind of you, Rae. I was just about to go home and get something to eat."

"No need for that," Rae said. "How are the calves doing?"

"Better than they were twenty-four hours ago. We only lost two last night, which was less than I expected." Faith bit into a waffle slathered in strawberries, maple syrup, and cream and almost moaned. "This is *really* good."

"You're welcome. I make the preserves myself," Rae said. "Eat up, Danny dear, before it gets cold. Your mother wanted to come and see you, but Jeff said the less of us coming out here the better, and for once I agree with him. She was hoping you'd be able to take a break today and meet her in town. She wants to talk to you about something."

"I'll check in with her after we've seen the state of play up here today, okay?" Danny was devouring waffles at a speed Faith could only envy. "I think I'll be able to get away. I need to talk to Fred down at the feedstore and see how bad the Brysons' bills are."

"Dave and Jenna are handling most of the veterinary business today so I can stay here for as long as you need," Faith said, speaking directly to Danny for the first time.

His slow smile made her want to reach across and lick the strawberry preserves from his lips, which she definitely couldn't do while his aunt was watching. The answering gleam in his eyes as he watched her made it hard to concentrate.

"I just had an idea!" Rae said brightly. "Why don't you and Faith go and do what you need to do while Dave and I keep an eye on the calves?" She held up a finger as

Danny went to speak. "I did live on a ranch for fifteen years, dear. I know how to hydrate a calf."

Danny looked over at Faith. "I could drop you home to get a change of clothes and pick you up after I've been to town?"

"Sounds good to me," Faith said as she regretfully eyed the remaining six waffles. "If we bribe Dave with this amazing food, he'll probably go for it if I'm back within two hours."

Danny stood, kissed his auntie Rae, and held out his hand to Faith. "I was thinking we'd just get going before he notices."

Danny looked over at Faith as they drove up to the front of the McDonalds' house. Despite the interesting start to their morning she was smiling and relaxed, which made him feel good about everything that had happened between them. While she drove, he'd texted his mom and checked in with Ben about whether his and Silver's charity foundation could help out with the rising costs at the Brysons'. Ben had sent a thumbs-up and his mom said she'd meet him in Yvonne's for breakfast.

"What time do you want me to pick you up again?" Danny asked.

Faith gave him an amused glance. "Seeing as you're driving my truck, I think you're the one who'll be waiting on me." She paused. "I thought that while Dave's out of the house we could both have a shower and change our clothes. I can quick wash and dry most of your stuff and you can borrow a pair of Dad's old work jeans."

Danny slowly smiled. "I like that idea a lot."

Of course, because the shower was big enough for

two, they spent way too much time in it making out and had to rush to get dressed and back out the door to go down to Morgantown.

"So, what's this foundation Ben's started?" Faith asked as she negotiated the sharp turn out onto the county road.

"It was Silver's idea, actually. She wanted to find a practical way to help out her new home. It soon became obvious that the ranchers in this valley, particularly the legacy ranchers, were under threat from developers. They've recently been helping the Garcia Ranch with refencing and renovating their place and they employ local people to do the work."

"That's awesome," Faith said. "And, Ben said they can help the Brysons?"

"They can certainly straighten out their current finances and help them start with a clean slate if that's what it takes to keep the ranch alive and kicking." Danny put on his sunglasses against the glare of the sun. "It might help Doug make a better decision about coming back as well."

"I hope so." Faith sighed. "Neither of them like me, but I don't want to see them fail."

"You're a good person." He pointed toward the parking lot behind the feedstore and lumberyard. "I need to talk to both these guys about the Brysons' accounts."

"Cool, because I need some supplies from Fred." Faith backed into a space in front of the feedstore. "I'll see you back here when you're done."

It didn't take Danny long to get the information he needed and send it off to Ben. The amount of debt the Brysons had accumulated predated the scours outbreak but was indicative in Danny's mind of why they'd ended up where they had anyway. Bad land management, impulsive financial decisions, and an unforgiving and changeable climate made successful ranching almost impossible. For the first time in a while Danny paused to consider how well his father had done to navigate his ranch through the last three decades. As far as he knew the ranch carried very little debt and Adam would be inheriting a thriving and forward-looking place.

Of course, his dad had the advantage of all that free labor in his own kids. . . .

"What are you smiling about?" Faith asked. She was sitting on the lowered tailgate of her truck, legs swinging like she didn't have a care in the world waiting for him.

"My dad."

"That makes a change."

"I was just thinking about how hard it is to keep a ranch going."

She sighed. "Tell me about it. Getting you guys to pay your bills in a timely manner is an uphill struggle."

"I bet." He set his purchases down beside hers. "I'm supposed to be meeting my mom at Yvonne's. Would you like to come with me, or do you have other stuff to do?"

"You're okay with me coming?" Faith asked.

"Didn't I make that clear earlier in the shower?"

She actually blushed as she poked him in the ribs. "You know what I mean."

"If we're both going to continue to live and work here, people had better start getting used to seeing us together." He searched her face. "My mom's thinking of coming back for good."

"I didn't know that." Faith hesitated. "Is it because of what happened to your dad?"

"I think that's part of it, but she wants to come back for herself. She grew up here. Her dad was a farrier. He had a shop right here." He pointed at the corner of the lumberyard. "It's been incorporated into their store now. I think she'd like to be friends with you, Faith, regardless, because she knows what it's like to try and come home again."

Faith reached for his hand. "Then let's go and see her. I could probably manage a second breakfast right about now, and I haven't heard anything from Dave."

Danny kept hold of her hand as they strolled along the raised walkway toward Yvonne's, tipping his hat to his neighbors, and trying not to smile at their various reactions to seeing him with Faith.

He opened the door into the coffee shop and saw his mom sitting right in the middle with Ellie at her side. She waved at him and he ushered Faith ahead of him.

"Hey, Mom. I hope you don't mind me bringing Faith with me. We've both escaped from the Bryson place for a couple of hours and she's my ride back."

"Of course not." Leanne smiled. "It's lovely to see you again, Faith. Did you enjoy the wedding?"

"It was wonderful." Faith sat down and Danny took the seat next to her, winking at his half sister, who was busy eating a pile of croissants. "Jackson's a good guy."

"He certainly understands Daisy." His mom looked inquiringly at Danny. "Do you want to get yourself some coffee before we start?"

"That bad is it?" Danny joked, and turned to Faith. "Can I get any of you beautiful ladies anything to eat or drink?"

"I'd like some coffee, please," Faith said.

"Ellie?"

"I'm good." His half sister spoke around half a croissant stuck in her mouth. "This stuff is awesome!"

When he returned, his mom and Faith were chatting

away like they'd known each other for years while Ellie alternated between eating and staring at her phone.

"So, what's up?" Danny asked as he handed Faith her coffee.

Leanne took a breath. "I've decided to buy the top apartment in the old movie theater Kaiden's been renovating just down the street."

"That's a great idea," Danny said. "It's got two bedrooms, right? Ellie can hang out there when she's not at college."

"That's the plan." Leanne fiddled with her coffee mug. "If everyone's okay with it."

"Why wouldn't they be?" Danny asked, genuinely puzzled. "It's a great location, it's newly renovated by your awesome son so you won't get any nasty surprises, and you're less than fifteen minutes away from the ranch."

"Your father thinks I should move in back there. He says that since half his family have moved out there's plenty of space."

Danny frowned. "The only person who's left is Ben and he's only a mile up the road. Kaiden and Adam might not be there all the time, but they still call it home as does Evan."

"That's exactly what I told him. And I don't want to live up there anymore. It's not convenient and I don't want to end up getting roped into working full time for your father."

"He'd definitely get you doing all the unpaid labor he could." Danny fought a grin. "You know what he's like."

"He's also trying to persuade me not to lend you any money to build your own place, but I told him straight out to knock it off or I'd buy you a nice condo in New York and he'd only get to see you once a year."

"Thanks, Mom."

She nodded and he marveled at the changes in her anew. When she'd left Morgan Valley, she'd been quiet and shy, but adversity had strengthened her in ways he couldn't even imagine and now she was full of confidence. He knew how tough it had been for her to move to a city and survive while constantly being rebuffed by her soon-to-be ex-husband and denied access to her children. Eventually, she'd met a man who valued her enormously, remarried, and ended up wealthy in her own right after his death.

Even if Jeff objected to everything Leanne wanted to do, he couldn't actually stop her. That gave Danny a lot of quiet satisfaction.

"I spoke to May, the architect for the movie theater conversion, last night and asked her if she'd be interested in working with you on your new house," Leanne carried on speaking. "She'd love to meet you and talk things through."

"Kaiden spoke very highly of her, when he was working on the project," Danny said. "I'd definitely be interested."

"Great!" Leanne held up her phone. "I'll give you her number. She's staying in town for the next few weeks to finalize some details on the top-floor apartment for me and make sure the rest of the building is ready for sale."

"Four new low-cost apartments to rent or get help buying." Danny turned to Faith. "Four more people who can stay and work in Morgan Valley."

"That's awesome. I'm thinking of starting a small animal clinic here in town, so that might help me get some staff," Faith said.

"I think that's a great idea, Faith," Leanne said enthusiastically. "If you need a business partner in that venture, do let me know."

Danny grinned at her. "If you're not careful, Mom,

you'll soon own the whole town and Dad will get super salty."

"More fool him," Leanne said briskly. "If he's going to make such a fuss he can stay up on his ranch and sulk all by himself. I love this town; I was born here and the idea of investing in it to make sure it survives another hundred years greatly appeals to me."

"Go, Mom!" Ellie piped up, and clinked her mug against Leanne's. "But I doubt Jeff will really get mad, he's way too sweet and cuddly to do that."

When everyone else at the table stared at her, her brow creased. "What?"

Faith drank her coffee and enjoyed the banter between Danny, his mom, and his sister. She'd managed to check her cell phone while Danny was getting the coffee and there were no further e-mails from Brandon or Callie and nothing from Dave. For the first time in a long while she felt like her feet were firmly on the ground and that everything was going to be all right. Aware that Dave's patience wasn't endless, and that he had surgery to do at the clinic, she surreptitiously checked the time.

Danny leaned in close and lowered his voice. "Do we need to go?"

"Soon. We can't leave Rae stuck with Dave for too long. That's not fair on anyone."

He chuckled and checked his phone. "No cries for help yet, but you're right, we should be heading back." He turned to his mom. "We need to get back to the Brysons. Are you two going up to see Dad or hanging out at the hotel?"

"We're going to the ranch. Evan's taking Ellie out with him."

"Evan is?" Danny paused.

Leanne patted his shoulder. "It's okay. He's promised to be on his best behavior."

"I know how to ride," Ellie said. "And I've got a really good sense of direction if he gets lost."

"Just keep him in sight at all times and tell him I'll kill him if he plays any pranks on you," Danny instructed her.

"Will do." She grinned. "How's it going at the Brysons'?"

"We're getting there." Danny glanced over at Faith, who was talking quietly to his mom. "Faith and Dave are great veterinarians. I'm just helping out."

"She's really nice," Ellie whispered. "And she's really into you. Maybe you should ask her out."

Danny concealed a smile. "I'll think about it."

Leanne turned back to him. "I was just asking Faith if she could come to dinner with us at the ranch at the weekend before Ellie goes. Do you think you'd both be able to make it?"

"It depends on the calves," Danny said diplomatically. "We're going to ride out and see if we've missed any today so that might change things up."

"I understand." Leanne nodded. "But if you both can make it, it would mean a lot to me to have the whole family around before Ellie has to go back to school."

Much later, after they'd checked over the calves, made sure they were all well hydrated and comfortable, Faith found herself riding out over the undulating fields with Danny at her side. He looked totally at home on a horse, his body swaying, his commands so unobtrusive that she only knew he'd done something when his mount completed the move. He wore a white straw hat, his favorite fleece-lined denim jacket, and boots that looked somewhere between completely comfortable and worn out.

"Do you think we'll find any more calves?" Faith asked eventually, unwilling to break the companionable silence.

"I've got no idea. Neither Bryson wants to talk to me so I'm doing this blind same as you." He shifted his weight backward in the saddle as they went down the slope. "I hope they had the sense to leave some of them out because if that's all that's left"—he jerked his head back toward the ranch—"I guess Doug's lost three fourths of his herd."

"That's awful," Faith said. "I mean, how can he recover from that?"

"I don't know." Danny grimaced. "I'm kind of seeing why he doesn't want to come back."

"Is there anything else Silver and Ben's foundation can do for them?" Faith asked as her horse picked its way through the boulders littering the slope.

"It depends whether Doug and Sue Ellen ask them for help. I suggested it to Dr. Tio, but from what he's said, they're really not interested. I'm guessing they might sell up."

Faith glanced over at him as they reached level ground and stared out over the field looking for any elusive cattle. "Any chance you could buy this place?"

He grinned. "I wish, but my savings and ranch wages at my dad's place aren't going to hack it."

"I'm still separating my finances out from the Humboldt clinic, so I don't have any money either," Faith mused.

"Were you thinking we could buy it together?" Danny stopped moving.

"No!" Faith protested. "I was just thinking out loud about . . . possibilities."

Danny continued talking like she hadn't spoken. "Because that's some jump from friends with benefits."

"Like I'd do that to you." Faith made a face at him. "We're taking this one day at a time, remember?"

"How could I forget when you remind me every day?" Danny countered. "And here's another thing. If you come to dinner, are we supposed to act like we're together or still just friends?"

"I don't know. What do you want us to do?" Faith asked as she suddenly realized he was being serious.

He looked away from her for the first time, his gaze settling on the distant pine trees.

"What?" Faith was determined to finish the damn conversation even if it killed her. "Just tell *me*, I promise I won't bite."

He slowly turned to her, his gray eyes steady, his expression calm. "I guess I need more reassurance than I anticipated."

"About what?"

"This." He gestured at them both. "Us. I know if we admit we're seeing each other there's going to be a lot of talk—"

"About me," Faith interrupted him. "You'll probably be fine."

"Is that what this is about?" Danny asked. "You're worried about your reputation being trashed again?" He grimaced. "I hadn't thought about it from that angle."

"Why should you?" She shrugged. "Everyone loves Danny Miller in Morgan Valley."

He frowned. "And that's a problem for you?"

"It might be when I'm always cast as the bad guy," Faith said.

He considered her for a long moment and then slowly

nodded. "Okay, let's keep it as we're just good friends in front of everyone for now. And, if anyone inquires, because you know they will, I'll stick to that."

"Thank you," Faith said, and meant it.

"Awesome." His slow smile of appreciation warmed her heart. "Shall we push on? I want to get back before it gets too hot out here."

There were no more cows or calves in the Bryson fields. By the time they turned back, Faith was overheated and dispirited about the future of the ranch. She might not have had a good relationship with either of the Brysons, but she didn't want them to fail. Every empty ranch was an open invitation to just the kind of development Morgan Valley had been trying to keep out. Was it worth asking Ben and Silver if they might buy the place or should she leave that up to Danny? If the Brysons ever found out she'd suggested such a thing, they'd never sell to the foundation.

"Will you ask Ben about the ranch?" Faith said.

"I don't think it will do any good, but sure." Danny leaned down to open the final gate into the yard. "The Brysons will still have to agree to it."

"Couldn't they buy it anonymously if they had an auction?" Faith asked.

Danny grinned at her. "Like anything in Morgan Valley could be kept a secret."

"I suppose that's true." Faith sighed. "Half the valley probably saw us sneaking up the back stairs at the wedding as well."

"No one's mentioned anything about that to me," Danny said as he dismounted and turned toward her, his arms held out. "Need a hand down?"

"Yes, please." She eased her booted feet out of the

stirrups. "I haven't ridden this much for years. I'll be sore in the morning."

He lifted her down with an ease she could only appreciate. "I've got some great cream for that. Emu or ostrich or something. HW Morgan got samples of it at the national rodeo last year."

"No, thanks." She looked up at him as he continued to massage her shoulder. "But I wouldn't turn down an actual massage."

"Yeah?" He raised his eyebrows. "I learned a lot about that at college."

"I thought you were doing an agricultural degree?"

"I was." His smile widened. "The massage techniques were for horses, but I'm sure they could be adapted for humans."

She went to swat his Wrangler-covered ass, but he kissed her instead.

When he raised his head, his expression was serious. "Can I ask you something?"

"Sure."

"There are . . . organizations around now where you can put your name if you're willing to be contacted by your adopted child."

Faith went still. "Is that something you'd want to do?"

He shrugged. "It's a long shot but I guess I like the idea that if Marcus did want to find us when he turned twenty-one, or even when he was older, that there might be a way for him to do it." He searched her face. "What do you think?"

"I . . . no, I'm not sure I'd want him to find us at all."

"Why's that?"

"Because what is he going to think when he finds out we were seventeen years old?"

"That we were human and made a mistake?" His brow creased. "From what I understand you can also leave details about your family and what you've gone on to accomplish in your life, if it matters that much to you."

"I just don't think it would be right to open that door," Faith said in a rush.

Danny's smile had completely disappeared now. "Because you're ashamed of who we were. I get it." He nodded. "Then I'll leave things alone." He took her horse's reins out of her unresisting fingers. "I'll put these guys away while you start on the calves, okay?"

Faith held her ground. "I'm not *ashamed*."

He looked back at her over his shoulder. "Sure sounds like it. Or are you just ashamed of me?"

"That's totally unfair!"

"Why? You're the one who's gone on to become a vet, and I'm the fool who stayed home and still lives with his dad. You're right." He clicked to the horses and started moving again. "What kid would want a father like that?"

"Why do you do this?" She stormed after him and headed him off in front of the barn. "Why do you constantly put yourself down?"

"Because I'd rather get it out there front and center before anyone else says anything?"

"You could've gone to college, Danny, like you planned," Faith said steadily. "There was nothing stopping you."

"Sure." He stared at her, a muscle flicking in his jaw, before shaking his head. "Nothing stopping me."

She had to hastily step aside as he came toward her and went into the barn.

"Like what are you trying to say?" she called out to him, but he pretended not to hear. "All you had to do was take up one of those scholarship offers you had and leave."

He set the saddle and blanket over the top of one of the stall doors and focused his attention on removing the bridle before briefly looking up at her. "There's no point in raking up the past right now, Faith. I shouldn't have said anything. Just let it go."

"You can't just say stuff and then tell me not to be concerned about it." Faith actually stamped her foot. "Because I'm beginning to feel like you're blaming me."

He led the horse into the stall, closed the door, and came back out to start on the second horse, his movements jerky and rushed, his attention anywhere but on her.

Faith advanced toward him. "You *do* blame me, don't you?"

"Just . . . drop it, okay?"

"Danny . . ."

He finally looked her right in the eye. "I don't think this conversation is helpful, do you?"

"I don't know." Faith raised her chin. "Maybe these things needed to be said."

"Says the person who likes to compartmentalize everything." Danny obviously wasn't having it. "How about you tell me how things really are between you, Brandon, and Callie, and I'll spill all the shit I had to deal with from our parents when you weren't around?"

"I was in a *coma*!" Faith shouted. "What the hell did you expect me to do?"

"See? You won't answer *my* question but expect me to listen to you defending yourself against what happened to *me*."

"That's . . . not fair."

"Life's not fair, Faith. We of all people should know that."

Her eyes filled with tears and the thought of letting him

see even one of them fall made her turn around and leave the barn. She'd go and check on the calves and hopefully by then her desire to murder Danny Miller would have receded.

Danny took his time in the barn rubbing down the horses, checking their hooves, and making sure they had plenty of water. He was half hoping Faith might have decided to leave, but when he came out of the barn into the circular driveway, her truck was still parked there. He rarely lost his temper and he wasn't feeling too good about his spat with Faith. She had always known him best—the good and the bad—and loved him for himself anyway.

Not that she loved him right now, but she sure did get under his skin . . .

He straightened his Stetson and went into the second barn where he found her in the feed room mixing hydrating solution up in one of the big plastic drums. He leaned against the doorway and observed the rigid line of her shoulders and the way she kept her face turned away from him.

"I'm sorry," Danny said simply. "I was out of line."

"Excuse me." She hefted the plastic drum back onto the table. "I need to get past."

"I can take that," Danny offered.

"I'm quite capable, thanks."

He made no move to let her get by and she sighed.

"Okay, I'm sorry, too."

He considered her for a long moment. "My dad refused to pay anything for me to go to college. And your dad said he would write to any college I intended to go to and ask them to rescind any scholarships because of my lack of moral character."

She went very still.

"I didn't want to get into that, because it happened a long time ago and I don't want you getting mad at your dad all over again," Danny explained. "He did what he thought was right to protect his daughter."

"Destroying your chance for a future?" She suddenly looked up at him.

"As my dad had already withdrawn his offer of financial help I wasn't going anywhere anyway," Danny reminded her, "your father's threat was just frosting on a cake that didn't even exist."

"Don't be nice about him," Faith snapped. "If he was here right now, I'd . . . brain him with this plastic drum."

Danny looked at the full container. "Good job he isn't, then, because that could do some damage."

She set down the drum and came toward him. He tensed, but she did nothing more threatening than walk into his arms.

"God, I'm so sorry." Her words were muffled against his chest. "For all of it."

He held her carefully, one hand smoothing over her back until she relaxed against him. Even as he soothed her it occurred to him that she still hadn't offered him any explanation about what was going on with Brandon.

Chapter Eighteen

They'd patched things up and continued working together, but Faith was supremely conscious of the rift between her and Danny. Her father was still proving evasive, and the more she heard about his decision-making, the more she understood why. She got that he'd wanted to do his best for her and that the shock of her almost dying must have been hard to deal with, but his deliberate attempts to make Danny bear the brunt of all the blame didn't sit well with her.

She checked the calves over, glad to see that most of them were on the mend, and heard a truck horn on the driveway. After carefully washing up, she went through to see that three vehicles had arrived with Danny. His brother Ben got out of the second one and walked over to her. Unlike Danny, who favored his father, he was not only tall but broad, and redheaded. His smile was the same though.

"Hey! I hear you need some new hands around here."

"You found some?" Faith asked.

"Yeah, I managed to persuade half of the Brysons' old crew to come back and Morgan Ranch offered a couple of guys, too. They all know the procedures for containing the scours outbreak. I guess you can keep them on their toes about that, too."

"We haven't had any new cases for almost a week," Faith said. "At the moment it's just a question of keeping the remaining calves hydrated, testing as we go, and rereleasing them into uncontaminated fields."

"Sounds like a good plan." Ben shaded his eyes and glanced over at the barn. "Okay if I come in and take a look while Danny organizes the guys?"

"Sure, be my guest."

Faith already knew that Ben and Silver's foundation had stepped up to pay the wages of the new crew and pay off the ranch bills, which meant if Doug and Sue Ellen did want to come back, they would be in a much better position to make a go of things.

"Any news from the Brysons?" Ben asked.

"Not a peep. They are both in Florida right now. Dr. Tio's the only person they'll talk to, which makes things a little difficult."

"I bet." Ben paused to look at the remaining calves. "You've done a great job here, Faith."

"With a lot of help from Dave and Danny."

"I think Danny's enjoyed it," Ben said thoughtfully. "It's good for him to get away from Dad and manage stuff on his own."

"Maybe if the Brysons decide to sell you should buy this place for him, then," Faith said lightly.

Ben looked down at her from his considerable height. Unlike Evan he'd never made her feel bad about the whole Danny thing and always treated her like a friend. "You think?"

She shrugged. "It's definitely an idea. He'd run it much better than the Brysons."

"Yeah, he would."

Ben lapsed into silence and contemplated the barn. He was a man of few words, so Faith didn't take it personally.

"I hear Mom invited you to Ellie's going-away dinner."

"Yes, she did." Faith wasn't sure about the abrupt change of subject, but she wasn't willing to challenge him on it.

"You're coming, right?" Ben walked over to the gate that stopped the calves leaving the barn. "You're good for him."

"For Danny?" Faith sighed. "We argue all the time."

Ben grinned. "As I said."

"I'm not sure he sees it that way," Faith said. "And, I don't want to fight with him. I want him to be happy."

"Being happy doesn't mean never being challenged, Faith. Sometimes it takes the bad shit to make you realize you *are* happy." He suddenly straightened up and looked over his shoulder. "I should stop talking. Danny's coming our way."

"We're all set up and ready to go, boss," Danny called out to them. "And, yeah, before you get any ideas, Ben, I am talking to Faith."

"She's definitely the boss." Ben turned around and looked down at Faith. "She's been awesome."

"She has." Danny's smile warmed her. "Thankfully, with these guys taking on the bulk of the work going forward, both of us can get on with our lives again."

"Yes, thanks for that, Ben." Faith patted his sleeve. "I can't wait to get back to the rest of the work that's been piling up around poor Jenna and Dave."

"No sleep for the wicked," Ben joked. "I bet Dad's got a mountain of chores for Danny to get on with when he gets back home as well."

"He'll never let me leave again," Danny groaned.

"At least Adam's back and Evan's stepping up," Ben

remarked as they walked back through the barn. "Dad's hardly shorthanded."

"Since I reorganized the way we use our manpower, I mean person power, and set up that new schedule for the entire cattle operation, even Dad acknowledges that things have been running more smoothly," Danny said.

"I wish you'd come on over and take a look at our operations, Bro," Ben said. "I'd really value your input."

"Only if you pay me a consulting fee," Danny countered with a grin.

Ben raised his eyebrows. "Of course I would. I don't expect to get anything good for free these days."

"See?" Faith pointed at Danny. "I told you this the other day. Set up a website and take on consulting work."

For once Danny didn't immediately shoot her suggestion down. He merely looked thoughtful. "I guess Daisy could help me with that."

Suddenly, Ben met her eyes and slowly winked before patting her on the shoulder.

"We should get going. There's a lot to do."

Danny pulled up outside the McDonald place and wondered again why the hell he'd accepted Faith's invitation to dinner. She'd said it was to celebrate their liberation from the Bryson place and he'd stupidly agreed. He checked the vehicles parked in the garage and was relieved to see that Dave was home.

He opened the passenger door to retrieve the flowers and beverages he'd brought with him and self-consciously checked the collar of his newly ironed shirt. After over a week in the same two sets of clothes that he intended to set on fire after the scours infection was finally gone, it was nice to wear something different.

Instead of sticking his head through the door into the mudroom and shouting just in case Dave decided to thump him again, he went up the path to the front door. He admired the slatted pine finish and the rocks pulled out of Morgan Creek that adorned the path and the walls. Ron Mac had done a great job on the design of the house. It looked like it had grown out of the hillside. The pine trees that surrounded the site offered shade and shelter and a stunning backdrop to the mainly wooden structure, which was currently lit up from within.

"Hey, are you going to stand there all day?"

Danny looked back at the door to find Dave regarding him.

"Sorry, I was just appreciating the place. I'm planning on building something for myself and I'm always looking for inspiration," Danny said as he went through into the house. "Your dad did a great job."

"He did." Dave gestured at the flowers. "Are they for me?"

"Maybe a couple of them. You did help out at the Brysons'." Danny grinned and held up the beer. "Although you might prefer this."

"I see you're trying to cover all your bases." Dave took the beer. "But it's okay, Danny. I'm over trying to murder you. I think I'll leave that to Faith."

They entered the kitchen and Danny had a moment to appreciate the sight of Faith as she rushed around the kitchen waving a spoon, her back turned to the door.

"Dave? Where did you go? You were supposed to be watching the sauce!"

"I was opening the door to this weirdo." Dave jerked a

thumb in Danny's direction. "He seems to think we asked him to dinner."

"Shut up. We did."

Faith smiled at Danny and something happened to his heart. He didn't care if they were at odds, he just knew that there would never be another woman who would mean the same as Faith did to him. It didn't even matter what happened between them, he just knew it was the truth. Maybe it was time to take a stand and find out whether there was any hope for them having a future together and not just a past.

"Hey." He held out the bouquet. "Dave thinks they are for him, but that's up to you."

"He's not having them." She took the flowers and hugged them to her chest. "I love them."

"It's okay, I got the beer." Dave set it in the refrigerator. "That's much more important."

Danny offered Faith the bottle of wine. "I brought this, too."

"Thanks. It'll go nicely with dinner. I'm making bacon, pea, and cheddar pasta carbonara."

"It smells great," Danny said appreciatively.

Faith smiled. "I know you usually make carbonara with ham, but I've got a load of really good local bacon from Roy up at Morgan Ranch and it goes great in it."

"I bet it does. Can I open the wine for you?" Danny asked.

Dave's phone buzzed and he groaned. "I hope this isn't who I think it is." He read the text and grimaced. "I've got to take this call. Don't wait for me to eat."

Faith frowned. "Is it something I can help with? I'm supposed to be doing the night calls for the rest of the month, remember?"

"Nah, I'm good. It's not work. You enjoy your dinner with lover boy." Dave walked out of the kitchen, the phone to his ear as he listened intently.

Faith sighed and turned back to the stove. "I cooked enough for a family of eight, but I suppose it will keep."

Danny cleared his throat. "I can go home if you'd rather do this another night?"

"Don't you dare go anywhere." She pointed the spoon at him. "I'm not eating alone after I made all this effort."

"Then I'll stay. Is there anything I can help you with?"

"You can put the salad and the wine on the table, and then I think we're good to go."

Faith watched Danny pull apart a piece of garlic bread with his strong fingers and remembered how they felt on her skin. He seemed to be enjoying the food and was making easy conversation, but there was something distant about him, like his mind was on other things.

"I think we can safely say the scours outbreak is now contained," Faith said, just in case that was what was worrying him. "No new cases even at the Brysons'."

"That's great." Danny wiped his mouth with his napkin. "I guess we still don't know whether the Brysons are coming back." He twirled his fork in his spaghetti and chewed slowly. "Ben asked me if I'd be interested in running the place if he and Silver bought it for their foundation."

Ah, maybe that was what was on his mind. Faith tried to look neutral. "What did you say?"

"I told him I'd need to think about it." He looked up at her. "Did you put in a good word for me?"

She shrugged. "I didn't need to. Ben was already on it."

"I'm not sure it's what I want," Danny continued. "With Dad's health, Adam needs all hands on deck up at our place to keep things going. I think I have the tools to make us more efficient and profitable and that kind of appeals to me."

"More than owning your own place?" Faith asked.

"You know as well as I do that running a ranch is damned hard work and how easy it is for a place to fail. Owning one outright is even worse."

"I'm pretty sure that wouldn't happen to you." Faith held his gaze. "You're more than competent."

His smile was warm. "Thanks for that. I guess I'm finally beginning to believe that's true."

"It's about time." Faith finished the last piece of bacon in her bowl and sat back with a sigh. "I'll definitely make that again. It's awesome."

"As you've probably got three more meals there, I don't think you'll have to worry about making it for a while." Danny reached across the table and took Faith's hand. "I need to ask you something."

"Okay." Faith set her fork down and braced herself for just about anything.

"I'd like to speak to your dad."

She immediately tensed. "Why?"

"I think it's time we cleared a few things up, don't you? Neither of us can move forward until we understand what happened back then, and your dad has all the facts."

"I've moved forward," Faith said.

"You've certainly done a great job of telling yourself that, but Faith, our parents made a whole series of decisions for us that we're only finding out about now. We don't even know whether Marcus was adopted in California or Nevada. Someone knows and my bet is it's your dad."

"Is this about you wanting Marcus to find us?"

"No, that's not on the table." His usual smile had gone, and his expression was uncompromising. "I'll never lie to you. If we don't both want that then it doesn't happen, okay?"

Faith swallowed hard. "Thank you."

He nodded, reminding her more of his father with every second. "You don't have to talk to your dad if you don't want to. Leave it to me. I just need you to make the connection."

Faith listened to the ticking of the kitchen clock as her thoughts chased each other around her head like spring lambs. Danny was patient enough to wait her out without any signs of irritation.

She sucked in a breath. "I think we should do it together."

"You sure?" His fingers tightened around hers.

"Yes, because you're right. We do deserve to know the truth."

"Okay."

She liked the way he didn't attempt to change her mind.

"In fact, why don't we try and get hold of him right now? They should be up by now." She rose to her feet. "Help me clear the table and make some coffee and we can call him."

Half an hour later they were sitting in her dad's study, her laptop open on his desk, staring at the screen which suddenly showed her father.

"Hey, Dad!" Faith smiled even as she realized she was trembling. "How's Paris?"

"Trey Bonnie." He smiled back. "Not much golf around

here, but your mom's enjoying the culture and I'm partial to the food. She's out shopping for breakfast right now. How's it going with you guys?"

"Well, we think we've contained the scours outbreak, which is awesome, so things are pretty much back to normal."

"Great! Is that Dave back there? Not like you to be so quiet, Son. Has your big sister got you running scared?"

Faith drew Danny forward. "It's not Dave."

"Hey, Mr. McDonald," Danny said. "Faith and I thought it would be a good idea to talk to you together about what happened when Marcus was born."

Her father's face sagged. "Really? Why, Faith? Why now?"

"Because Danny and I need to move past this, and you can help with that," Faith said firmly. "This isn't about you, Dad. It's about us. Please just listen for a minute."

Danny took his cue. "We just want to know whether Marcus was adopted in California or Nevada because each state has different rules about adoptions and what information can be shared or kept secret. Basically, we want to make sure we're ready if Marcus tries to contact us through the state adoption agencies."

Her father sighed. "He won't do that."

"How do you know?" Faith asked.

"Because we didn't go through the state. It was a private adoption. I guess they must have sent in paperwork at some point to change his birth certificate and all that stuff, but—"

"Hold up a minute, sir," Danny interrupted him. "What do you mean by private?"

"Well, your mother and I knew a family who were looking to adopt a kid and when all this happened, we decided the easiest way to give Marcus a good home was with them."

"You *knew* them?" Faith's voice rose with every syllable.

Her father's eyebrows rose. "How do you think we got all the pictures?"

"Through the adoption agency agreement," Faith said. "Are they local?"

"Not anymore. They moved a couple of years ago because their eldest was off to college on the East Coast. The mom's family were from there and she decided it was time for her kids to get to know that side of the family."

"Are you saying I could've bumped into this kid anytime in the last fifteen or so years?" Danny asked. "I coached Little League, I helped out with Bridgeport High football."

"Yup, I suppose you might have done." Faith's dad nodded. "Imagine that!"

"You're not helping, Dad." Faith grabbed hold of Danny's hand. "Does Jeff Miller know about this?"

"No, I didn't trust him not to go around there and start telling them how to raise his grandson. You know what Jeff's like. And he might have told Danny, sorry, son, which wouldn't have been good."

"Did Mom know?"

"Yes, of course."

Faith struggled to think what to say next. She was way beyond anger and into middling panic.

"Why didn't you tell me all this?" Faith asked.

Her dad frowned. "Because up until now, you never wanted to know. We thought you were okay with everything and that the less said the better. When we tried to broach the subject after you recovered, you said you wanted to get on with your life and go to college. We took you at your word." He paused. "Is Danny pressurizing you to do this?"

"No, not at all," Faith answered. "It was a joint decision."

Danny's arm came around her shoulders and she leaned back to hear as he whispered in her ear. "Do we want to ask for the name of this couple?"

"I'm not sure."

He nodded and turned back to the screen. "Thanks for sharing all this information, Mr. McDonald. We appreciate it."

"Just remember we found that baby a loving home with parents who were grateful to receive such a gift. Maybe we should've insisted and told you earlier and then we wouldn't have to be having these discussions today." He leaned forward. "We tried to do what we thought you wanted, Faith. I hope you know that."

"Thanks, Dad." Faith leaned forward and abruptly turned off the screen before getting to her feet and walking over to the window to stare out into the darkness.

"You okay?" Danny asked softly.

She glanced over her shoulder at him.

"Not really."

"We know more than we did before, right?"

She swung around. "Why aren't you angry?"

"At what exactly?" He frowned. "Marcus grew up in a family who loved him and who had a connection with your parents. Isn't that a good thing?"

"I wasn't talking about that." She raised her chin. "Why aren't you angry with *me*? Apparently, I'm the one who shut down any attempt by my parents to tell me what was going on back then. *I'm* the one who decided it was more important to go to college than come home and face what I'd done."

"Faith . . ." He slowly stood up and held out his hand. "Don't—"

"Don't what? Weren't you the one saying I compartmentalized everything? That I locked things away because I didn't want to deal with them? Well, you were right, weren't you? I did that to my own son. I don't know how you can bear to even look at me."

His brow creased. "Because you're beating yourself up about something that isn't your fault."

"It was my fault!" She only realized she was shouting when he backed up a step. "I didn't want to hear anything!"

"You nearly died, you'd just had a baby, and you were seventeen. You were hardly in a good place emotionally, physically, or mentally," Danny said evenly.

"Didn't you also tell me that I didn't have the right to use that as an excuse to avoid things?"

"Now you're just twisting my words." Danny's expression tightened. "And, I'm not the enemy here. I'm on your side."

She turned away because she couldn't bear to see the compassion and understanding in his eyes. Things she definitely didn't deserve.

"I think you should go."

His breath hitched. "*What?*"

"You've got what you came for. You know where Marcus is, you also know your family had nothing to do with that, and you know I let you down. Isn't that enough?"

The silence behind her grew like a living thing so much so that she braced herself for impact.

"I'll go, but I want you to know something before I do," Danny said slowly. "I don't blame you one bit for what you did or didn't do back then. I didn't exactly cover myself in

glory either and I have too many regrets to count. You did
the best you could at the time, Faith. We both did, so please
forgive yourself, okay? And if you want to come find me
and talk it through, this time I promise I'll be there for you
whatever it takes."

He waited but she couldn't turn around even as his
words sunk into her soul. She didn't deserve them. She
didn't deserve him.

Eventually she heard the door click closed behind him
and she finally gave in to her need to cry.

Chapter Nineteen

Danny set out the water glasses and napkins on the table, which Daisy had decorated with vases of vibrant flowers, and went back to get the silverware. The house was full of Millers including his mother, his half sister, all his siblings and their better halves, and even a kid. Adam and Leanne were cooking in the kitchen and Danny was doing whatever he was told. The problem was it didn't matter how busy he kept himself, all he could see was Faith's back turned to him and her complete dismissal of everything he'd tried to say to her.

He got that she'd been shocked to hear that she'd been the one refusing to hear any details about the adoption, but he also knew she'd been in a bad place for a seventeen-year-old. And he bet her parents hadn't pushed that hard to make her change her mind. Less said soonest mended was probably the McDonald family motto. He even understood her father's reluctance to lay that on her, but she'd asked, and after prevaricating for weeks he'd finally answered her honestly.

What really frustrated him was that he couldn't make

things right for her and that at this point she wasn't even letting him in to try.

"Danny?"

He looked up as his mother set a pan full of roast pota- toes on a trivet. "Can you call everyone in for dinner?"

He went outside and shouted toward the barn where Roman was proudly showing off his calf to as many people he could persuade to go and see him. Then he went back into the long connecting hallway and shouted down there as well. Within seconds, Millers appeared from every- where and converged on the table. Of course, Daisy was a Lymond now and Leanne and Ellie had a different last name, but they still counted.

To his surprise even before they all sat down, Daisy banged on the table for attention.

"Hey! We have news!"

"You pregnant already?" Kaiden asked, and received a death glare that didn't deter him in the slightest. "Fast work, Jackson. I didn't know you had it in you."

"Shut up, Kaiden," Daisy said. "The first thing is that the coins Cauy and Jackson found in the old Morganville Mine on their property were sold at auction yesterday!"

"That's taken a while," their father commented. "Did you make any money?"

"Yeah." Jackson grinned like a fool. "A whole shitload. Enough to fix up our place and then some."

Everyone whooped and banged on the table as Kaiden shouted, "Drinks are on Jackson for the next year, okay?"

"Sounds good to me." Jackson turned to Daisy. "Now tell them the most exciting part."

"You're having triplets?" Kaiden yelled.

Daisy ignored her brother. "My company's being bought out!"

"Is that good?" Jeff looked dubious. "I thought you were planning on going public or something."

"Well, we were, but one of our big competitors came in with a bid to buy us outright. It was a good bid." She swallowed hard. "Like a multimillion-dollar bid."

Silence fell around the table as they all stared at Daisy. As usual, it was down to Kaiden to break the spell. He looked across the table at his girlfriend, Julia.

"Hey, I think we need to up our game here, honey, don't you?"

"Shut up, Kaiden." This time there was a chorus of voices.

"That's wonderful, Daisy," Leanne said. "We're all so proud of you."

"Well, we've got to pay Chase Morgan's investment back and the rest gets split between the four of us, but none of us will ever have to worry about money again," Daisy said.

"That's awesome! You two will have so much cash you'll be swanning around like Silver and Ben and forget all about us little people," Evan, who was seated next to Danny, said.

"Hey," Ben called out. "We don't swan, we fly."

"On your own private jet," Evan countered. "Are you going to get one of those, Daisy? You could keep it here."

"*So* not happening." Daisy sat down, her face flushed, her hand tucked tightly into Jackson's.

For a second Danny almost resented their happiness and togetherness before he shut the feeling down. Daisy and Jackson deserved everything they had. The real issue was his lack of satisfaction with his own life, not them.

"Did Faith get held up at work?" his mom called out to him as she took her place at the foot of the table.

"Yeah, she sent her apologies. She might not be able to make it," Danny replied.

"That's a shame. I was looking forward to talking to her." Leanne smiled sympathetically before turning to Ellie, who sat on her right.

"Why did Mom invite Faith?" Evan asked Danny. "Like, she's not family or anything."

Danny shrugged. "How should I know?"

"You didn't ask her to?"

"Why would I?" Danny met his brother's gaze.

"Because you're totally gone on her?" Evan rolled his eyes. "Maybe she didn't come because she knew everyone else wouldn't be pleased to see her."

"Like you, you mean?"

"I like her, but as I told her it doesn't mean I like her messing with your head again."

"You told her that? To her face?" Danny asked.

"You're my favorite brother." Evan frowned. "Of course I did."

"You thought it was okay to interfere in my relationship with her?"

"Whoa." Evan held up a hand. "Back off, Bro. What relationship? I did it for your own good."

"Like you'd know what was best for me?" Danny was only aware that his voice had risen when he realized the whole table had gone quiet. "You know nothing, Evan."

"I know you're keeping secrets from this family and that Faith walked out on you. Isn't that enough?" Evan wasn't backing down.

"You also know why Faith did that, so maybe you should shut the hell up right now before you say something you shouldn't," Danny snapped. "Grow up, Evan. This isn't some stupid TV drama. It's my goddam life!"

"Evan . . ." Their mother attempted to intervene. "I don't think this is the time or the place for this, do you?"

"Why not?" Evan looked around the table. "We're all here. Maybe it's time to talk about why you're all suddenly okay with Faith hanging around Danny after everything she did to him? I remember how gutted he was. Don't you? Like he'd lost his way? And you're all okay about her doing that to him *again*?" He slapped the table with his palm. "Come on!"

Something inside Danny shifted and he rose to his feet, his gaze meeting his father's, who gave him an imperceptible nod.

"Maybe Evan's got a point and you should all know the truth about why Faith left."

"You don't owe anyone an explanation, Danny." Adam immediately jumped to his defense.

"Thanks, but I can't sit here and let you all think badly of Faith anymore." He took a steadying breath. "We ran away to Vegas to get married because she was pregnant. We didn't realize we were too young to do that without parental consent. While we were there, Faith went into premature labor and I had to call her parents. She ended up in the hospital having an emergency caesarian, went into a coma after the birth, and almost died. Meanwhile, Dad arrived, I was bundled back home like I didn't matter, and Faith's parents made some decisions about the baby that neither of us had any control over."

He studied the horrified faces of his audience.

"Part of the deal was that if Faith wanted her parents to

support her then she couldn't come home until she'd at least qualified. As it turned out she didn't come home until her parents needed her here because she didn't want to upset my life again." He stared down at Evan. "So, if any of you want to talk shit about Faith, come and talk to me, okay?"

Leanne raised her hand. "We have a *grandchild*?"

Danny nodded. "Yup, his name's Marcus, unless they changed it, which is highly likely. He's seventeen and he lives on the East Coast with his new family."

"Have you met him?"

"No, and we don't intend to. He's happy, and he has parents who love him. What would happen if we turned up now and disrupted his life for no purpose?"

"But he's your kid," Kaiden said slowly. "Don't you think he has a right to know where he came from?"

"If that's something he wants to find out when he's older, he can do that," Danny said. "But until then, I think he deserves to live his life in peace, okay?"

There was a lot of consternation on some of the faces, but he got that. He felt it himself.

"Did you know?" His mom had now turned his attention to her ex-husband.

"I knew the basics." Jeff shrugged. "I was the one who had to go all the way to Vegas to bring Danny home. He was in a terrible state. I did what the McDonalds asked me to do, brought him safely back here, and kept his secrets."

"And you never bothered to tell me?" Leanne asked.

Jeff held her gaze. "I promised Danny and the McDonalds I'd keep my mouth shut and I have. Not that I wanted to— but a promise is a promise." He took a sip of water. "I saw the boy once or twice."

Danny stared at his father. "*You* did? Ron McDonald said he didn't tell you."

"He didn't, and I certainly didn't go looking for him." He shrugged. "The mother came up to me once at one of the 4-H events and thanked me. I had no idea what she was talking about at first and almost told her to back off until the penny dropped. Her kid looked just like you, Son, so I had no reason to doubt her story. She seemed nice if a bit overemotional."

"I thought you said they lived on the East Coast, Danny?" His mother frowned.

"They do now," Danny confirmed, and held up his hand before his father could speak. "I don't want to know any names, okay? If you two want to discuss this, can you do it after we eat? All this good food is going cold and we're here to celebrate Ellie, Daisy, and Jackson, not rake over old family scandals."

"Yes, let's eat." As usual Adam came to his rescue. "Dad, do you want to say a quick prayer?"

Much later, Danny went out to the barn to make sure Roman had secured his calf safely for the night. He tended to get excited and forget to shut the gate before he left. Danny also needed a moment of peace. Between the deafening silence from Faith and the whole dragging out of his private life into the family spotlight he was off-kilter. No one had asked him anything about Faith or Marcus after they'd eaten, which he'd appreciated. Evan had tried to apologize, which Danny respected, but he wasn't ready to forgive him just yet. Evan's ability to just blurt stuff out was legendary, but it sure wasn't helpful and he was way too old to get away with it.

He checked Applejack's foreleg and reminded himself to give Andy a call to come and put the regular horseshoe back on. He spent a while feeding apple cores to his horse as the solid stillness of the night curled around him. The sigh of the wind in the pine trees, the occasional shifting of a horse's hoof against the concrete barn floor, and the scrabbling of the rodents along the draining gutters was a well-loved rhythm that somehow soothed him.

He wasn't aware exactly when his mother appeared because she didn't say anything but simply joined him staring out at the star-filled sky. Eventually she did look up at him.

"Are you okay?"

"I'm hanging in there."

"I wish I'd known sooner about what you and Faith went through."

"You couldn't have done anything."

"I could've been there for you—stood up to the Mc-Donalds because I know what Ron's like, argued that you and Faith should be given the chance to make your own decisions together when she got well again."

Danny shrugged. "They didn't know if she would survive. She was in a coma."

"Then they should've left the decision up to you."

"I would've kept him," Danny said. "That was the whole point of going to Vegas in the first place. I thought that if Faith and I were married no one would be able to take our kid away from us."

"It was a good plan." His mom nodded. "It's a shame it didn't work out."

"It was a terrible plan." Danny half smiled. "I panicked. Faith told me I was making things worse and then . . .

when she got sick, I felt I'd really screwed everything up forever."

"You can't predict what life is going to throw at you, Danny. Sometimes you just have to take the knocks, pick yourself up, and move forward." Leanne nudged him. "Ask me how I know."

"But you got your happy ending with Declan, and now you and Dad are getting on fine, right?"

"*Yes,* because I didn't give up."

Danny shook his head. "Faith's decided everything was her fault and that she doesn't deserve forgiveness. I've tried to tell her that's not true, but she doesn't want to listen."

"She sounds just like me when I met Declan," Leanne said. "I blamed myself for everything that went wrong between me and Jeff. I didn't think I deserved to be happy, let alone be loved by a decent man like Declan. I pushed him away for years."

"I guess Faith shoved everything into a box and tried to forget about it, but coming back here and facing me suddenly made it hard to keep the lid on everything."

"I think you're right," Leanne said. "You're the kind of person to work things through, but not everyone can do that. I certainly couldn't."

"What made you change your mind?" Danny asked, his gaze on the crescent moon and the distant peaks of the Sierra Nevadas. "How did you forgive yourself?"

"Time." She shrugged. "A growing acceptance of who I was, what I wanted to be in the future, and the solid support of a man who wouldn't let me shoulder all the blame. Declan had been there with the death of his only son. He knew what I needed."

"Which was?"

"One, to forgive myself, and two, Declan's unconditional acceptance and love. The first was up to me, the second came from him. Eventually, I began to believe he meant it and that I was worthy of that love."

Danny considered her words for a long while. "That's what I want to do for Faith."

She elbowed him in the side. "Then why are you standing here talking to me? Go and tell her."

"Aren't you supposed to be at that Miller thing?" Dave asked from his position on the couch.

"I decided not to go." Faith ate another handful of chips from the bag. "I didn't feel up to dealing with all the Millers at once."

"Understandable." Dave yawned until his jaw cracked.

They had the TV on, but neither of them was really watching. It occurred to Faith that her brother looked almost as miserable as she did.

"Why aren't you out and about yourself?" Faith asked. "It's the weekend."

Dave shrugged. "I thought you were going out, so I asked someone over."

"You can still do that. I can go up to my room," Faith said encouragingly.

"He couldn't come anyway."

"Was that the phone call you had yesterday?" Faith ate more chips.

"Yeah, usually his grandmother goes to play bridge tonight, but it was called off, so he had to stay home."

"That's a shame." Faith studied her brother. "You could go over there."

"I'm always over there." Dave hesitated. "He thought it might be a good idea to tell her about us."

"Ah, okay." Faith nodded. "I can see why he might want to do that alone." She gestured at his phone. "Are you expecting him to call you?"

"I guess." Dave shifted restlessly against his pillows. "I don't think I'll be able to settle down and do anything until he does."

"I'm sure it will be fine—"

Even as she spoke, Dave's phone beeped, and he held it up to his ear. "Hey." He nodded. "Okay, I'll see you in ten." He ended the call and looked over at Faith. "He's coming over."

"How did he sound?"

"His usual charming self."

"That's good, right?" Faith reluctantly closed the bag of chips. "I'll get out of your way."

"Can you stay until he gets here?"

"If you like." Faith subsided into the couch, aware that she was in her jammies and hadn't washed her hair that morning. But it wasn't as if Dr. Tio would be looking at her anyway. "Shall I make some coffee?"

"I'll get on that. I need to do something." Dave shot to his feet and dusted down his Cheetos-coated T-shirt. "Or maybe I should take a quick shower."

"How about you do that, and I'll deal with the coffee?" Faith offered.

If she could do one thing in her life to make someone else's happy-ever-after come true she was all for it.

"Okay, I'll be quick." Dave shoved a hand through his

hair. "Just pretend everything's normal if he gets here early, okay?"

Faith had never seen her brother so flustered and shut down her usual smart sisterly remarks. "Sure."

She'd barely had time to make the coffee before the doorbell rang and she went out to answer it. Dr. Tio looked like he'd run all the way from his house in town. His smile faltered slightly as he looked hopefully over her shoulder.

"Hi! Is Dave in?"

Faith had barely stepped aside to let him in when Dave came thundering down the stairs. Even as Faith was shutting the door, her brother and Tio were hugging things out, which made her want to cry stupid happy tears. She didn't say a word as they disappeared toward the back of the house where, she assumed, they wanted some privacy.

The sound of another truck pulling up made her hesitate by the front door. Had Tio's grandmother come after him? It seemed somewhat unlikely. She cautiously opened the door again and saw Danny coming toward her, his expression so serious that she considered backing up and pretending she wasn't home.

He looked up and saw her silhouetted against the light of the house and went still.

"Hey." He gestured at the steps. "Can I come up?"

Faith nodded, turned on her heel, and left the door wide open for him. She went into the kitchen and stood by the coffee maker while she tried to collect her scrambled thoughts. He came in, took his Stetson off, and placed it carefully on the countertop.

"How are you doing?" Danny asked.

"I'm sorry I didn't come to the dinner tonight," Faith said. "I just couldn't . . . face everyone."

"That's not like you."

She shrugged. "I guess I'm feeling a tad vulnerable right now."

"Well, you didn't miss much," Danny said. "Daisy's sold her company and she's now a multimillionaire. Jackson and Cauy sold the buried coins from Morganville Mine and made a fortune. And I got mad at Evan and told everyone what really went down in Vegas." He paused. "I also told them that if they had any questions, they should talk to me and not you."

Faith blinked and studied the hard set of his jaw.

"You look just like your father right now."

"Maybe it was time to show my Jeff side. Whatever happens I never want you to feel like you can't live in your own hometown."

"Thanks for the heads-up." Faith tried to gauge how she thought about all the Millers knowing about Marcus and couldn't quite get her head around it. "I appreciate it."

He stared at her for a long minute and reached for his hat. "I guess I should let you get on—"

"No! I mean, would you like some coffee?" Faith blurted out. She really wasn't at her best right now, but she'd have to bumble through. "I just made it."

"You sure about that?"

"It's definitely fresh."

He sighed and let go of his hat. "That's not what I meant, but why not? I didn't get any at home because I didn't want to hang around."

Faith poured two mugs and added cream and sugar to hers, sugar to Danny's, and slid the mug across the counter-top to him.

"Thanks." He took a sip and then set it back down. "The thing is—"

The doorbell rang.

Faith gave him a distracted look over her shoulder as she headed toward the hall. "I just need to check who this is." Maybe Tio's grandmother really had come after him.

She opened the door and frowned.

"Callie?"

"Oh, thank God you're here, Faith." Callie swept into the house. "I was so afraid you wouldn't be home, or that I'd get the wrong house. It's so dark out here and the roads . . ." She stopped to unwrap a scarf from around her neck. Her short blond hair was in disarray and her expression tragic. "Wow, what a beautiful house."

"Thank you," Faith said. "What the hell are you doing here?"

"Can we go through to the kitchen? I'm dying for a cup of coffee." Callie headed off down the hallway. "I'm so sorry to intrude like this, but I didn't know what else to do."

"Callie . . ." Faith followed her old colleague and her ex-husband's new wife into the kitchen where Danny sat at the countertop. "I still don't know why you're here."

Callie pulled up short. "Oh, God, I didn't realize you had a visitor."

Danny held up a hand. "Don't mind me. I'll be out of here as soon as Faith asks me to go."

"Don't go." Faith looked at him and then back at Callie. "I'm not comfortable with you being here at all."

"But you're the only person who can talk some sense into Brandon!"

"I've already told him that I want nothing to do with this," Faith said.

"He *told* you? He expected you to help him?" Callie snorted. "That's just so typical!"

The doorbell rang again, and Danny slid off his stool. "I'll get it."

"Don't—" Faith held out her hand, but it was too late; he'd already gone. Somehow, she wasn't surprised when he reappeared with Brandon in tow.

Brandon went straight to Callie. "Why the hell did you come here? What were you trying to achieve?"

"I was trying to make some sense out of your stupid decision to divorce me!" Callie fired back. "I thought that Faith might help me explain to you why me being pregnant doesn't have to be a deal breaker!"

"Faith doesn't want to be involved!" Brandon fired back.

"And you only know that because you went behind my back and asked her to intervene on your side!"

Danny came over and stood slightly behind Faith, his expression a combination of awe and deep interest.

"Excuse me," Faith tried, but they were too busy glaring at each other to take much notice of her. "Excuse me!" This time she shouted. "This is not okay. Neither of you should be in my house right now."

"But Faith." Callie turned to her, her voice wobbling. "I know you and Brandon had some problems trying to conceive, but that's hardly my fault, is it?"

"*Some* problems?" Brandon spoke up. "Three years of absolute hell while we tried every test and every procedure known to man!"

Faith held his gaze. "I can assure you it was far worse for me than it was for you, Brandon."

He had the grace to blush. "Okay, maybe, but you can't deny that it eventually sunk our marriage."

Danny's hand came to rest on Faith's shoulder, grounding her.

"Then why can't you be pleased that I got pregnant

without even trying?" Callie asked him. "I changed from one brand of birth control to another, got the flu at the same time, took antibiotics, and ended up pregnant."

Brandon stared at her, his mouth open. "You might have mentioned that part sooner, Callie. I thought—I believed you'd done it deliberately."

"I didn't want you to know I'd messed up!" Callie said. "I thought—after everything that happened with Faith you'd be thrilled!"

"Hold up a minute," Danny said slowly. "You thought your husband would be thrilled that you could do something Faith couldn't?"

Callie's guilty gaze flicked toward Faith. "I didn't mean it quite like that."

"It sure sounded like it." Danny wasn't having it. "I might just be a bystander, but how come you two think it's okay to turn up in the middle of the night and air your dirty laundry in front of the woman you both betrayed?"

Brandon went to stand beside Callie. "That's hardly any of your business."

Faith cleared her throat. "You made it his business by bringing your marital problems into my home. How *dare* you?" She turned to Callie first. "You were my friend. I told you *everything* and guess what? It does look like you thought you could do better than me and give Brandon a child."

"That's not fair! You said you were okay with everything, that we were still friends," Callie cried.

"What choice did you give me about that, Callie?" Faith asked. "If I had any chance of getting away, I had to work with you both to keep the clinic running until I could buy myself out."

Faith turned to Brandon. "And you think it was bad for

you? I was the one who had to record my temperature, keep all those damn charts, rush off to the doctors to get blood taken and hormone levels checked and . . ." She waved a hand. "Then I find out that you've been telling Callie how awfully hard it is on you, and suddenly I'm the bad guy? You both betrayed me and I'm tired of trying to pretend that *any* of it was okay."

She pointed to the door. "Now, you can both get out of my house and please don't ever come back."

"Faith, I think you're being a little unfair here." Brandon took Callie's hand. "I didn't physically cheat on you while we were still married—I . . ."

"No, you did something far worse, Brandon. You both betrayed me mentally and emotionally," Faith said, refusing to look away. "And then you tried to make me feel bad if I didn't go along with it. Well, I'm done being nice."

Callie drew herself up and faced Faith. "I'm sorry that you feel this way, Faith, but it's not our fault that you can't have kids, and I won't be made to feel bad because I can."

When Faith opened her mouth to speak Danny suddenly moved in front of her. "Can I see you both out? There's a hotel down in Morgantown if you need somewhere to stay for the night."

He escorted them firmly but politely to the door, offered vague instruction about how to get to town, and just about resisted the urge to kick them down the steps before shutting the door behind them. When he got back to the kitchen, Faith was standing with her back to him staring out the rear window. Her stance reminded him forcibly of the last time they'd spoken, which wasn't good.

"They're still by their cars arguing, but I turned off all the outside lights so hopefully they'll get the message and leave," Danny reported back.

"You should have sent them up to the ghost town," Faith said.

"I didn't think of that," Danny said thoughtfully. "Not sure if the Morgans would be happy with trespassers on their land, but I'd quite like to see them being run off."

"I don't care." She swung around to face him, her arms folded under her chest, and her head held high.

"Neither do I. What a pair of shits." Danny went and poured them both more coffee. "I'm impressed that you put up with them for as long as you did."

Inside, his heart was aching for what she'd been through, but he waited for a signal from her to understand what she needed from him right now.

"I didn't feel like I had any other choice. I had to save the business."

"So you said." Danny focused on the coffee. "Still."

"I did what I normally do, packed all the hurt away in a box, sealed it up, and got on with my life while telling myself that everything between us was fine when it obviously was not fine." She blew out a breath. "In a weird way it was good to get that off my chest."

"I bet." He slid the coffee over toward her. "After facing down my entire family at dinner I'm beginning to think my dad might be right about letting it all out sometimes."

She shuddered. "Not all the time."

"Definitely not." He met her gaze and took a deep breath. "I admire you for saying what you did. I think it's one of the reasons I still love you."

"What did you say?" Faith whispered.

"You heard me." Danny sipped his coffee like he had all the time in the world and his heart wasn't thumping fit to burst.

"We—" She waved a hand at him. "Of course you loved me. I loved you, too."

"I'm not talking about the past and you know it," Danny replied. "I guess, what I need to know is whether you love me, too."

"Didn't you just hear all that?" she asked. "Haven't I already proved I'm not good enough for you?"

"I think you're just fine the way you are. I always have," Danny said. "You've had a whole load of shocks to deal with recently, and I know you hate that. How about when you sit down and think things through you give yourself some credit, accept that you are instantly forgivable, and come around to my way of thinking?"

"About what?"

"Deciding whether you're in love with me." He shrugged. "It's an easy question. Once you answer that then we can deal with everything else together."

"It's not that simple," Faith protested.

Danny set his coffee down and picked up his hat. "Yeah, it is."

"Where are you going?" she demanded as he set off for the door.

"To make sure those fools are off your land and to lock the gate behind me so they can't get back in again."

"But—" She came toward him, her voice rising.

"You know where I live." He looked down at her. "As I said, come and give me an answer. I can take it."

"Danny . . ."

He gently dropped a kiss on her nose. "'Night, Faith. Give Dave and Tio my best."

Chapter Twenty

"So Tio's grandmother was all, like, don't you think I'd noticed? And Tio was all, but are you okay about it? And she said she totally was and hugged him and they both cried."

Dave was regaling her with way too many details about what had happened between him and Tio the night before, but Faith nodded and smiled as she ate her way through a massive bowl of frosted cereal with marshmallows that was supposed to brighten her day. He looked so happy that she didn't have the heart to stop him.

"That's awesome." Faith ate another spoonful of cereal. "I guess Mom and Dad know already?"

"Yeah, they worked it out a year or so ago."

"Well, I'm really happy for both of you," Faith said. "He's way too good for you, of course, but—"

"Ha, ha." Dave pointed his fork at her. "Seeing as you're hanging out with Danny Miller again maybe we balance each other out."

Faith ate more cereal and checked the time. She was due up at the Brysons' for one last check before they could relax the quarantine. The two fields where she suspected the cows and calves had first contracted scours were currently cordoned off and would be dealt with when the Brysons came back.

If they came back.

She looked up to ask Dave and found he was still staring at her.

"What?"

"You didn't immediately deny you weren't seeing Danny."

"So?"

"I guess that's progress." Dave filled his flask with the rest of the coffee. "Admitting you have a problem is the first step toward recovery."

"What if I don't want to recover?"

He smiled. "Then I suppose you're addicted?" He got off his seat and came around to her side of the counter. "I'm good with it."

"Like I care what you think," Faith groused.

"How could you not care? I'm your adorable baby brother." He gave her a noogie. "I just want you to stick around and be happy, Sis. See you at the clinic when you get back."

Faith finished her cereal, the sound of her crunching loud in the silence. She wondered whether Callie and Brandon had gone back home, or if they'd stayed the night somewhere. Reluctantly, she got out her phone. There was nothing from Danny, but there was a message from Brandon asking if she'd be willing to speak to him and Callie at the hotel in town before they left at lunchtime.

Faith considered her options. *Was* she willing? Did they deserve any more of her time? She'd think about that while she drove up to the Brysons'.

It was a beautiful clear day, the sky an endless blue without a cloud in sight, heat already shimmering off the roads and heating up the rocks. She loved Morgan Valley. The thought of settling down with her family within reach and the potential of expanding the business appealed to her greatly. She'd have to work things out with her parents before she made any final decisions, but they weren't the only people who had made mistakes, and she knew in her heart that they'd only wanted the best for her.

And then there was Danny . . . she sighed as she turned into the Bryson driveway. He was as strong and reliable as the mighty Sierra Nevadas that enclosed the valley and just as full of contradictions. He was waiting for her to make her mind up about their relationship and she already knew he had the patience of a saint.

She pulled up in front of the barn alongside an unfamiliar car and looked cautiously around.

"Hey."

She almost jumped when Sue Ellen appeared in the doorway of the house. She was almost unrecognizable having lost so much weight.

"Hey!" Faith held up her bag like a shield. "I'm not trying to intrude, Sue Ellen. I just need to make some final checks on the calves and then I'll leave you to it."

"Don't worry. I'm not going to jump down your throat." Sue Ellen cleared her own throat. "I hear you did a really good job keeping things together for us. Thanks."

"It wasn't just me. Dave and Danny Miller were here a lot as well," Faith said. "How's Doug? Is he here?"

"He won't come back." Sue Ellen shifted her position slightly and pushed open the door. "Come in and have something to drink, will you?"

"Sure. Thanks."

Faith entered the shadowed house, took off her boots, washed up, and went through into the kitchen where Sue Ellen was setting out a jug of iced tea on the table. She accepted a glass of tea, winced slightly at the sweetness before deciding it went well with the marshmallows, and downed half the glass.

Sue Ellen appeared lost in thought, her gaze drifting around the kitchen as if she was trying to recognize something unfamiliar. Reluctant to disturb the silence, and still unsure of Sue Ellen's motives, Faith stayed quiet.

"Ben and Silver made me an offer for the ranch," Sue Ellen finally said.

"Is that something you'd be interested in? Selling up I mean?"

Sue Ellen shrugged. "I can't run this place by myself."

"If you wanted to, I'm sure Ben and Silver could make that happen," Faith said gently. "You're more than capable."

"I've kind of lost heart." Sue Ellen sighed. "All those dead calves . . . and all because Doug and I were too proud to ask for help. I think we both need a new start and the money would mean we could go anywhere, or just travel the world for a while. We've been stuck here for years."

"Ranching is hard," Faith agreed, and hesitated. "Have you thought of maybe taking a year off to think about things and then making a decision? I'm sure Ben and Silver would keep this place going for you while you were away."

Sue Ellen frowned. "I hadn't thought of that. I don't think Doug will go for it, but everyone keeps telling me not to make such an important decision too quickly."

Faith didn't say anything but sipped her tea.

"Dr. Tio said the only reason we have any cattle left is because of you and Danny."

"Danny was amazing. He put in more hours than any of us," Faith said. "Have you spoken to him?"

"I'm kind of embarrassed," Sue Ellen said slowly. "He was the one who found me in the barn completely failing at everything."

"One thing I can tell you about Danny Miller is that he has an amazing capacity to forgive people," Faith said. "Ask me how I know."

Sue Ellen smiled for the first time. "He's still sweet on you."

"Then I'll take advantage of that and make sure you get to speak to him soon." Faith finished her tea, aware that they were heading toward dangerous ground. "I'd better get on. It was nice visiting with you, Sue Ellen."

"It's okay, I'm not going to shout at you about Danny anymore either. Doug and I really need to let it go."

"That would be awesome." Faith still stood up. "I'll go and call Danny, okay?"

"Tell him I'm going back to Florida tomorrow to tell Doug about Ben's offer." Sue Ellen met her gaze. "Thank you again, Faith. I really mean it."

"You're more than welcome." Faith set the glass in the sink. "I'll come back and give you an update before I leave."

She went out into the light and blew out a long breath. That had gone way better than she had expected. The thought of the Brysons walking away from the ranch they'd farmed for three generations still made her sad. At least she'd suggested alternatives to Sue Ellen giving it all up too fast and then regretting it.

She sent a text to Danny but didn't wait for an answer. He'd either turn up or he wouldn't. She'd done her part.

An hour later, after she'd given her report to Sue Ellen, she was back at the clinic where she took over from Dave, who had to deal with an emergency. The place was running way more smoothly now with patients able to book appointments online as well as by phone and, even better, everyone was on board with it. The old ways of turning up unannounced at the clinic, or at the house, or meeting up with her dad at the golf club weren't going to hack it anymore.

Her parents were due back in four weeks. She wondered what her dad would think of the rest of the improvements she'd made to the business. He'd certainly appreciate the increased revenue stream. Faith's phone buzzed and she saw another text from Brandon, whom she'd totally forgotten about.

> We are leaving Morgantown at noon. Have decided to get counseling together. I apologize for descending on you like that and hope we can repair the damage at some point.

"Not if I have anything to say about it," Faith muttered, channeling her best Jeff Miller. "The nerve of some people."

She checked in with her techies and admin and decided to walk back up the slope to the house to get some lunch. She needed to think, and the house was empty enough for her to do that in private. The walk helped clear her head

even more although she was still puffing when she reached
the side door and looked for her key.

"Faith?"

She almost squawked when someone spoke from
behind her.

"Brandon . . ." She spun around only to find Evan
Miller behind her, hat in hand. "What do you want?"

"I just wanted to talk to you for a minute." He smiled.
"I didn't mean to give you a heart attack."

"Then don't creep up on me." Faith opened the door and
beckoned him inside. "I'm just about to make some lunch.
Would you like something?"

"Like food?" Evan asked as he followed her lead, took
off his boots, and sauntered into the kitchen.

"No, like poison." Faith wasn't in the mood to be lec-
tured by Danny's baby brother right now. "Have you come
to tell me to leave Danny alone again?"

"Nope." Evan studied the hole in his sock. "Actually, I
wanted to apologize."

Faith leaned back against the counter, amazed at her
second unexpected apology of the day, and regarded him.
"About what?"

"Last night at dinner I kind of got into it with Danny,
and he ended up telling everyone about you and the baby."
He grimaced. "It was my fault, and I wanted you to know
that before you thought Danny did it to spite you or something."

"Danny hasn't got a spiteful bone in his body," Faith
pointed out.

"Well, I know that, but—"

"Evan, I know Danny pretty well," Faith said gently.
"You don't have to explain him to me."

"Yeah, well, he's kind of my favorite brother, and I kind

of blew it, and I just wanted to make sure it didn't get any worse because he'll kill me if you get upset again." His gaze drifted toward the door. "I guess I should be getting back."

Faith patted the nearest stool. "Why don't you sit up here and I'll make us both a sandwich?"

"You sure about that?"

Faith met his gaze. "I know how much you care about Danny, and I get that you want to guard his back. Dave does the same for me." She turned to the refrigerator. "I've got chicken, mayo, and salad. Will that work for you?"

Ten minutes later, Evan was starting on his third round of sandwiches, which he'd made himself while Faith ate her first.

"You know he's in love with you, right?" Evan looked up. "Like seriously."

"He did mention something to that effect," Faith admitted.

"Do you love him back?"

"That's the million-dollar question, right?" She held his gaze. "I also think that's between me and Danny."

"Okay." Evan held up his hands. "I get it. I'll shut up."

Faith was just showing Evan out the door, with an extra bag of chips tucked under his arm in case he got hungry on the way home, when his brother's truck parked up in the driveway.

"Crap," Evan breathed. "Don't tell him I was here."

"Unless he's suddenly lost his sight, he can see you right now, you idiot," Faith said. "If you don't want to talk to him, I suggest you make a run for it."

"Will do. Thanks for lunch."

Evan dived to the right and hightailed it around the

bushes to his truck while Danny made his leisurely way to Faith's side.

"What's with him?" He pointed as his brother's truck made a loud turn and roared away.

"No idea. Did you speak to Sue Ellen?" Faith asked.

"Yeah, I was just up there." He searched her face. "Is everything okay?"

She smiled way too brightly. "I hope it will be. Can you come in and talk, or do you have to get back?"

"I'm here, aren't I?" He followed her into the house. "I hope Evan wasn't making trouble."

"He was totally fine," Faith assured him as she gathered up the plates and put them in the dishwasher. "Coffee?"

"Sure." Danny still didn't look convinced about Evan's innocence. "Have you heard any more from Brandon and Callie?"

"Just a text to ask if I'd be willing to talk to them and when I didn't reply, one to tell me they were leaving town."

"Good riddance."

"I feel kind of free of them now," Faith admitted. "Their marriage is nothing to do with me and I won't be dragged back into it."

"Awesome."

Faith drew a resolute breath. "I need to talk to you about something Brandon said."

Danny leaned back against the countertop and nodded. "Shoot."

"And I want you just to let me get to the end of it before you say anything," Faith added.

"Got it." He drew his finger across his lips.

"Okay. When I married Brandon, I was keen to start a family and he was totally on board, but things didn't work out naturally. After a couple of years, we ended up seeing

a bunch of specialists and things went downhill from there."
She grimaced. "You know me well enough to understand
that failure was not an option and it became my life's purpose to get pregnant, which wasn't healthy."

She met Danny's gaze. "I think some of it was tied up
with what happened with Marcus. Some stupid idea that
this time I could do it *right* and that would make up for
what I'd lost, but along the way it morphed into an obses-
sion. I can totally see why Brandon wanted out. He tried
to tell me, but I didn't want to hear him, so he went off and
complained to Callie behind my back. And then, of course,
it came down to the fact that medically he was totally okay,
and I . . . wasn't."

Now came the hard part. She gathered her courage.
"The specialist finally obtained the surgical records of my
emergency caesarian and subsequent full-blown eclampsia
and coma from Vegas. She said I would never be able to
carry a baby again."

Danny stayed absolutely still.

Faith sucked in a breath. "I thought you should know
that."

"Because?"

"Obviously, I can't have kids."

"Okay."

"Doesn't that bother you?" Faith asked. "Like if we
were to get back together then we wouldn't be able to have
another child."

His slow smile was a beautiful thing to see. "*If* we get
back together? Are you trying to tell me something here?"

"Danny Miler." Faith almost stamped her foot. "I'm
trying to give you an out!"

He came toward her, framed her face in his hands, and

bent to kiss her nose. "We of all people know that there are plenty of kids in this world who need parents."

"You're saying . . ."

"Well, unless you've got a plan for stealing Marcus back, I guess I'm saying that if we can't have our own, and it's something we both want, we can certainly look at adopting."

Faith's eyes filled with tears. "I do love you."

"I know." He kissed her properly this time. "You just needed to find a way to say the words."

"I just needed to believe that we could have a future together as well as a past," Faith said. "Do you think—?"

"Yeah, I do," Danny said firmly. "Now hold me tight because I'm shaking, here."

She went up on her toes and wrapped her arms around his neck. "I love you, Danny Miller. I always have."

A little while later, when she was sitting on his lap on the couch and things were getting heated, she remembered she was supposed to be back at work, grabbed for her phone, and texted Dave.

Hey, I might not make it back until 3. Can you cope?

Sure. What are you up to?

You don't want to know. ☺

Eew, GROSS. Give Danny a kiss from me.

Will do x

Actually, why don't you take the rest of the day off and I'll see you in the morning?

Faith turned to Danny, who'd been reading the texts over her shoulder.

"What do you think?"

He got out his own phone. "I think we need to take advantage of this free time and make a plan."

Faith frowned. "A plan to do what?"

He grinned at her, set her on the couch, and stood up. "Wait and see. Hang on while I just make a few calls."

Three hours later Faith was still staring at him like he was nuts, but at least she'd been willing to go along with his crazy idea. After calling his mom, who was the only person in his family who could keep a secret, he'd persuaded Silver to lend him her private jet and pilot and they were on the move.

"Please return to your seats. We will be landing in five minutes."

Danny took the seat beside Faith and held her hand as he craned his head to see the lights of Vegas and the mind-boggling view of the Strip come into view.

"You still good on this?"

"It will certainly save us having to answer a lot of questions."

He squeezed her fingers. "And this time, we'll get it right. I promise."

A private limo met them at the airport and whisked them away to one of the nicer and pricier of the Vegas hotels. At her insistence he'd left certain matters in Silver's capable hands and was interested to see what she'd managed to achieve in the two hours head start she'd been given.

They were bowed into the hotel like royalty and taken up to what looked like the penthouse suite. There was certainly enough room for about fifty people in the place.

"The documents you requested are on the desk, sir, along with a copy of the preapproval you completed online. I will send someone up at six to escort you down to the wedding chapel. Ms. Meadows has ordered you a sumptuous repast that will be delivered to your suite after the celebration."

"Thank you." Danny went to tip the guy, but he held up his hand.

"No need, sir. All taken care of." He gestured at the master bedroom. "I believe there are a variety of garments laid out in the dressing area if you wish to change for the ceremony, madam, and of course, complimentary robes courtesy of the hotel."

As Danny closed the door behind the hotel guy Faith was already making a run for the bedroom. He grinned as he heard her gasp.

"Silver's . . . amazing."

"So Ben keeps telling me."

Danny leaned against the doorframe as Faith stared openmouthed at the beautiful clothes hanging on the stand-alone rack. There were shoes, hats, bags, and all kinds of jewelry laid out on the coffee table as well.

"How did she know my size?" Faith spared him a brief glance.

"She asked. She also wanted to know if you needed a makeup artist and hairdresser, but I said you'd be okay without them." Danny shrugged and strolled over to inspect his own rack of clothes. "Now, those are some fancy cowboy boots."

"But how am I going to repay her?" Faith asked. "I mean, what if I spill red wine all over myself, or rip my hem, or—"

Danny handed her the notecard propped up on the sink and let her read it out loud.

"'Dear Faith and Danny, please take what you want and consider it our wedding gift to you, love Silver and Ben xx.'"

"Sometimes it must be nice to be married to a millionaire movie star," Danny murmured as he looked through the shirts on the rack. "Let me see what you're going to wear, and then I can coordinate my look to yours."

"Nope. I want to keep it a secret for as long as possible." Faith set the notecard down on the table. "You pick exactly what you like, and I'll tell you which accent color you need."

"What does that even mean?" Danny pretended to complain as she hustled him toward the enormous bathroom and the slightly intimidating twenty-second-century shower.

"You know. Knock before you come back in to get changed and I'll make sure I'm already out of your way."

"Don't you need a shower, too?"

She raised her eyebrows. "There are his-and-hers bathrooms in this suite. I'll be fine."

She picked something classic in cream with a soft little sparkly knitted shrug to go around her shoulders. The dress was V-neck and A-line with a rustling petticoat underneath. She'd gone fancy with her sparkling beaded teal shoes and a flower crown of sapphires and wildflowers. She looked like a million dollars and, as she currently felt like she was living in a dream, she intended to own it.

Despite the sudden decision to come to Vegas she knew in her soul that she was making the right choice. Danny wasn't just her past, but her future as well, and there was no one she would rather have by her side in the upcoming years. They'd proved they could weather the worst of times, now hopefully they could enjoy the best.

"Faith . . ."

She turned to see Danny in the doorway. He wore a shirt in his favorite blue, cream pants, and the fanciest cowboy boots she had ever seen. He'd also replaced his battered straw cowboy hat with a new white one and carried a sports jacket over his arm.

"You see?" She pointed at his attire. "I knew you'd pick blue."

"You look beautiful." He came over and took her hands. "You still okay with all this?"

"Yes." She smiled into his eyes. "After all the crap our families have put us through, I'm more than happy to get one over them for a change."

His gray eyes crinkled at the corners as he grinned at her. "That's my girl."

"I think I always will be." She squeezed his fingers. "Now, shall we go and get married?"

"Yeah. We've waited seventeen years for this." He gently kissed her nose. "Now let's do it right this time and make it forever."

RECIPE

FAITH'S
BACON, PEA, AND CHEDDAR CARBONARA
FOR DANNY

Ingredients:

  4 eggs
  2 ounces strong cheddar cheese, finely grated
  1 pound spaghetti
  10 ounces frozen peas (defrosted)
  8 slices of bacon, roughly diced into inch cubes

Method:

Whisk the eggs in a small bowl, mix in grated cheese, and season with black pepper.*

Cook the pasta as directed on packaging, add in peas for last 2 minutes to cook through.

Fry the bacon pieces for about 5 minutes until golden and crisp. Remove pan from heat.

When the pasta and peas are cooked, drain, reserving ½ cup of water. Add pasta, peas, and water to the bacon pan and toss together.

Pour in the egg and cheese mixture, toss through and stir for 2 minutes to allow the residual heat from the pasta to cook the eggs. Serve immediately.

* If worried the eggs will curdle, add 2 tablespoons of heavy cream to the egg and cheese mixture before mixing into the pasta.

Connect with Us

Visit us online at
KensingtonBooks.com
to read more from your favorite authors, see books
by series, view reading group guides, and more.

for sneak peeks, chances to win books and prize packs,
and to share your thoughts with other readers.

facebook.com/kensingtonpublishing
twitter.com/kensingtonbooks

Tell us what you think!

To share your thoughts, submit a review,
or sign up for our eNewsletters, please visit:
KensingtonBooks.com/TellUs.